Wings over
the Rift Valley

Janet E. Green

Wings over the Rift Valley

Where Unexpected Evil
Lurks in the Shadows Beneath

Wings over the Rift Valley

Janet E. Green

ISBN 9798871365779

Cover design and typeset by www.greatwriting.org

The author thanks and acknowledges Jim Holmes of www.greatwriting.org for assistance in preparing this book for publication.

A
HABARI
PUBLICATION

www.janetegreen.org

Contents

In memory of

my dear friend Virginia,

with whom I had many flying adventures

Wings over the Rift Valley

Having been subjected to a heartbreaking incident, Georgia is now determined to move forward, concentrate on her future, work hard at her chosen career and make a success of her life. She does not expect to find the happiness that suddenly and wonderfully comes her way. But unfortunately, lurking in the shadows beneath, there is evil that unexpectedly takes her by surprise.

Prologue

1969

Reflecting sparkles of sunlight from its shiny surfaces, the little red and silver Cessna 150 aeroplane could be clearly seen buzzing around south of Lake Elmenteita in the clear, sunlit, pristine air above the area known as the Highlands of Kenya. To those who may have been casually watching from the ground, it would be apparent that the pilot was putting the aircraft through a number of different manoeuvres as the wings dipped this way and that, causing the reflected sunbeams back to earth and into the eyes of the watcher as the aeroplane was put through its paces. It would be unsurprising if the onlooker thought that whoever was flying the little aeroplane was having the time of their life as they enjoyed the freedom of the wide uncluttered sky to dive and swoop, turn and spin, without a care in the world. Nothing could have been further from the truth.

The young lady in the left-hand seat of the Cessna 150 was in the process of sitting her private pilot's licence flight test, and she was completely focused as she strived to get each manoeuvre perfect. The concentration was making her sweat a little because she was well aware that the examiner, who sat on her right, was a stickler for perfection and he would knit-pick and fail a candidate for the smallest reason. Furthermore, he was not a fan of women pilots! She had been dismayed when she heard that it was to be he who would be coming to Lanet from Nairobi to conduct the practical flight tests that she and the Sikh were hoping to pass that day.

The examiner had been almost as dismayed as the candidates when he had learned, earlier in the week, that it was his turn to conduct the flight examinations in Lanet. The three men qualified to do practical flight examinations in Kenya all resided in Nairobi, and they took turns to go to the far-reaching places around the country to oversee flight examinations. The examiner who now sat in the Cessna 150 with the young lady enjoyed his job within the urban area of Nairobi, but he disliked the more rural places where he felt standards were never as high as those maintained in the capital. Lanet, in particular, was his bugbear.

Earlier, having grumpily decided that he would be utterly ruthless and uncompromising when it came to small mistakes, the examiner was now feeling slightly disappointed that the girl had, thus far, not done a thing wrong. She had a light touch on the controls but flew with confidence. She also kept a constant lookout for other aircraft while she executed the manoeuvres he asked her to perform, even though there was only a small chance of another aeroplane being in the vicinity. When she rolled into a turn, she used the rudder to overcome adverse yaw and kept the aeroplane in balance, so she smoothly and accurately arrived on the required heading.

From past experience, the examiner knew that the Lanet Flying Club normally produced a never-ending stream of farmers who wanted to gain their flying licence, and these fellows seemed to think they could handle aeroplanes and flying in the same manner as they operated their tractors on the farm! In his eyes they were yokels, the whole lot of them! They scrambled into the aeroplane with manure on their boots, while the smell of the farmyard still clung to their rumpled clothing. They had no idea of the finesse required to fly correctly, or the safety criteria that had to be strictly adhered to when in charge of an aeroplane. Even those who scraped a pass soon resorted to their cowboy standards, in this examiner's opinion.

The examiner was meticulous when it came to his own appearance. The creases in his trousers were always sharp, his snowy white shirt was freshly laundered and he wore a smart sports jacket and a coloured cravat. His dark hair was swept back and kept in place with Brylcreem, and he always made sure he applied deodorant and aftershave before he went flying. He felt a pilot should always be well presented and he kept up his own strict standards. In his opinion, a person who was careless when it came to his appearance often turned out to be a messy, disorganised pilot.

Being forewarned that the examiner liked his candidates to dress well, the young lady had discarded her normal attire of shorts, a T-shirt and rubber flip-flops, and dressed instead in a pair of black jeans, a collared, button up, red blouse and blue trainers. She had applied a little makeup to her face in an attempt to appear more grown up, and her honey blond hair was tied neatly back in a ponytail. Even so, she felt that the examiner's appraisal of her when they first met had been disapproving.

Once in the air the girl concealed how nervous she felt and calmly executed the steep turns, stalls and spins that the examiner asked her to perform. Right from the start of the test, she had taken her time and was organised. Her pre-flight checks had been meticulous and so scrupulous that it seemed to the examiner that she had checked every rivet on the aeroplane before take-off! She methodically followed each checklist that she had painstakingly committed to memory, and everything she did was measured and correctly performed. All the time she had kept the examiner engaged with what she was doing by vocalising her actions, but she never rambled on or said anything unnecessary.

The examiner had indeed looked at the girl disapprovingly when they first met, but it was because he did not think it right that a woman should learn to fly—especially one as young as this. She looked very youthful and vulnerable and had he not checked her age he would have estimated she was thirteen or fourteen years old. He liked to think of women pursuing womanly pursuits, and for a moment his thoughts had drifted to his own wife at home in Nairobi. She was expecting their third child and would be pottering about in the kitchen, most probably making him a delicious meal for when he arrived home that evening. That's what women should be doing, he thought, taking care of the children and looking after their husbands! The girl in the left-hand seat looked little more than a child herself—what could her parents be thinking letting her train for her private pilot's licence? But now he had to admit she was proficient when it came to flying so far and he couldn't fault her.

Without warning the examiner leaned forward and pulled the throttle into the idling position. 'Engine failure,' he said shortly.

The girl's eyes immediately sought a field in which to land even while she launched into her emergency checklist. She pointed out to him what she perceived to be a good place for a forced landing, and explained that she was using a spire of smoke that rose from the ground to determine in which direction the wind was blowing. She attained the best glide-range airspeed and trimmed the aircraft so it would maintain the desired airspeed without constant adjustment from herself. As they neared the ground she used the flap control intelligently and as each stage of flap was lowered, she readjusted the nose attitude to maintain airspeed. With calm determination, she glided the little aeroplane towards the field and manoeuvred it so that the landing would be within the area she had specified, while at the same time she simulated a distress call.

'Good. Overshoot now,' commanded the examiner once it was obvious that had the engine failure being genuine, she would have successfully landed in the field.

The girl, a little flushed in the face now from her effort, opened the throttle smoothly and climbed upwards into the sky.

The rest of the flying examination went well, and when they landed back on the Lanet airstrip the girl dropped the aeroplane onto the ground like a bit of thistledown. The examiner still didn't approve of female pilots, but he was a fair man and he had been impressed by the girl's confident, faultless performance. He was glad to be able to tell her, after the debriefing, that she had passed the test with flying colours.

Now, the examiner planned to have a cup of tea and then it would be the turn of the Sikh. He was glad there were no farmers to be tested that day and was happy to note that his next candidate was immaculately dressed, from his shiny black shoes to his snowy white turban. He looked like an intelligent young man and the examiner hoped he would be every bit as good as the girl had been. He was looking forward to wrapping up the day's work and returning to Nairobi and his wife.

Chapter 1

Charles

When the Mercedes Benz swept around the corner at the top of the Nairobi escarpment Charles Lenten, who was in the passenger seat, had his first view of the Great Rift Valley. As Howard Young carefully negotiated the bends on the rather narrow tarmac road, Charles gazed with delight at the breath-taking panorama that lay before his eyes. The valley was dappled in a chequered pattern that was caused by the shadows of the high, cumulous clouds that sailed serenely above, but Charles's eye was drawn to the colossus that dominated the surrounding landscape in the valley. Mount Longonot rose blue and mysterious to a height of 750 meters from the floor of the valley, with larva canyons on its steep slopes and a circular caldera over a kilometre in diameter.

'The last time Mount Longonot erupted was in the mid-1800s,' Howard told Charles as he drew to a stop in a lay-by at the edge of the escarpment. 'It's been dormant since then.'

When Charles got out of the car, he found the highland air to be deliciously bracing, and the purity and quality of the light over the valley was quite staggering. As he stood breathing in the indefinable fragrance of Africa that suggested dust, wood smoke and obscure scents that Charles was, as yet, unable to identify, he felt his spirits rising as an ecstasy of wellbeing seemed to wash over him.

'What a fantastic view,' Charles murmured in an awed voice.

'Yes, you don't get anything like this in England, do you?' Howard said a trifle smugly. 'You'll find we have many magnificent views to enjoy in Kenya—you won't be disappointed when it comes to views!'

Howard had been born in Kenya and had lived there all his life. He had no wish to live anywhere else. Now in his middle years, his suntanned face was deeply grooved with wrinkles and his rather frizzy hair was greying, but he kept himself trim and made sure his hair was kept under control by using liberal amounts of Brylcreem. He was fastidious when it came to dressing, always choosing his clothes carefully and he radiated a sartorial elegance. Having worked as an accountant all his life he was now a senior partner in a firm of accountants in Nakuru, and Charles was sure the shrewd eyes that glinted behind Howard's large square glasses missed very little.

Now after many years of hard work, Howard led a very comfortable lifestyle. He had a loving wife and enough money to afford a beautiful home, a good car and an aeroplane that he kept at the Lanet airfield. Since being voted in as the chairman of the Lanet Flying Club, he was determined to uphold the standard of the club and make it a successful institution for those who wished to learn how to fly.

Charles, who was a qualified flying instructor of light aircraft, had earlier been met at Embakasi Airport near Nairobi by Howard. The younger man had flown in on a B.O.A.C. airliner from Heathrow, London, and the flight had been long and uncomfortable, so he was glad when he had finally reached his destination. As a pilot himself, Charles hated flying on airliners, because he had no control if things went wrong. He much preferred to be in charge whilst in the air and he felt relieved as he walked down the steps of the aeroplane. It was mid-afternoon and the sun shone down hotly on his curly fair hair out of a clear blue sky. It was nice to be away from the depressing January rain in England and as Charles inhaled a great lungful of clean African air, he felt glad he had got away and left all his problems and humiliation behind. This was to be a new chapter in his life and as his intelligent blue eyes took everything in, he felt, for the first time in ages, optimistic and enthusiastic.

Charles was not particularly tall and stood at five feet nine in his socks, but he had the strong sinewy body of an athlete and the features on his face were chiselled and held a determined set. It had been a stroke of luck that he had seen the advertisement placed in one of the flying magazines by the Lanet Flying Club. They were looking for a flying instructor to come and work for them on a three-year contract. If he could get the job, he thought as he scrutinised the advertisement, it would be a chance for him to get away from England, away from his misery and embarrassment and start again. Charles had never travelled further than Europe, so going to Africa would be an adventure for him and he hastened to apply for the position immediately.

Howard had flown out to England to interview the many hopeful candidates who had answered his advertisement, but it was Charles who had got the job. Howard had hoped to employ someone a bit older than Charles, who was 24. He had envisioned a man of about 35 years of age who had possibly had some military experience. He wanted someone clean-cut and organised, someone who would stand no nonsense and be able to sort out the problems that had arisen in the club. Charles had not met the complete criterion, but Howard was impressed by the young man's attitude and his obvious penchant for doing things the correct way. He also had a fair amount of experience and had flown a number of different aircraft, including gliders. So, despite his age and the fact that his fair hair curled around his collar, Howard had decided he was the right man for the job. He gave Charles a month to wind up his affairs in England and he promised to meet him at the airport when he eventually arrived in Kenya. Now they were travelling from Nairobi on the road that led to Nakuru and the Lanet Flying Club.

'There's an interesting little church almost at the bottom of the escarpment,' Howard told Charles when they had resumed their journey. 'It was built by the Italian prisoners of war during the last conflict. They were made to build a road in this rather treacherous environment up the escarpment and the prisoners asked for permission to build a church as well. It's a Catholic church of course, but it's become famous now and people of all dominations or none at all stop to pray there—or just to look at it.'

When they got to the church, Howard pulled in so that Charles could get a good look at the building.

'It's tiny, isn't it?' Charles remarked as he looked at the picturesque little church set into the escarpment.

'Yes, and some people say that it's haunted. Apparently, one of the Italian prisoners of war fell to their death while working on the road, so now the many accidents that occur around here are attributed to the ghost of that fellow getting revenge for being made to work and die here. Pah! It's a load of rubbish of course,' Howard pushed his glasses up his nose and looked disgusted at the thought of belief in ghosts. 'The accidents are caused by people who are not concentrating as they drive down this rather treacherous stretch of road,' he concluded.

They drove on and were soon approaching Naivasha. Lake Naivasha could be seen glinting through the acacia trees as they approached the small town. Charles caught a glimpse of a family picnicking in the shade of the trees as they sped past.

'We'll stop at the Bell Inn for a coffee,' said Howard. 'It's very convenient as it's on the main road through the town—and the coffee is rather good!'

When they had been served their coffees, Howard said, 'This place is always associated with the history of Happy Valley in the 1920s 30s and 40s, and all the depravities and shenanigans that went on during that period. Visitors from Nairobi would call into the Bell Inn and take a stiff gin and tonic as they waited for a horse-drawn carriage to whisk them off to the Djin Palace for a weekend of parties, which included drugs and sexual orgies, if what I've read is true!' Howard looked very disapproving as he sipped his coffee.

'Really?' Charles was intrigued. 'Who were these people?'

Howard waved his hand contemptuously. 'They were mainly the aristocracy from Britain, although some of them came from other European countries. You'll hear all the gossip about them in time, I don't doubt,' he growled. 'They were a disgrace to the country, if you ask me!'

Charles wished that Howard would be more forthcoming as

what little he had said had intrigued him, but Howard obviously didn't want to talk further about the people who had so disgusted him. Charles decided he would just have to find some books on the history of Kenya and discover what had happened during that period.

Once they had finished their coffee and were back on the road, Howard started to fill Charles in with the plans that he had for the future of the Lanet Flying Club.

'We already have a basic clubhouse,' he told Charles. 'There's not much to it and it could do with sprucing up, but the building is there. We also have two Cessna 150s and a Cessna 182. There's a good long grass runway and a shorter cross runway. We also have a large hangar and since there's more than enough space in it for our aeroplanes, we rent out space to other owners of aircraft who operate from Lanet. At the back of the hanger there's provision for an aircraft engineer to maintain aircraft, and recently a fellow by the name of William Murray has set up business there and he services our aeroplanes, together with others who require his skills. So you see all the basics are in place.

'The problem is everything is a bit rudimentary and unfortunately the Lanet Flying Club has got the reputation of harbouring a bunch of flying cowboys! Not every pilot who flies out of Lanet is a cowboy, mind. It's just a few who, being away from the watchful eye of the aviation authorities in Nairobi, take advantage of the fact that they can get away with things out here in the country. Tear away cowboys—that's how I think of them!'

Howard took his eyes off the road for a moment and glanced at Charles.

'This is where you come in. I want the standard of flying around Lanet and Nakuru to improve and you have my full backing to question and stop any dangerous or inappropriate flying practice that you see around here. I want Lanet to gain the respect of the aviation authorities in Nairobi; I want it to be the hub of respectability and impeccable flyers. I know it will take a bit of time, but that's my vision for the club.'

'The fellow who was instructing up until recently—did he not try to improve the standard of flying around here?' Charles inquired.

'Martin Taylor was the last in a line of instructors who were, in effect, tear-away cowboys themselves—and Martin was the biggest cowboy of them all!' Howard said, a deep frown wrinkling his brow. 'He did as little as possible and seemed to spend all his time flying up to Eldoret to play rugby and visit his girlfriend! If anyone gave the Lanet Flying Club a bad reputation, it was Martin!'

'So, where's Martin now?'

'He went to England to pursue a career as an airline pilot. God help the people who try and train him—they'll need His help to get Martin to become responsible enough to fly an airliner! Look, Martin is a nice enough chap in himself—all the previous blokes were as well, in all honesty. But the problem is these colonial lads lack discipline, that's why I decided to recruit an instructor from Britain.'

'So, what's the background of the majority of the people who want to learn to fly at Lanet?'

'We have quite a few young farmers who want to learn how to fly, but there're others as well from Nakuru and other more distant areas. Most are white males, but we do have some Asians as well.'

'Any Africans?'

'No, not yet; I think that's because most of them can't afford flying lessons. There are some of the wealthier ones learning in Nairobi which is a good thing, I think. Now that the country has got independence, the Africans should learn how to do everything the white man has previously been doing. I'm sure we'll get some Africans coming to us soon.'

'Do you think having a bad reputation at the Lanet Flying Club has put people off wanting to learn there?'

'Not at all; since Martin left, I've had a number of enquiries and they're all as keen as mustard to start once you're settled in. I told them we were getting an experienced instructor from England and the standard of flying would be very high, and word has got around so I think you'll be very busy.

'Look, it's not just the flying standard that I want to improve; I want to develop and enhance everything about the club,' Howard continued enthusiastically. 'I want to do up the clubhouse, make a nice garden around it, provide a place that flyers want to drop into for a meal or even a bed for the night. I know it'll all take money, but we can raise money by putting on events—dinners, dances or discos as they now seem to have evolved into. Flying competitions, airfares. . . there's so much we can do to raise funds. Already we have a contingent of gliders at Lanet and sometimes we get skydivers coming down from Nairobi as well—we need to exploit both of those so that we can make money whilst providing a sport that the people are demanding.'

'So how many of us are there to make all this happen?' Charles asked.

'Well, we have all the people on the board and the club members,' said Howard. 'But the main movers and shakers will be me and you! Hans Schmidt has his assistant flying instructors rating, so he'll be able to help you with those who are learning to fly, but he'll be returning to Germany in a few months. It doesn't really matter; I'm sure by then we'll have another assistant flying instructor trained up,' he said optimistically.

When they were nearing the airfield Howard told Charles that before he took him to the club, he was going to show him the house that came with the flying instructor's job. It was in Lanet not far from the airfield, and when they arrived Charles saw it was a small house set in a garden that mainly consisted of lawn. Howard parked in front of the house and then he helped Charles to carry his luggage inside.

'As you can see the house has all the basic furniture,' said Howard. 'You can add pictures or anything else to make it more personal. Meanwhile, there's bedlinen in the airing cupboard and you'll find all the stuff you need for the kitchen in the draws or kitchen cupboards. I think my wife, Mary, took the liberty of putting a few groceries in your fridge and pantry as well.' Howard opened the fridge door and peered inside. 'There're milk and eggs and bread and butter in here,' he said. 'Let's see what's in the pantry. . . looks like there's breakfast cereal, jam and some tins of meat and vegetables; just enough to get you started.'

'It was awfully good of your wife to do this,' said Charles.

'Oh nonsense! I expect you'll be eating most of your meals at the club, anyway. We have an excellent cook there. By the way,

Mary has asked me to invite you to dinner with us tonight, so you don't have to worry about a meal this evening.'

It was now dusk and Howard wanted to take Charles around to the club to meet some of the members before he took him home to introduce him to his wife.

'There's the runway,' Howard said as they drove past the threshold of the grass strip on the way to the clubhouse. Charles could see it was wide, long and looked well kept.

'There's no control tower?' inquired Charles.

'Oh no, nothing like that here! We do have a radio in the club house that picks up all incoming traffic, but that's about it. There's the hangar—looks like William is working late this evening. We'll just stop here so you can meet him.'

When they walked into the brightly lit area where the aircraft engineer worked, Charles saw a man working on the engine of a Cessna 206 that had had its cowling removed.

'Good evening, William,' Howard hailed him.

William turned from the engine he had been working on and Charles could see he was a rather rotund man in dirty blue overalls who was bald and had a pencil stuck behind one ear and a cigarette behind the other.

'Hello there,' he replied, as he picked up a bit of cotton-waste on which to wipe his hands.

'I'd like you to meet Charles Lenten, our new instructor,' Howard said.

'Good to meet you,' William offered his still rather oily hand. 'I'm William Murray.'

'Working late this evening?' Howard enquired.

'Aye, had a lot on this week and needed to get it done. But I'll be up to the club for a dram very shortly, so I'll see you there.'

Howard and Charles left William to finish off and made their way to the club. The clubhouse stood rather forlornly all by itself not far from the runway, and Charles could just make out a drooping windsock in the gathering darkness. There were several aeroplanes standing on the apron in front of the clubhouse, all carefully tied down.

'The Cherokee 180 is mine,' said Howard proudly. 'The Cessna 180 belongs to Neil and Hamish McDonald—they're brothers who farm at Solai and they also have land elsewhere in the country, I forget now in which part. The Piper Cub has just been purchased by a couple who have recently learned to fly here, Jasmine and George Pearce—George has a somewhat chequered history, but I'm sure you'll learn all about him in club gossip! I think they have a farm near Nyeri. The two Grumman Ag Cats are crop-spraying aeroplanes owned by Scott Egerton of Egerton Agric. They're piloted by an American and a German. The German is okay—a quiet sort of chap who doesn't speak much, but the American is completely barking mad! The Dragon Rapide belongs to Mark Fleming who has an electrical shop in Nakuru. He hardly ever flies his aeroplane and it just stands there on the apron doing nothing. I don't know why he doesn't put it in the hangar. The two Cessna 150s and the Cessna 182 that are standing in a group belong to the club, and the other Cessna 182 standing to the left of them is owned by Patrick Reeves who has a farm near Elementaita.'

'There seem to be quite a few people who use the airfield,' Charles commented.

'Yes, there are others as well who have put their aeroplanes in the hangar.'

They drove into the club carpark that appeared to be empty and Howard looked around with surprise. 'That's funny,' he said. 'It's Friday evening and I expected to see a lot of people here.'

Charles followed Howard into the club house thinking it was rather a bleak little building. Inside there was a large room with a fireplace around which some easy chairs were placed. There was a black and white cat curled up in one of the chairs, but no cheerful fire burned in the hearth. At one end of the room there was a long dining table and chairs, and at the other end there was a bar behind which stood an elderly African man whose hair was peppered with curly white strands.

'Good evening, sir,' said the African, smiling pleasantly at them as they walked in.

'Good evening, Sam,' responded Howard. 'This is our new instructor, Charles Lenten. Charles, this is Samuel Wangi, our barman.'

'Pleased to meet you, sir,' said Sam, flashing his radiant smile on Charles.

'Sam, where is everyone?' asked Howard. 'I expected a crowd to be here since it's Friday evening.'

'Most of the young people have gone to the disco at the Oyster Shell in Nakuru, sir,' responded Sam. 'It's a bit early for the older members, but I expect they'll be in later. Can I get you a drink, sir?'

'What would you like?' Howard asked Charles.

'Just a beer please, if you have one,' said Charles.

'Tusker?' Sam asked.

Charles didn't know any of the beers served in Kenya, so he just nodded his head. 'That'll be fine.'

'I'll have my usual,' Howard told the barman. Then turning to Charles, he said, 'I'll just show you around the clubhouse while Sam is sorting out our drinks, it won't take long.

On the right of the passage leading off the main room there were two bedrooms. Howard opened the door of one of them and when Charles peeped in, he was surprised at how austere and spartan the room appeared. There were three black metal beds inside with kapok mattresses on them, a small cupboard with an ill-fitting door that enabled Charles to see bedlinen and towels stacked inside, and a table with a mirror affixed to the wall above it. The windows were covered by curtains made of rough white cotton material and the concrete floors were unadorned.

'I know,' said Howard gloomily when Charles made no comment. 'More like a prison cell than anything else! But we only charge people a pittance to stay in one of these rooms overnight and they're on my list for improvements.'

'Are all the bedrooms the same?' Charles asked.

'Yes. Well, the one next door is, but the one on the other side of the passage is occupied by a long-term resident and I think it's been done up a bit.'

Oh, I didn't realise you had long term residents; I thought you said the rooms were mostly for those caught out and unable to fly on to their destinations for one reason or another.'

'Yes, that's right, but we've made an exception. And having the room rented to a long-term client does insure a steady income from that room.'

At the top of the passage there were the Ladies and Gents

restrooms. Each had two toilets, a basin and a shower. Again, they were very basic.

'The only other rooms are the office, lecture room and kitchen,' said Howard. He opened a door to a large room with a blackboard along one end. 'This is supposed to be the lecture room,' he said, 'but it's not used for that purpose anymore.'

Someone had drawn a picture of an aeroplane on the board with diagrams depicting the principle of roll, pitch and yaw, but that was the only indication that the room was used for learning. At the other end of the room all the chairs were stacked up neatly, and in the middle of the room there was a table-tennis table on which lay two rather worn looking bats and a ping-pong ball.

'Why isn't this room used for lectures anymore?' Charles inquired.

'Well, our last instructor wasn't up to giving lectures. He was unwilling . . . and unable to help the student pilots with their theory. So now everyone goes to Daniel Carrington in Nairobi. He holds theory classes for students at Wilson Airport and gives them one on one instruction. He has a pass rate of about 99 per cent, and they can do their radio/telephony exam while they're staying in Nairobi at the same time, so it suits people very well.'

Next to the lecture room there was a small office with a telephone standing on the desk. It was neat and tidy and Charles guessed correctly that Howard was the one who made sure the paper work was done properly and then stored in the filing cabinets that stood against the far wall.

Howard then took him to meet the cook in the kitchen. Solomon Chege, a large rotund man from the Kikuyu tribe, called himself a chef, but in reality he was just an mpishi, a cook who only had the basic skills when it came to cooking. But what he could do, he did well and he was a jolly fellow who endeared himself to all whom he met.

'Welcome Bwana,' Solomon boomed in his deep voice when he was introduced to Charles. 'Can I cook you some supper?'

'No, not tonight,' Howard answered for Charles. 'He's coming home with me for a meal.'

Charles and Howard then returned to the bar where Sam had set out their drinks. Charles found that Tusker beer was a light larger served ice cold. Howard had a glass of whisky and they chatted as they sipped their drinks. It wasn't long before William joined them, he had taken off his overalls and cleaned himself up a bit, but his fingernails were still stained black by the oil. Charles found him to be an engaging Scotsman and immediately liked him. After a while other people came drifting in singly and in couples and Howard introduced Charles to all who arrived.

Meeting everyone en masse was rather confusing and Charles wondered if he would be able to remember everyone's name. However, they all appeared delighted to meet him and kind offers from people to whom he was introduced came rolling in.

'You must come around for a meal sometime.'

'We have a barbeque about once a month and everyone's invited, so make sure you come.'

'I have my own aeroplane and you can come up with me if you like and I'll help you to familiarise yourself to the country.'

'If you're looking to get a dog, my bitch is having puppies. You're welcome to have one if you can provide a good home for it.'

'If you feel like a break you can go to Lake Rudolph and stay in our lodge there. There's good Nile Perch to be caught in the lake.'

Charles felt quite dizzy as the generous offers from people he had only just met were showered upon him.

'Come on,' said Howard eventually. 'We must be going or Mary's dinner will be spoilt.'

Howard lived on the other side of Nakuru in a large and pleasant house. His wife, Mary, had a good-humoured but rather wrinkled face, and the dark curls that danced around her head were liberally sprinkled with grey. Charles could see she was a kind, motherly person as she made him very welcome.

'Is this your first time in Africa?' Mary enquired. When she learned that it was, she told him he must not hesitate to come to them for advice if he ever had an African related problem that perplexed him. 'Things are run a bit differently to Britain here in Kenya,' she explained. 'But you'll soon get the hang of things.'

The delightful aroma of roasting meat wafted in from the kitchen making Charles's mouth water. Luckily, he didn't have to wait too long before the meal was served and they were all tucking into roast lamb and all the trimmings.

'When do you actually start your job at the club?' Mary asked when they were all sitting drinking coffee after the meal.

'More or less straight away,' said Charles, glancing at Howard for confirmation.

'Yes, you need to get settled in first and it's important you have a car of your own,' said Howard. 'When I interviewed you in England you agreed that you would buy a second-hand car when you got here and I've taken the liberty to look for a suitable one for you. I know one of the car dealers in Nakuru quite well and he's got a Ford Popular on his forecourt that I thought might suite you. It's reasonably priced, hasn't got a lot of mileage on the clock and it looks in good condition. I could take you to see it tomorrow morning, if you like?'

'Yes, thank you, it sounds ideal,' said Charles. 'But will they be open on a Saturday?'

'Oh yes. Old Rajan is open every day of the week,' Howard assured him.

'You'll need to get a house servant as well,' said Mary.

'A house servant?' Charles had never thought to ever employ a servant.

'Yes, someone to keep your house clean and wash your clothes.'

'Well . . . I hadn't really thought about that . . . will I really need one?'

'Well, there's no washing machine in the house,' said Mary. 'You could buy one of course, but I think getting a house-servant would be cheaper and definitely easier.'

'Everyone has a house-servant, old boy,' said Howard. 'They don't cost you a lot and you'd be giving a man a job. Also, they're better value than a washing machine because they can clean your house as well, cut your grass and wash your car!'

'Well, I suppose I'll have to think about getting one,' said Charles, wondering how one would go about it.

'As it happens, Kamau, our house servant, has a cousin who's looking for work,' said Mary. 'I could send him around to your house tomorrow morning if you like and you can interview him. If you don't think he's suitable we can always look for someone else.'

'Okay, but I'm going to look at the car tomorrow morning.'

'I'll be picking you up at about ten o'clock,' said Howard. 'Tell Kamau to let his cousin know that he should be at Charles's house early, Mary, then Charles will have time to interview him before we go.'

Later that evening when Howard was preparing to take Charles back to his house in Lanet, Mary pressed a tin into Charles's hands. 'I've baked you a house warming present,' she said smiling at him kindly. 'I do hope you enjoy fruit cake.'

When Charles was at last alone in his house, he made himself a cup of coffee from the provisions that had been left for him and cut a slice of the delicious looking cake. He'd had a busy and exhausting day and now he had a lot to reflect upon. The culture and way of life in this country was certainly going to be very different from what he was used to, but everyone he had met had been so nice and welcoming. Granted, he hadn't yet met any of the 'tear away cowboys' that Howard had mentioned, but if they were even half as nice as the other folk he'd met, it was going to be difficult to be strict enough to lick them into shape. Maybe that was why the previous instructor hadn't bothered. He'd probably decided that if he couldn't beat them, he would join them! Charles knew it wouldn't be like that for him. Order and correctness had been hardwired into his character by his strict upbringing and now he was a stickler for doing things properly. He wondered if he would be able to make people come around to his way of thinking; if they were unwilling, he might find that he made some enemies, which was the last thing that he wanted. Well, only time would tell, Charles decided, as he staggered wearily off to bed, leaving his dirty cup and plate to be washed up in the morning.

Chapter 2

Georgia

Charles was exhausted by his long journey over from England and then meeting so many new people. He fell into bed and slept like a log until seven thirty the next morning when he was awakened by someone knocking on his front door. He looked at his watch in a panic, thinking he must have overslept and Howard was at his door, but when he saw the time, he knew it was too early for Howard and it must be someone else. Hastily, he wound a towel around his waist and rushed to open the door.

'Good morning, Bwana,' said the African man standing on his doorstep. 'I am Emmanuel Njoka.' He flashed a radiant smile at Charles.

Charles looked at him in confusion—who on earth was Emmanuel Njoka and what did he want? He was a middle-aged African dressed immaculately in dark trousers and a white shirt.

The African saw the confusion in Charles's eyes and said, 'I have come about the job as a house-servant.'

'Oh yes,' said Charles, suddenly remembering he had agreed to interview someone for the job this morning. 'You're a bit early!'

'Yes sir; I was told to come early,' Emmanuel replied.

'Okay, no problem, come in. You'll have to wait a while until I'm ready though.'

Charles couldn't even contemplate interviewing this smart

looking African man while he himself was only clad in a towel! He led the man in and invited him to sit down in the sitting-room.

Emmanuel gave Charles a strange look, 'I will wait in the kitchen,' he said firmly.

Charles didn't argue, he rushed off to have a quick shower and shave and put on some clothes. When he had finished his ablutions, he found Emmanuel had washed up his cup and plate that he had left from the previous evening and was now sweeping the kitchen.

'Right,' said Charles, feeling surprised that Emmanuel had already started work. 'We can begin the interview now.'

Emmanuel put the broom aside and looked expectantly at Charles, but Charles suddenly didn't know what to say. He had never thought to employ a house-servant before and didn't know what sort of questions he should be asking. After a minute Emmanuel seemed to grasp the fact that Charles was completely clueless when it came to conducting interviews, so he came to the rescue.

'I am very experienced in housework, Bwana. I am very good,' Emmanuel said. 'I will keep your house clean, do your washing and also wash your car. I can do a little bit of cooking and since you are one man, so not too much work, I can also cut your grass and do the gardening. I have been working for many years in house work. I have only left Mr Andrews, my old employer, because he has gone back to England with his memsahib and watoto, but I have a good reference. Let me show you my reference, Bwana.'

Charles read through the reference that Emmanuel dug out of his pocket, and his previous employer confirmed that the African was good at his job and was loyal and honest. Charles asked Emmanuel what he had been earning.

'Right,' Charles said when he realised he would easily be able to pay Emmanuel what he wanted. 'You can have the job, but where're you going to live?'

'You have servant's quarters on this property, sir.'

'Oh, sorry; I didn't realise that, I only moved in yesterday evening.'

'They are behind this house at the bottom of the garden on the other side of the bananas.'

'Good. So how about you move in this weekend and start work on Monday?'

'Yes sir; that would be very good. But I need the key for the servant's house because it is locked.'

'Oh. I wonder where it is? Help me to look for the key, Emmanuel, it must be somewhere around.'

Both men started to look for the key and Emmanuel found a whole lot of keys in one of the kitchen draws. They decided to take them all out to the servant's house and see if one would fit the lock. Charles realised that he hadn't been aware there was a facility for the servant because it was well concealed behind a large clump of banana trees. They soon discovered which key fitted the lock and Charles swung the door open and looked inside.

'It's rather small,' he said dubiously. 'Do you have a wife? It'll be a bit of a squeeze if two of you live here.'

'I have a wife and seven children,' Emmanuel told him proudly. 'But they will stay in the village and I will be here alone. It is all right for me.'

'Well, if you're sure. . . '

'I am sure, Bwana,' said Emmanuel, smiling broadly. 'I will move in this weekend and start work on Monday.' He was feeling extremely pleased because securing a job with a single bwana to look after was a coup. He had enjoyed working for Mr Andrews who had been a good and fair employer, but he had a wife and three children so it had been a lot of hard work. Now he wouldn't have a memsahib on his back with her high exacting standards, nor would he have the mess made by the three children to clear up. Also, he felt drawn to this young bwana who was so obviously unsure of the procedure of engaging a house-servant.

'How did you get on interviewing the prospective house-servant?' Howard enquired as he drove Charles to the car dealer to view the Ford that he had for sale.

'It went well,' said Charles. 'I liked the chap and he's agreed to start work on Monday.'

'Good. Well, we seem to be sorting you out gradually,' said Howard with satisfaction. 'I hope you'll like the car I've found for you as well.'

Later, Charles followed Howard to the Lanet Flying Club in the Ford Popular he had bought. He was pleased with the car; it had been less money than he had been expecting and it ran beautifully. It was late-morning by then and as they drove past the boundary of the airfield, Charles saw that there was a bunch of people standing on the end of the runway and a glider was being readied for launch. He slowed so that he could see what was going on and was surprised to see the glider was a T21 model, which he guessed must be over twenty years old. As he drove slowly by, he could hear the glider instructor giving instruction to a young man who was obviously the next person he was going to take up. The instructor was a large man who had flaming red hair and a red beard. He also had a very loud, booming voice which Charles could hear clearly even as he drove past. The Chevy V8 that they were using to launch the glider was further up the runway already in place to start the launch, and Charles saw that it had been painted bright red with patterns of white squares and stripes on it.

'As you probably surmised, our gliding instructor was the big bloke with the red hair and beard,' Howard told him when they had both arrived at the clubhouse and were walking in. 'His name is Bruce Little and he's very experienced and has glided all over the world, but he says that this is the best country in which he's ever glided because of the strong thermals.'

When they walked into the clubhouse there were many new people for Charles to meet. Those with whom he had socialised the previous evening had mostly been farmers, many of them social members, but today he could meet the flying enthusiasts. They all welcomed him warmly and Charles thought there couldn't have been a nicer bunch of people. He wondered how many among them Howard would class as 'tearaway cowboys'.

Howard ordered them both a cup of coffee and then took Charles to the office so that they could go over the paper work. It was lunch time when they had finished.

'Let's go and have a bite to eat,' suggested Howard.

After ordering a sandwich and a cup of tea, they went to sit outside on the veranda. Charles looked over at the runway to see what the gilding enthusiasts were up to, and saw that they had pushed the T21 up above the threshold of the runway and were now piling onto the back of the Chevy.

'I expect they've stopped for a while so that they can have a spot of lunch,' said Howard following his gaze.

He was right, once everyone had climbed aboard, the Chevy headed back towards the clubhouse. Charles watched with interest as they jumped off and then he stared in amazement as the driver of the car got out.

'Good God! That little girl wasn't driving the car and launching the gliders, was she?' he asked in astonishment.

'What? Oh, that's Georgia Thorne, she's older than she looks,' said Howard.

'But she can't be more than about thirteen years old!'

'No, she's seventeen or eighteen—old enough to have a driving licence anyway. That old Land Rover in the carpark belongs to her.'

At that moment Sam came to call Howard away for a telephone call that had come through for him, so Charles covertly studied the girl whom he immediately put down as a groupie. He knew all about groupies; they had had them at the club in England of which he had been a member and his mouth turned down at the corners when he recalled them.

Looking at the girl, Charles could hardly believe that she was seventeen or eighteen. She stood at about five foot three or four and had a slim boyish figure. He could see she had small high breasts concealed in her T-shirt and a tight little bottom under her shorts. Her long, honey blond hair was tied back in a pony-tail and when she turned in his direction, he saw that her face still retained some of the roundness of childhood, while her greenish eyes framed by long black lashes held a look of innocence under the delicate lines of her brows. It was her mouth that reminded Charles of someone else—it was wide and her soft full lips looked as though they could easily fall into a pout. Charles gave a little shudder.

'Hi, I'm Hans Schmidt,' said a voice, bringing Charles out of his reverie.

The assistant flying instructor put his plate of sandwiches and a bottle of Coke on the table and sat down. He had a beautiful even tan that set off his very fair hair and brilliant blue eyes, and he spoke perfect English with only the hint of a German accent.

'So, you have come to sort out the flying club for Howard,' he said after they had introduced themselves. His blue eyes twinkled with amusement.

'Is the standard of flying really as bad as Howard says it is?' Charles asked.

'Howard is a first-class man,' said Hans, 'but at the same time he's a bit of a granny! No, the standard here isn't that bad—there have been a few incidents, but no major accidents. The last major accident was years ago when Howard was a young man himself. One of his contemporaries managed to crash into the Nairobi escarpment and he and his wife were killed. Since then, no-one has done anything so silly, but Howard is all about perfection; maybe when you work with figures all day like he does it makes you that way.'

'Well, I'm glad to hear that it isn't as bad as I feared,' said Charles. 'I was beginning to think I had bitten off more than I could chew!'

Hans laughed loudly. 'There are one or two hoodlum pilots who may need some steadying words in their ears but on the whole, I don't think you have much to worry about. Howard is convinced that the standard of flying in and around Nakuru is poor, but I don't think it's any worse than Nairobi. Martin wasn't a bad instructor; he just lost his way a bit at the end of his time here and that's why he fell out with Howard.'

'Lost his way?'

'Not literally!' Hans laughed again. 'Martin loved to play rugby and he would fly to Eldoret as there was a good rugby team that he played for there. That was fine; he did it on his day off and paid for the use of the aeroplane. But then he met a girl called Lisa in Eldoret and started to fly there more and more often. Sometimes he got stuck there due to the weather conditions and couldn't get back to Nakuru to teach those who had booked flying lessons. Some people had driven quite considerable distances for their lessons and I couldn't fly with them as I had my own students, so that's when things started to go wrong between Howard and Martin.'

Charles felt relieved that there didn't seem to be such a big problem as Howard had suggested and later when Hans had gone to give one of the students a lesson, he decided that he would only insist on having a check flight with those who had recently qualified as private pilots.

'Come on, I'll take you up in my Cherokee and you can familiarise yourself with the area,' Howard said when he appeared again.

Once they were airborne, Howard pointed out the landmarks to Charles.

'Those are the Aberdare Mountains,' he said pointing to the imposing range in front of them. They're about 100 kilometres long from north to south and form the easternmost wall of the Great Rift Valley.'

Then, as he turned right a glittering body of water appeared under the right wing; it shimmered pink around the edges and sparkled in the sunlight.

'That's Lake Nakuru and the pink is caused by flamingos on the lake,' Howard told Charles. 'It's a soda lake and the abundance of algae in the water attracts them there as they love to eat it. It's a sanctuary for other birds as well; there're masses of species that live on the lake and in the surrounding area. There's also a lot of game around the lake because it's situated in a National Park.'

'What does the name Nakuru actually mean?' Charles asked.

'I believe it's a Masai word that means Dust or Dusty Place,' said Howard as he turned and headed away from Nakuru towards the Menengai Crater.

'Menengai is another good landmark,' Howard remarked as they flew over the massive crater. 'There hasn't been any volcanic activity for hundreds of years and it's considered extinct, but there are some hot spots on the floor of the crater where steam jets sometimes fill it with vapour. The farmland that flanks the crater consists of rich volcanic loam soil and there're some very productive farms there.'

'What's that body of water I can see in the distance?' Charles asked pointing.

'That's Lake Hannington. There're hot springs and geysers there and lots of flamingos!'

Howard then headed to the town of Thomson's Falls, where he pointed out the pretty fall of water.

'Thomson's Falls is an attractive little place to visit in the Highlands,' Howard told Charles. 'It's quite cool there because it stands at the elevation of 7,740 feet above sea level, but on a warm sunny day it's really lovely. The falls are on the Ewaso Ng'iro River, and hippo from the river often come up into the suburbs of Thomson's Falls at night to feed on the vegetation that they find in people's gardens!'

'Are they dangerous if you come across them in your garden?' Charles asked curiously.

'Very dangerous,' Howard assured him. 'They are herbivores so they won't kill you for food, but if you annoy them by getting between them and the water, they can be very aggressive. One chop of their huge jaws is enough to cut a man in half!'

As Charles was digesting this bit of information, Howard turned and flew towards Naivasha. When he got there, he dropped low over the lake. 'Look on your right and you'll see the infamous Djin Palace,' he told Charles.

Charles saw a white, ornate, castle like building as they flashed past and wondered again what had gone on there. Then Howard was climbing up again and heading for Nakuru.

'Have you decided on a plan of action to improve the standard of flying from Lanet?' Howard asked Charles when they had landed and were having a cool drink at the bar.

'Well, I thought I'd insist on having a check flight with all those who had recently qualified as private pilots,' said Charles. 'That way I can check on their standard of flying and nip any "tear away" tendencies in the bud; as for the others who've picked up bad flying habits over time, I'll have to pull them up as and when I see it happening and have a quiet word in their ears.'

'Yes, well, that seems like a good start,' said Howard. 'And there's your most recently qualified pilot coming in right now. Why don't you arrange a time to have a check flight with her now?'

Charles was surprised to see that it was Georgia walking in. He had put her down as a groupie and hadn't realised she had obtained her private pilot's licence.

'Georgia, come and meet our new chief flying instructor,

Charles Lenten,' Howard said to the girl.

A small smile flitted over Georgia's face when she was introduced to Charles, but it disappeared when he told her he would need to do a check flight with her.

'It's nothing personal,' Charles tried to reassure her when he saw her expression. 'I intend to do a check flight with all newly qualified pilots. Howard has just mentioned you're the most recently qualified, but there'll be others.'

'Fine,' Georgia said shortly, but her displeasure was reflected in her greenish eyes.

'Can I buy you a drink?' Charles asked, feeling he had got off on the wrong foot with this pint-sized woman. He thought she was going to say no, she would buy her own drink, but she obviously decided to try and be polite and accepted his offer. Sam immediately produced a bottle of Coke and after opening it, he handed it to her with a straw.

'Thank you,' she said to Charles. He thought she looked more like a little girl than ever as she sucked up her Coke through the straw.

As Howard had wandered off Charles made an effort to make conversation with Georgia. 'When did you sit your PPL flying test?' he asked.

'Last week.'

'How did it go?'

Well, I passed,' said Georgia a little defensively.

Charles realised that the girl was more than a little displeased with the idea of having to be subjected to another check flight so soon after she had passed her flying test, but he persevered with the conversation nonetheless.

'Were you the only one to take the test last week?'

'No. The examiners come up from Nairobi and they'll only come if there are two or more students to sit the test. Amar Singh also sat his test on the same day as me, but he failed.'

'Oh, I'm sorry to hear that.'

'Well, it wasn't unexpected.'

'Amar Singh was put up for his flying test and not expected to pass?' Charles was astonished. He never put students up for their test unless he was 99% certain that they would pass. He thought it would reflect badly on him if one of his students failed, and so far, he was proud to have a hundred percent pass rate.

'I wanted to sit my flying test before Martin left and there was no-one else ready except Amar. He was desperate to do his test, but he tends to get stressed and panic, so. . . ' Georgia shrugged her shoulders.

'Are you saying he was only put forward to do his flying test so that there would be two people for the examiner?' Disapproval was obvious in Charles's face.

'Amar is more than capable of passing his flying test,' said Georgia firmly. 'He wanted to have the chance to prove he could pass it and Martin thought he could as well. Martin knew Amar might bottle it due to his nerves, but he thought the worst that could happen was that he would fail. He never thought Amar would actually crash the aeroplane!'

'He crashed on his flight test?' Charles was aghast.

'Well, I guess "crashed" is too strong a word for it,' said Georgia. 'The examiner wanted to simulate an engine failure after take-off, so as they were climbing away from the airstrip, he pulled back the throttle and told Amar that the engine had failed. Amar knew exactly what to do because he'd practiced it many times before. He pushed the nose down into a gliding attitude and said he would have to land straight ahead because he didn't have the height to turn back to the airfield. But when he should have simulated turning off the petrol and ignition, he panicked and actually turned off the petrol and switched off the ignition and then he pulled out the keys and threw them on top of the instrument panel!'

A little smile broke out on Georgia's face.

'Of course, it was the turn of the examiner to panic then, and he tried to grab the keys that had slid towards the windshield and at the same time turn the fuel on again, because Amar was now busy unlatching the door, but by the time the examiner had got the keys in the ignition the wheels of the aeroplane had gone into the wheat in the field ahead of them and basically that was it.' Georgia giggled.

'You think it was funny?' said Charles who was horrified by the story.

'Yes,' said Georgia giggling again, 'I do. Everyone thought it was hilarious, everyone except Amar and the examiner—oh, and Godfrey Appleton of course, who wasn't impressed at all.'

'Godfrey Appleton?'

'Yes, he's the farmer who owns the field of wheat in which they crashed.'

'What an absolute disaster,' said Charles, who looked appalled.

'No one was hurt and the aeroplane wasn't damaged either, because it dropped into the wheat so gently,' said Georgia. 'Amar's family are as rich as Croesus and they were able to compensate Godfrey, so it wasn't such a disaster.' She was obviously very amused at the incident.

Howard came and called Charles away as he wanted to discuss some fund-raising ideas, so nodding to Georgia, Charles went off thinking that Howard was probably right to think there were a number of "tear away cowboys" in the club if everyone thought that such a serious incident was hilarious. Later that evening, Charles noticed Georgia sitting on the steps of the veranda with a Sikh and wondered if it was the infamous Amar Singh.

'I can't go into the clubhouse and show my face,' Amar was saying to Georgia. 'I feel so ashamed.'

'Don't be silly, Amar, everyone makes mistakes,' Georgia replied.

'Yes, but not great big huge mistakes like landing in a wheat field during your PPL flight test!' Amar wailed. 'They must all be thinking I'm very stupid.'

'No, you're more like a hero, Amar.'

'A hero? Why?'

'Because there isn't one person in the club who wouldn't relish the opportunity to make Mr kinky clean Stewart, the examiner, get wheat chaff in his turn-ups and blackjacks all over his pristine sports jacket—but you actually managed to achieve that!'

'It was a bit funny seeing him trying to dust himself down and get the blackjacks off when he walked out of the wheat field,' chuckled Amar. 'He was definitely more worried about his sports jacket and trousers than he was about the aeroplane!'

'It was hilarious,' agreed Georgia giggling. 'He was still trying to pick the blackjacks off even as he left in a huff for Nairobi!'

'I'm just glad you did your test first, because I'm sure he would have failed you if he'd had to fly with you while there were blackjacks in his jacket.'

They both laughed again and then Amar grew serious. 'My father thinks I'm a failure,' he said. 'He was so cross when he heard what had happened, and as the only son of my father I feel I've let him down really badly.'

'Don't be so hard on yourself, Amar.'

'But my father is now saying that it was a waste of money paying for my flying lessons. You know he has a number of butcheries in various locations around the country and he has to fly the meat out to them in his Cessna 182—well, I was supposed to be getting trained up so I could do that for him; now that I've failed so miserably he is talking about getting my cousin Raj trained up instead, so he can do it.' Amar looked really miserable. 'He thinks I'll never be able to make the grade and maybe he's right. I should probably just give up!'

'That's just ridiculous! You've already passed the written exam and the radio/telephony test, so you're already two thirds of the way there. You *can't* give up now!'

'But I don't seem to be able to pass the flying test.'

'Well, you've only had one go at it—and lots of people fail the first time they sit the flying test. Then they do it again and pass, and I'm sure you will as well.'

'I'll have to convince the new instructor that I'm ready for the test, first,' said Amar. 'Have you met him yet?'

'Yes; he seems a bit of a prat to me, he's very uptight!'

'I'm doomed then,' said Amar miserably.

'No, you're not! Look, maybe I can help. If your father lets me check out on his Cessna 182, I could do the meat runs for him. You could come with me and share the flying—although you'll have to sit in the right-hand seat since I haven't got an instructor's licence. Then slowly you will regain your confidence and eventually taking your flying test will be a piece of cake.'

'You would do that?'

'Yes, it would benefit us both and your father. I'll be able to build up my hours, you'll have a chance to regain your confidence and flying skills, and your dad won't have to pay a thing to me because I haven't got my commercial licence yet!'

Amar suddenly looked a lot happier. 'Yes, that could work,' he said enthusiastically. 'I'll speak to my father tonight.'

'Good, now come into the clubhouse and I'll buy you a drink.'

Later that evening Charles was sitting in the office alone, reading an old diary about the club that someone had written not long after the war had ended. It was meticulously written and illustrated, and there were one of two newspaper cuttings stuck in about the airfield and the aeroplanes that had operated from Lanet at that time. He became so engrossed he didn't notice the passage of time, and only when he realised that everything had gone very quiet did he glance at his watch and see it was almost ten o'clock.

Locking up the office with the keys Howard had given him, he went out into the lounge. At first, he thought there was no one there, but then he suddenly saw Georgia curled up in one of the easy chairs reading a flying magazine. The cat was on her lap and neither of them noticed Charles.

'Haven't you got a home to go to?' Charles enquired when Georgia suddenly became aware of his presence.

'Not one that I want to return to at the moment,' she replied.

'Well, I'm off then, see you tomorrow,'

'Night.'

Charles made his way to the carpark thinking that Georgia had probably fallen out with her parents. Her old Land Rover was the only car in the park apart from his, and he noticed it was battered and scratched, while the canvas covering was frayed and didn't look particularly watertight. Charles wondered why she chose to drive around in such a scruffy old vehicle. It would have been better suited to a farmer, he thought.

Chapter 3

Dissention

When Charles arrived at the Flying Club the next morning at eight o'clock, he noticed immediately that the old Land Rover that belonged to Georgia was already in the carpark and one of the club's Cessna 150s was not in its place outside the clubhouse. He went at once to the log to confirm his suspicions as to who had taken the aeroplane. When he saw it was Georgia, he felt annoyed. He had told her he wanted to do a check-flight with her, but she had come in early and taken the aeroplane before he'd had a chance to check her out. According to the log, she had taken off shortly after seven that morning and was flying to Thomson's Falls.

'Do you know why Georgia has gone to Thomson's Falls?' Charles asked Sam after he had ordered a coffee and sat sipping it at the bar.

'Yes, she's gone to visit her uncle on his farm near Thomson's Falls,' said Sam helpfully.

'Is there an airstrip there?' Charles couldn't remember seeing one when he had overflown Thomson's Falls with Howard the previous day.

'I think you can land on the track where they do the horse racing in Thomson's Falls,' said Sam. 'But Miss Georgia has gone to her uncle's farm.'

'Does he have an airstrip on his farm, then?'

'No, I don't think so.'

'So where will she land?'

'I don't know. Perhaps he has a field that she can land on.'

'Do you know if she's ever flown to his farm before?'

'No; she told me this morning that this would be the first time.'

Charles felt angry and worried at the same time. Would Georgia realise that the Cessna 150 would be underpowered when it came to taking off from an altitude of over seven thousand feet above sea-lever? She may well manage to put the little aeroplane down on a field, but if it wasn't very long, she would most definitely have a problem taking off again! It would be just great if the girl managed to write-off one of the club's aeroplanes on the very first morning that he started working there, he mused angrily.

'Do you know when she'll be back?' he asked Sam.

'No sir. But she has booked the aeroplane for the whole morning, so I think she will be back by lunch time.'

Charles felt sure that Georgia had deliberately got to the club early before he started work so that she could cock a snook at his check-flight, and it really annoyed him.

'What time did she arrive here this morning?' he asked Sam.

Sam looked confused for a moment and then he said, 'Miss Georgia lives here, sir.'

Charles remembered Howard had told him that one of the rooms was rented out on a permanent basis, but he hadn't realised that it was Georgia who was in residence at the club and now that he did, he found it irritated him. From what she had said the previous evening she did have a home but didn't want to live there, so she must have decided to take advantage of the very cheap rooms at the club and moved in. He suspected that she must have fallen out with her family and that was entirely her own business—but he felt she shouldn't be allowed to use the club as a refuge.

Charles had students to teach in the other Cessna 150 that morning, so there was nothing he could do except get on with his job and hope that Georgia would get back without mishap. In between teaching secessions when he went up to the Gents rest-room he noticed that the door to Georgia's room was open.

Glancing in, he saw the cleaner was in there vacuuming the carpet. He noticed it looked like a Persian carpet and there were brightly coloured curtains up at the windows and a patchwork bedspread on the bed. There was also a dressing table and a desk in the room and a couple of chairs. It all looked very snug and comfortable.

'So, she's really made herself at home,' Charles muttered to himself, feeling irritated.

At twelve o'clock Georgia landed gently on the runway and taxied to the clubhouse where she manoeuvred the Cessna into its designated parking spot before shutting everything down.

'Switches off, petrol off, throttle closed, radio and rotating beacon off, gyro instruments caged and master off,' Georgia muttered. Then she got out of the aeroplane, tied it down, put on the pitot cover and straightened the propeller. When everything was to her liking she sauntered over to the clubhouse where she was met by Charles, who had a face like thunder.

'I thought we agreed that I would do a check-flight with you,' Charles said without preamble.

'Sure, we can do it any time you want,' said Georgia who seemed surprised to see Charles looking so annoyed.

'I wanted to do it before you were let loose on one of the club aeroplanes!'

'What do you mean—let loose on one of the club aeroplanes? I'm a qualified private pilot now; I don't even know why you're insisting on a check flight. I actually find it quite insulting since I've been passed by one of the strictest examiners in Nairobi.' Georgia said defensively as two spots of colour rose in her cheeks.

'I did explain to you that I was going to do a check flight with all those who had recently qualified,' said Charles. 'I thought you agreed and that we would do it before you flew on your own again.'

Georgia just shrugged. 'We can do it now if you insist,' she said sullenly. 'I've booked the 150 until one o'clock, so we have more than enough time if you're free.'

'Right, we will. But first there's another thing I need to talk to you about. I understand you've just flown to your uncle's farm near Thomson's Falls?'

Georgia nodded.

'Is there an airstrip on his farm?'

'Not exactly.'

'So where did you land?'

'There's a perfectly good field near his house that I landed on.'

'Georgia, as a newly qualified pilot, you can't just fly off to places and land on fields that you imagine will do for an airstrip—it's an absolute recipe for disaster!'

'I'm not stupid, Charles,' Georgia replied hotly, her cheeks now a flaming red. 'I didn't just fly to the farm, see a field and land in it. I drove to the farm last week and found what I decided was a suitable field on which to land. Then I had my uncle put the gyro mower over it, I checked it for holes and stones and decided in which direction the prevailing wind came from. Then when I went there today, I flew over field several times to check there was nothing untoward before landing on it. This is Africa and you don't always have a nice runway on which to land like you probably do in England!' She glared at Charles.

'Well, it's lucky nothing went wrong,' said Charles giving her a look that said he thought she had taken a huge risk. 'You have very little experience and although landing in a short space isn't impossible, taking off again could be—especially at that high altitude.'

'Oh, for goodness' sake!' Georgia felt very frustrated at his attitude and she was doing her best not to lose her temper. 'Come on then, are we going to do this check-flight now or what? You better give the aeroplane a good going over before we fly just to make sure I didn't damage it landing on that field,' she added caustically.

Charles felt quite disappointed that he couldn't fault Georgia when it came to her flying. The girl irritated him and he would have loved to be able to criticise her on some point, but she flew confidently with a light touch on the controls and performed every manoeuvre he requested with precision.

'You'll do,' Charles said grudgingly when they eventually landed. 'I would suggest though, that you wear more suitable footwear when you're flying. Some aeroplanes have heel brakes rather than the toe brakes that the Cessna has, and you wouldn't be able to operate them properly if you were wearing rubber flip-flops.' He was aware he was knit-picking and knew he deserved the withering look Georgia gave him.

'Fine, I'll remember that,' was all she said as she went to fill in the log.

During the afternoon, Hans came in and told Charles that he was going to check Georgia out on the Cessna 182 that belonged to Zail Singh.

'She's going to do his meat run for him when she's checked out,' Hans explained.

'His meat run?'

'Yes, he owns a number of butcheries dotted around the country and flies frozen meat to them from his depo in Nakuru. His son, Amar, was going to take over the delivering duties but he failed his flight test, so I think Zail has come to some agreement with Georgia.'

'Well, I hope she realises that she can't take payment until she gets a commercial licence!'

'Of course, she knows that. She just wants to build up her flying hours so she can sit her assistant flying instructors' licence, and it will be a good opportunity for her to do that. She'll also be able to gain valuable cross-country flying experience,' Hans's expression indicated that he thought it was a very good move on Georgia's part. 'I expect she'll eventually take over my job when I leave for Germany,' he added.

'Right.'

The idea of having Georgia as his assistant didn't fill Charles with joy, but in the short term, if she was busy flying Zail's aeroplane it would at least keep her out of his hair, so that was something for which to be thankful.

Charles was kept busy during the afternoon giving lessons to three new students. He didn't see anything of Georgia until the evening when he went to have a beer with Sean, who was his last student for the day. Georgia was sitting at the bar sipping a Coke through a straw while she talked with Hans and a handsome Sikh whom Charles correctly guessed was Zail. There were also a number of social club members who had come in for a drink and most of them sat chatting around the bar.

'I'm sorry my last landing was so disastrous,' Sean apologised to Charles when they had ordered their drinks. He was feeling frustrated at his lack of ability. 'I just don't seem to be able to get the hang of landing an aeroplane.'

Sean was a very likable farmer who came from Ol Kalou. He was in his mid-forties, a bit older than most of the students, but he was determined to learn to fly.

'It'll come Sean, but you must stop trying to look over the aeroplane's nose when you land. Look to the front on your left, then you can judge your height from the ground and know when it's the right time to round out.'

Just then the radio that was situated in the corner of the room crackled. This was usually an indication that someone approaching the airfield was going to announce their arrival, but instead a harsh staccato sound boomed out of the radio. 'Taka, taka, taka taka, got ya, ya dirty Kraut!'

'That's just the crop sprayers coming back,' Hans told Charles when he saw the astonishment on the other man's face. One of the Ag Cats is flown by Klaus Aust, a German pilot, and the other by Randall Freeman who comes from America. If, by chance, they both arrive back here at about the same time, Randy always pretends to shoot Klaus down because Klaus flew for the Luftwaffe during the war and Randy won't let him forget it!'

The gruff roar of the two approaching Grumman Ag Cats could now be heard and everyone rushed outside and looked up at the bi-planes looming out of the dusk. In the clubhouse they could still hear Randy's voice coming through the radio. 'Taka, taka, taka, taka!'

The first Ag Cat seemed to be heading straight for the clubhouse and the second one was right on his tail. Everyone instinctively ducked as they went over because they were so low and the noise of the engines was excruciatingly loud. Then Klaus pulled up sharply, and doing a 'crop-spraying turn' he spun on his wingtip and then dropped towards the airfield and landed firmly in the middle of the runway. Randy was right behind him and they taxied towards the clubhouse together.

Everyone laughed and then gravitated back to the bar, but Charles remained outside. This was the first 'tear-way cowboy flying' he had witnessed and he knew he had to say something to the two men who were now walking towards him. He noted that one of them was in his mid-forties and had a thick drooping moustache on his upper lip. His eyes, under his heavy black brows, were dark and piercing and there was an arrogance about his mouth and a suggestion of stubbornness in his jaw. The other man was much older, probably in his early sixties. His dark hair was now peppered with grey and everything about him indicated that he had been an officer in the Luftwaffe, from the immaculate Hitler-like moustache to his precise confident steps as he marched towards Charles. There could be no doubt that he was a man who had served in the military forces.

'Good evening,' Charles said as they approached. 'I'm Charles Lenten, the new chief flying instructor.'

'Oh yes, we heard there was to be a new man from England, no less,' the American drawled, holding out his hand. 'I'm Randall Freeman—Randy by name and randy by nature,' he let out a loud guffaw. 'And this old bastard is Klaus Aust,' he added.

'Guten Abend,' said Klaus, clicking his heels. He then made as to go into the club.

'Wait a minute,' said Charles. 'I just want to have a word with the two of you.'

'Never try and get between a Kraut and his beer!' said Randy laughing as Klaus ignored Charles and continued to walk into the clubhouse. 'Come on, Charlie, I'll buy you a drink and you can let us know what you have on your mind while we're drinking.'

Charles though it would be much more diplomatic to chastise these two men in private, but it didn't seem he had any say in the matter because Randy followed Klaus to the bar.

'Good evening, all,' said Randy expansively when he walked in. 'Sam, a beer for Mr Aust, a Bourbon for me and whatever Charlie boy would like to order.'

'Yes sir.' Sam hastened to get the drinks.

'Ah—there you are me darlin' I hoped I'd find you here,' said Randy when he spied Georgia sipping her Coke. 'I'm still waiting for you to accept my offer to come and have a flight in the Ag Cat with me!'

'As I've mentioned before, Randy, I can't accept your kind offer because there's only one seat in the Ag Cat,' said Georgia with a giggle.

'That isn't a problem,' Randy assured her. 'You can sit on my knee; a little thing like you will easily be able to squeeze into the cockpit with me!' He wiggled his bottom on the barstool as he thought, with pleasure, of her sitting on his knee.

'No way Randy—it's not going to happen. Dream on!' Georgia giggled again.

Randy shrugged and turned to Charles, 'Now, Charlie me boy, what's the problem?' he took a huge swallow of his drink, downing at least half of it.

'Basically, I wasn't very impressed at the way you flew in this evening,' said Charles. 'There's an accepted procedure for joining the circuit that should be adhered to when flying into any airfield, and you certainly didn't follow the guidelines this evening when you landed here.' Charles tried to look severe.

'I didn't?' said Randy looking incredulous.

'You know you didn't,' said Charles. 'And furthermore, you both flew very low over the clubhouse which was a very dangerous manoeuvre, and you were also using the radio inappropriately. I don't know what games you and Klaus like to play, but I can't have you endangering people here in the club.'

'My God, this chap *is* in a bad mood,' said Randy turning to all those who were listening with interest to the conversation. 'It was you, Georgia, wasn't it?' he said, twisting to face her. '*You* put him in a bad mood! I've never met a woman who could put a man in a bad mood as quickly as Georgia can!' He went on, 'She has only one word in her vocabulary and that's no! Isn't that enough to put any man in a bad mood?' He gulped down the rest of his drink. 'Sam, another Bourbon please,' he banged his empty glass onto the bar.

Georgia was giggling again and some of the others were sniggering as well, but Charles couldn't let it go at that.

'Look, I don't want upset you or Klaus, but I must insist on better flying practices around here now that I'm in charge.'

'Tell *him* then,' said Randy, pointing his chin towards Klaus.

Klaus had been sitting quietly at the bar drinking his beer and didn't seem to be taking any notice of what Charles was saying, but now he raised up an almost empty mug and said, 'Zum wohl!'

Then he took the last swallow, got up and marched smartly out of the clubhouse.

'F-ing Kraut,' said Randy affectionately. 'When he doesn't like what you're saying to him he pretends he can't understand a word of English! Sam—another Bourbon!'

Sam brought the drink and Randy swallowed it down in two gulps. 'Right folks, I'm off to find a woman who doesn't say no all the time,' he gave Georgia a ferocious look and she burst into giggles again. Then Randy got up, saluted everyone in general, and walked off.

'Well, that went well,' Charles murmured as he watched the American disappear out of the door.

'Don't take it personally,' said Hans,' taking pity on Charles. 'Those two are a law unto themselves. If you want to get through to them, you'll have to complain to their boss, Scott Egerton. He owns Egerton Agric and he'll tell them to pull their socks up or he'll fire them!'

When Charles got home that evening, he did wonder if he had bitten off more than he could chew. Teaching people to fly wasn't going to be a problem, he enjoyed doing that and people seemed to respond well to his teaching techniques. The new students with whom he'd flown had all seemed promising, and he'd met many nice people who frequented the club. But obviously there were some people who needed to be pulled into line and he wondered if he was capable of doing that. If this evening was anything to go by, he wasn't!

Then there was Georgia—why did she irritate him so much? She seemed to think the brash American was really funny and for some reason Charles found that very annoying as well. Oh well, he thought eventually, I'll just have to see how it goes.

Chapter 4

Adapting and moving forward

Georgia relaxed as she let Amar fly his father's Cessna 182 from the right-hand seat. She had executed the take off and marvelled again at the increased power that the Cessna 182 had over the Cessna 150. Very quickly they had reached their cruising height and once she had levelled off, she had passed control of the aeroplane to Amar. He had taken the controls gingerly, but now, after a few minutes, he had relaxed as all the training he had been given flowed effortlessly from his brain and he flew the 182 with confidence.

They were on their way to Kisumu and Georgia couldn't help feeling grateful for living in a country that had such wonderful flying conditions for the majority of the time. The little aeroplane was buffeted gently as they flew through updrafts and downdrafts caused by air heated at ground level rising up in bubbles and causing mild turbulence, but the visibility was perfect in every direction. The whole of Kenya seemed to be rolled out below them, brown and yellow countryside interspersed by patches of brilliant green and crisscrossed by paths or roads. The vast landscape stretched endlessly toward the bluey/grey horizon.

Georgia had agreed with Zail that she would fly with Amar on Mondays, Wednesdays and Fridays and they would deliver meat to his butcheries that were situated in various places around

Kenya. So long as she was sitting in the left-hand seat, she could log the hours in her log-book, but she would share the actual flying with Amar so that he could regain his confidence. She knew that he would be perfectly competent when he wasn't under any pressure, but she made sure he understood that she would take control if anything untoward occurred.

Before they left from Lanet, Zail would take the back seats out of the aeroplane to make more room for the meat. It was always frozen and packed in cardboard boxes for transportation. Both Georgia and Amar would be present when the aeroplane was being loaded so that they could made a loading graph and be sure everything was secured properly before taking off. When they landed at their destination, they would be met by one of Zail's butchery vehicles that would take delivery of their share of the meat, and then they would fly on to the next place.

Georgia liked the young Sikh. Amar had a slight build and he was always dressed immaculately. His long black lashes interlaced over his dark flashing eyes and he had neat tidy features with a mouth that would often break into a grin. Georgia thought he radiated a wholesomeness that she hadn't found in European males of his age, and she was impressed that he was always so spotless and smelled deliciously of aftershave.

'How long has your family been in Kenya?' Georgia asked Amar as they flew over the sunlit open spaces of Kenya.

'For a very long time,' Amar told her. 'My great-grandfather and his brother came here in the last century and they worked on the Uganda/Kenya railway in 1898. We have an old diary at home written by my great-grandfather that details the events that happened at Tsavo when the lions kept attacking the workers.'

'Gosh, that must be interesting! What a marvellous piece of history to have.'

'Yes, but it was a terrible time for all the workers. More recently, it has been said that the man-eating lions that preyed on the workers developed a liking for human flesh because Tsavo had been used as a dumping ground for corpses over the years. But at the time no one knew that and they couldn't understand why the lions would want to hunt man when there was an abundance of game in the area, which would normally be their natural diet.

'My grand-father wrote in his diary that every evening they would be exhausted from the day's work, but when they retired for the night, they were terrified of being attacked. They would lie in trepidation, dreading the pandemonium that would ensue if the lions struck. He said it always seemed to him that just as he had managed to fall into an uneasy sleep, the shrill screaming of one of his colleagues would jerk him awake and in the morning, they'd find the remains of the poor man's shredded body. It must have been horrible!' Amar shuddered. 'Nothing they did, from building massive fires to surrounding their encampments with fences of thorns, kept the lions from attacking them. Eventually, the workers started to think that the lions were demons in the form of lions and they named them "The Ghost" and "The Darkness". Many of the workers felt that these demons would not cease preying on them until every last man had been killed, and they deserted and fled for their lives. It was then that the work on the railway all but came to a halt.'

'It must have been absolutely terrifying,' said Georgia with feeling. 'But the lions were killed in the end, weren't they?'

'Yes, eventually an army lieutenant called John Patterson shot them, but hunting them wasn't easy. To start with, he wounded the first lion when he tracked it and tried to kill it. The lion then turned and stalked him even as he continued to hunt it! In the end it took several shots for him to kill it! And the second lion wasn't easy to kill either; Patterson shot it five times and it still tried to charge him. It took another three shots to finish off the beast!'

'Goodness! It sounds as though John Patterson wasn't a great shot! But how many people did the lions kill before he did eventually shoot them?'

'Well, Patterson claimed that 135 workers were killed in that nine-month period, but the figures have been disputed and some say it was only about 35.'

'Well, I'm glad your grand-father and his brother weren't killed!'

'Yes, otherwise I wouldn't be here today! But it wasn't only the lions that caused death. Many of my grandfather's contemporaries died of malaria, dysentery and other tropical diseases. Working on that railway was pretty brutal!'

'Gosh yes,' agreed Georgia. 'We tend to forget the adversities of those who worked so hard to get a railway in place when we jump on a train and go off to the coast or somewhere else!'

'How about your family, Georgia, have they been in Kenya for long?' Amar wanted to know.

'No, nothing like as long as yours; my father and mother moved here after the war. Dad worked as a spy in Germany during the war and after it ended, he felt he had made dangerous enemies who could very possibly put his life in danger, so he decided to get out of Britain and Europe and go farming in Kenya. He came from farming stock you see; his father had a farm in Devon and Dad had worked on the farm before the war started. Mum followed him out to Kenya because they were engaged, so they got married in Mombasa when she arrived off the boat and nine months later, I was born!'

'What did your father do that caused him to have enemies after the war had ended?' Amar asked curiously.

'I don't know. I do know he was parachuted into various places in Europe at night and he had to infiltrate the Nazi party, but everything was hush, hush. Dad spoke German fluently so that's probably why he was selected to be a spy, but he also had Jewish blood in his veins, so he knew the penalty he would face if he was ever found out. After the war ended, he didn't tell anyone about his experiences; he didn't even tell my mother what had happened because he wanted to forget all the awful things he'd seen.'

They were now approaching Kisumu so Georgia took control of the aeroplane.

To his relief, Charles had not seen either Randy or Klaus for a couple of days. He had rung up their boss, Scott Egerton, and told him he couldn't have his two pilots flying like madmen over the airfield and explained that when he'd tried to talk to them, they had basically ignored him. Scott had seemed surprised by his call at first and then amused. But he had assured Charles that he would have a word with his two pilots.

'Where have the two crop-sprayers got to?' Charles asked Sam. Already he'd learned that Sam was the man if you wanted to know anything. The barman would listen into all the conversations as he served behind the bar and knew just about everything that was going on.

'They've got a big acreage to spray at Kitale, so they are going to be staying up there for a while until they finish it,' Sam told him.

Charles wondered how they were going to react to him when they returned. He really didn't want to make any enemies, but he couldn't have people blatantly flying like madmen around the airfield, putting peoples' lives at risk. He hoped that they, and the people who flew from Lanet, would respect him for trying to improve the safety of the airfield. He hadn't come across anyone else flying with such reckless abandon so far, and the steady stream of students that were coming to learn to fly all seemed level headed and willing to stick to the accepted procedures.

Feeling something rubbing his legs, Charles looked down and saw the cat was looking for attention.

'Hello,' he said, stroking the cat. 'What's your name?'

'His name is Beano and he belongs to Georgia,' Sam informed him.

'Georgia brought a cat to come and live here with her?' Charles was surprised.

'Oh yes, sir. It's a very good thing because we had a problem with mice and rats before, but Beano has killed them all!'

Charles was going to ask Sam why Georgia was living at the club when she had a home elsewhere, but the cook called to Sam and he disappeared into the kitchen. Then Charles's next student appeared, so the moment was lost.

'How're you getting on?' It was Friday evening and Howard and Mary had come to have a drink and bite to eat at the club.

'I'm getting on well, thank you. I'm beginning to find my feet and getting to know everyone, and also I'm becoming familiar with the area as well. We've had a number of students sign up for flying lessons and those that I'm teaching seem to be progressing okay. It's actually a pleasure flying here, because the weather seems to be good all the time.'

'Well, not all the time,' said Howard. 'It can catch you out sometimes, and you have to be aware of the low cloud that often comes right down onto the top of the escarpment when you're trying to fly into Nairobi.'

'Is your house-servant working out all right?' Mary asked.

'Yes, Emmanuel is always there, always smiling, and he keeps my house spotless, my clothes clean and ironed, and my car washed. He also says he'll cut the lawn when I get a lawnmower.'

'Does he cook?'

'Oh yes, he can do simple things. He cooks me breakfast, but I tend to have all my other meals here. I don't know what I'd do without him now!'

'Yes, it's very easy to fall into colonial ways,' said Howard with a laugh. 'Now, I have some good news. Someone has made a generous donation to the club and so I'd like to do up the club house, especially the bedrooms, and also get the garden started. Then once we have this place in shipshape, I think we should have a fly-in.'

'A fly-in?'

'Yes, I thought we could organise some events and invite all the members from the different flying clubs that are dotted around the country—and, indeed, anyone who owns an aeroplane, to fly in and enjoy the weekend with us. They could arrive on Friday evening or Saturday morning, and we could put on some competitions during Saturday, you know, bomb dropping, forced landing competitions, things like that. Everyone likes to participate in a competition! Then on the Saturday evening, we could have a bit of a shindig. Everybody in the area would be invited for that and I bet it would be well attended and we'd make a lot of money! On Sunday we could put on some displays—perhaps the crop-sprayers could be persuaded to do something and we could invite the skydivers to come and perform as well. I might even be able to convince Dave Hill to fly in from Nairobi in his Chipmunk and do some aerobatics, because everyone loves a good aerobatic display.'

'Yes, that sounds like a wonderful idea,' said Charles. 'Who did you say owns that old Dragon Rapide that's parked on the apron, Howard? Maybe we could get him to come and give joy rides on that weekend as well, or if he gives me permission, I could fly it as

I've flown one many times before.'

'Excellent idea,' said Howard looking pleased. 'The Rapide belongs to Mark Fleming who owns the electric equipment shop in Nakuru. I'll get onto him next week.'

'We could also do taster secessions for those thinking of doing their PPLs,' said Charles. 'If we did them on the Sunday when hopefully a lot of people come to watch the displays, I've sure we could hook a few new students!'

Charles and Howard bounced ideas off each other for a while and then Charles said, 'Where're all the people who fly in going to stay? We've only got three rooms here, one of which is occupied. It's a pity that you've agreed to rent out that room on a long-term basis, Howard, because if we're going to be putting on a number of events it would be useful to have it free.'

'Yes, well, we're not going to put Georgia out, are we? She's a good girl—had a bit of a tough time lately—so she stays. But as to the problem where the other people can stay, well, we'll have to lay on transport to Nakuru and they can book into the hotels there. Also, we'll ask club members to offer up their spare rooms and invite people to stay. People around here are very accommodating and I'm sure we'll get everyone a bed for the night.'

Howard and Charles continued to discuss the proposed fly-in for a while as they sipped their drinks and then Howard said, 'Now, I need to speak to you about young Amar Singh. Has he signed up for any flying lessons with you yet?'

'No. I've seen him going off in his father's 182 with Georgia, but he hasn't spoken to me yet.'

'Well, I wonder if you could make the time to have a word with him, old boy. I expect he's still feeling very embarrassed about what happened during his flying test, that's most probably the reason why he hasn't approached you as yet. But I know Zail wants the lad to get his licence and I'm hoping you will be one who gets him through.'

'Okay,' said Charles slowly, wondering why Howard was so keen to push this risky student forward.

'It was Zail who gave the generous donation to the club, you see,' Howard explained. 'Apparently, he offered money to Georgia when she said she would fly his meat to his various butcheries around the country—and at the same time take Amar along so that he could regain his confidence. She told him she couldn't accept any money because she didn't have her commercial or instructor's licence yet, but if he liked, he could give a donation to the club. So, I suppose we should be thanking both Zail and Georgia! But I think we could show our appreciation to Zail by encouraging Amar to get his licence.'

Charles nodded his head uncertainly.

'Anyway,' said Howard, changing the subject, 'I've organised a gang of labourers to come and start work on the garden on Tuesday morning, so you'll have to put a bit of time aside to organise them. I've already drawn up a plan of the prospective garden, but you're welcome to make any suggestions or changes.'

Howard pulled the plan of the garden out of his pocket and handed it to Charles. It was quite straightforward. He had marked off an area for a lawn around the clubhouse and pencilled in where the flower beds should be. There was also to be a small fence around the perimeter of the garden.

'I thought a fence would nicely separate the clubhouse premises from the apron,' said Howard. 'At the moment it looks as though the clubhouse was accidently built in the middle of the area designated for the parking of the aeroplanes!'

'Yes, having a demarcation around the clubhouse premises will improve things markedly,' agreed Charles. 'What about the bedrooms, have you thought what you're going to do to improve them?'

'No, I'm going to leave that to Mary. She says she's going to enlist the help of Georgia, who has managed to make the room she rents very presentable. I've also asked various members of the club to lookout for any pictures or flying memorabilia that would be appropriate to hang in the club house. It's going to be much improved once we've finished with it! Now, I need to speak to Sam, but don't forget to have a word with young Amar, will you?'

Charles felt a bit uneasy about encouraging Amar to continue with his flying lessons just because Zail had given a generous monetary donation to the club. It all seemed too much like bribery to him and he really wanted no part in it. Also, he wasn't prepared to put forward for a flying test anyone whom he wasn't one hundred percent sure would pass, and the young Sikh seemed to him to be a bit of a loose cannon. However, he couldn't disregard everything Howard had said to him, so on the Monday morning when he arrived at the flying club and saw Amar and Georgia having a coffee before they took off for Nanyuki, he went to have a word with the young man.

'Uh-oh, danger at one o'clock,' muttered Georgia when she saw Charles approaching. 'He's probably coming to give us hell for not wearing the correct footwear for flying!'

But Charles was smiling when he walked up to them and after a few pleasantries he enquired politely whether Amar would like to continue with his flying lessons.

'I do want to continue, of course,' said Amar, sounding rather flustered.

'Well, you shouldn't leave it too long,' advised Charles. 'You need to get back into the saddle straight away when you fall off a horse, and it's the same with flying.'

'I know, you're right; but I have got back onto the horse in a manner of speaking, because Georgia lets me share the flying when we deliver the meat.'

'I hope you're not trying to give Amar instruction?' Charles asked Georgia, frowning. 'You're not qualified to do that and if anything happens, you, as captain of the aeroplane, will be held responsible.'

'Of course, I'm aware of that,' Georgia sounded exasperated. 'I do know the rules, believe it or not! And I don't try and instruct Amar, I just give him advice and let him fly some of the time so that he can build up his confidence. If, at any time, things get tricky, he knows he must hand over control to me.'

'That's right,' said Amar. 'Georgia has been very kind and already I'm feeling a lot more confident.'

'Good,' said Charles giving Georgia a disapproving glance. 'So perhaps now would be a good time to book in for some more lessons?' He herded the reluctant Sikh over to the booking sheets and Georgia was left fuming by herself while Charles encouraged Amar to sign up for several lessons in the coming week.

'Actually, Charles seems okay,' Amar said to Georgia once they had taken off and were heading for Nanyuki. 'He doesn't seem to despise me for landing in a wheat field during my test, he just seems to want to help me achieve my dreams and get a PPL.'

'I should hope so,' said Georgia. 'That's what all good instructors should want to do. But personally, Amar, I think the man's a bit of a prat! He seems to think he's so superior to us just because he comes from England!'

❖

The next day when Charles arrived for work in the morning, he found the materials for the garden fence had arrived, and the gang of labourers that Howard had laid on was waiting for him to give them instructions. He had just greeted them when Georgia appeared.

'Yes Georgia, can I help you?' Charles asked rather shortly.

'No, I thought I might be able to help you, though,' replied the girl.

'Thank you, but I'm quite capable or organising this lot; I don't really think I need any help.'

'Fine, but I hope your Swahili is good, because not one of these chaps understands English,' Georgia replied a trifle smugly. 'Howard suggested to me that I could act as interpreter for you—if you needed me to.'

Charles felt annoyed. He really didn't like Georgia and didn't want to accept her help. He was sure he could have got Sam to be the interpreter, if necessary, but it would seem churlish to refuse her help now, so he nodded. 'Okay, thanks.'

Howard had left Charles the plan so he handed it over to Georgia and asked her to explain to the workers what they would have to do. He couldn't understand what she said, but he was aware that she was asking them to do the job rather than telling them. She also seemed to be asking their opinion on certain matters and he could see her diplomatic approach was engaging them; they laughed a lot and seemed keen to help and get the job done. They soon had the garden area marked out and started digging the flower beds.

Charles's first student arrived, so he had to leave the gang to their work and go and give a lesson. When he got back things were progressing well, but there was no sign of Georgia or her Land Rover. I suppose she got bored and left when she could no longer lord it over me, Charles thought unkindly. But a few minutes later she drove back into the carpark and called one of the labourers to help her unload some sacks.

'I've just been collecting some kraal manure from Godfrey's farm,' she told Charles.

'Kraal manure?'

'Yes, it's basically cow dung mixed with soil and is a very good fertilizer. It will help the shrubs and flowers we plant to grow, once we've got them in the ground. Godfrey says he has some turf we can have as well, so when we're ready for it in a day or two I'll go and get it—that is unless you want to collect it?' Georgia was very aware that Charles had reservations about her helping in this project.

'Er, no,' said Charles, thinking that the last thing he wanted to put in his Ford was a load of turf. 'If you could collect that as well it would be very helpful.'

'Good. I'll also collect the plants and shrubs if you like. Mary told me she has a friend who has offered to donate loads of plants and things, but we need to go and dig them out and collect them ourselves.'

The garden around the club house took shape very quickly due to the hard work of the labourers and Georgia's enthusiastic help and ideas. Very soon the fence was erected, the beds were planted up and the turf was laid. Charles had to admit to himself that he had provided very little input into the project in the end, but he didn't disclose this to Howard when he came to inspect the work at the end of the week.

'My goodness, what a difference this is making already,' said Howard as he looked at the new garden. 'When the turf settles and the shrubs and plants start to grow properly it's going to look amazing!'

Charles had also noticed that Mary and Georgia had started on the bedrooms, and curtains, carpets and other soft furnishing had appeared and been incorporated in the rooms. Meanwhile, people had been donating pictures and William Murray had brought a magnificent wooden propeller that was now hanging above the fireplace.

'Well, it's all beginning to look splendid,' said Howard with satisfaction. 'What we'll do now is settle on a weekend for our fly-in; we'll give it another month or six weeks so people have plenty of notice, and that will give the garden time to settle and grow properly as well.

Chapter 5

The Vegetable Run and Night Flying

As the weeks went past, Charles settled into his job as chief fly-ing instructor of the Lanet Flying Club. Despite the fact that he made it quite clear that he would not tolerate any dangerous flying in the vicinity of Lanet, he soon became a respected and popular member of the club. Randy and Klaus did not resent him for complaining to their boss about their flying practices, and the others with whom he wasn't happy slowly fell into line after he had reprimanded them.

Charles had become accustomed to Georgia buzzing around the club, always busy and helpful, but by unspoken mutual consent they tended to avoid each other most of the time. He knew she was keen to build up her hours and that was why she made herself available to fly anything or anyone anywhere they wished to go. He could understand why she needed to gain experience, but sometimes he felt irrationally irritated at the way she scavenged for free flying hours all the time. However, other people didn't seem to mind and it was always Georgia to whom they turned when they needed someone to ferry something somewhere by air.

'Georgia, I wonder if you would consider doing the supplies run up to my lodge at Elyie Springs on Lake Rudolph?' Howard asked her one day. 'I've been doing it in my Cherokee, but I just don't have the time anymore. I'd pay for the hire of the club's Cessna 182 and you could fly the groceries to the lodge in that aeroplane every couple of weeks or so, if you'd like to.'

Of course, Georgia was willing to do this, especially as she could fit it in with the other flying she did for Zail.

Early on the morning of her first run to Elyie Springs, she helped Howard to remove all the groceries he had bought for the lodge from his car and pack them in the Cessna 182. William Murray had removed all the seats as requested, leaving only the pilot's seat so that they could maximise the space, and Georgia made sure everything was secure and the weight came within the loading graph.

'Now listen,' said Howard when they had finished loading the 182. 'If you fly directly to Eliye Springs from Lanet, you'll have to go over the Loriu Range and some very rough and inhospitable country. If you were to have an engine failure over that sort of wilderness you wouldn't have a chance of getting the aeroplane down in one piece and surviving. So, what I do, and what most of the more experienced pilots do, is fly a slight dogleg and go up the Kerio Valley so if anything were to happen, we'd have a better chance of a forced landing with a good outcome.'

Georgia nodded, but she had already plotted her course in a straight line from Lanet to Eliye Springs and didn't really think it was necessary to change it. In her opinion, a forced landing was very unlikely and if it did occur, she would deal with it when it happened. Life was too short to be worried about engine failures, she decided!

Lake Rudolph, also known as the Jade Sea because of the remarkable, almost incandescent colour of its waters, was a massive inland sea. At about 4,349 square miles it was the largest desert and alkaline lake in the world. Fed by the rivers Omo, Turkwel and Kerio it was home to the Nile crocodile and many large turtles, and it lay within the sweltering brown and grey lava deserts of northern Kenya.

The flight to Lake Rodolph was long and boring. Georgia missed the company of Amar, because they chatted together when they flew Zail's meat around the country and it helped to make the time pass. An open box of tomatoes had been laid on top of the other groceries to prevent them from being squashed and Georgia helped herself to a tomato and ate it slowly, relishing the tangy sweetness of the fruit. If I did have a forced landing in a remote area, I'd be able to live like a king until I was rescued, Georgia thought as she glanced at all the stuff stacked in the aeroplane. Hopefully though, if I do have an engine failure it will be on the way to Elyie and not on the way home, because all I would have on my return journey are the emergency rations!

When Georgia flew over the Loriu Range she had to concede that the terrain was so rough and hilly it would be impossible to find a place to do a forced landing if the engine failed. Everywhere was rocky and steep with vales and valleys and precipitous drops. Shrugging her shoulders, Georgia selected another tomato and looked ahead towards Lake Rudolph.

Eventually, the lake came into view looking blue and inviting. When Georgia reached Elyie Springs she buzzed over the lodge to let them know that she had arrived with their provisions and as she circled around, she saw their Land Rover setting out on the road to the airstrip. By the time she had landed the Land Rover had arrived and her load was immediately transferred to the vehicle.

'Are you going to come and have some lunch at the lodge?' The African driver of the Land Rover enquired. 'The manager, Mr Bailey, told me to invite you to come and eat. Since Mr Young rang him to say you were going to take over delivering the groceries, Mr Bailey has been looking forward to meeting you.'

Georgia hesitated; she didn't want to be rude and she knew from speaking to others that the lodge was an attractive oasis in the arid countryside situated on the banks of the lake, and a lovely place to visit. But she wasn't particularly hungry and didn't really feel like socialising and making polite conversation with a stranger.

'Please say thank you to Mr Bailey,' she said after a moment. 'But I've got to get back to Lanet for an appointment this afternoon; another time maybe?'

'Okay, well, thanks for bringing the provisions. I need to get them back to the Lodge quickly before they get too hot, but if you go to the fuel shed, John will be there to help you refuel.' With that he jumped into the Land Rover and drove away into the heat haze.

Georgia saw through the wavering heat waves that there was a shack towards the end of the runway in which she assumed she would find John and the fuel. Wiping the sweat off her forehead, she climbed back into the cockpit to taxi to the shed. The heat was searing and already everything in the cockpit was red hot. What a climate to live in, Georgia thought.

John appeared from behind the shack as she drew up. He was a small, muscular African clad only in a pair of grubby shorts, and after greeting her he proceeded to pull a drum of fuel out of the shed. Once he had it in position, he produced a hand pump with which he could pump the fuel up into the wing tanks of the 182. Georgia climbed up the steps John had provided and held the nozzle in place while John did the pumping. She felt she was being flayed by the sun, but decided she had a better deal than John, who had runnels of sweat running down his face and torso as he vigorously pumped the fuel into the wing tanks.

'Do you have to stay here all day in case someone flies in and needs fuel?' Georgia enquired as she produced the carnet that ensured payment for the fuel.

'Yes, all day,' said John sighing. 'My home is too far away so I have to be here. Sometimes I wait all day and no one flies in, but there is no way to tell if anyone is coming or not, so I stay here.' He indicated a plastic chair that was set up in the shade cast by the shed. It must be a very hot and boring job, Georgia reflected as she did the pre-flight checks.

'Memsahib, next time you come maybe you bring me something?' John suggested as he stood watching her.

'What sort of thing?'

'Coca Cola? Sweets?' John looked hopeful.

Georgia had brought a cold Coke, a sandwich and a Mars bar in a cooler-bag for her lunch, but now she thought that John deserved them more than her. She pulled them out and handed them to the delighted man. His pleasure and happiness at that small gesture was more than enough to make up for the loss of her lunch. The lake had looked lovely as she flew in, but here, a couple of miles inland, the dry arid countryside that danced in the heatwaves felt almost hostile in the unrelenting rays of the sun. She was glad she didn't have to sit in the heat waiting for someone to fly in; it would be an awful job! She felt relieved when she eventually took off and cooler air started to filter through the vents and lower the temperature in the cockpit.

After arriving back at Lanet without mishap, Georgia headed straight for the bar. 'Can I have the coldest Coke you've got please, Sam, I'm absolutely parched!' She felt dehydrated and not at all hungry, but a drink was a must!

She was sitting on the floor sipping her Coke through a straw and making a fuss of Beano when Charles came in and she could see he was looking for her. She quickly scrambled to her feet wondering what she had done this time to upset him, but then she noticed he wasn't looking cross.

'Hello, you look hot and tired,' said Charles. 'Did you have a good trip to Lake Rudolph?'

'Yes, no problems.'

'Good. I've heard a lot about the place and hope to go up there soon, maybe for a weekend.'

'Well, make sure you pack you swimming trunks because the only place that you can keep cool is in the lake!'

'In the lake? But what about crocodiles?'

'Well, there're Nile crocodiles in the lake of course, but they don't seem to bother anyone too much. I saw people swimming in the lake when I flew over the lodge, and there were a couple of mini-sails out on the water as well.'

'Well, I'm not so sure I'd like to risk it!'

'Oh Charles, life's too short to be worried about what might happen all the time! If you went to Lake Rudolph and stayed for more than a couple of hours and you didn't go in the lake, you'd probably die of heat stroke!'

'Right. Anyway, I saw Hans a short while ago and he suggested that it would be a good night tonight to do some night flying as it's going to be clear with a full moon. Is that something you'd be interested in doing?'

'Yes,' said Georgia enthusiastically. 'I do want to get my night-rating.'

'Good. The course is five hours of flying training and will highlight the additional pre-flight considerations and differences involved in operating an aeroplane at night, and you'll learn all the specific handling techniques required. Of the five hours, at least three will be with instruction and you'll have to do a one-hour cross-country navigation and five solo take-offs and five full-stop landings.'

'Okay, that's great. No-one has done any night flying from Lanet for simply ages, so I'll go and find the Hurricane Lamps that are used for the flare-path and check the wicks and fill them up with paraffin. I'll put them in the back of my Land Rover ready to be taken out later.'

Charles watched as Georgia placed her empty Coke bottle on the bar and then skipped into the kitchen to go and locate the lamps. He couldn't help thinking she looked exactly like a child who had been promised an unexpected treat!

Later that evening when all the lamps had been put in position, Hans took Clive Player, who also wanted to add a night rating to his PPL, up in one of the Cessna 150s and Charles and Georgia were in the other one. Four other people who also wanted to do some night flying stood at the end of the airstrip, and a small group of the club members had also gathered there to watch, many of them clutching drinks in their hands as they sat on the sweet-smelling grass in the brilliant moonlight.

'The moonlight is so bright we hardly need the flare path,' said Georgia as they lined up for take-off.

'Yes, but it's probably a good night to start with. Later, we'll pick a really dark night so you can gain additional experience.'

Georgia had to reluctantly admit to herself that Charles was professional and skilled when it came to giving instruction. She had always felt he was a bit of a prat who was overcautious and inclined to see danger lurking in every corner, but on this evening his instruction was concise and clear as he expertly directed her in the art of night flying.

They flew around the area to start with so that she could familiarise herself with the night time landmarks. There was a little cluster of lights around Lanet and further on the brighter lights of Nakuru could be seen. Georgia could visualise the Nairobi/Nakuru road when she saw the odd car travelling along it, their headlights beaming ahead of them, and Lake Nakuru was shining in the brilliant moonlight.

When they joined the circuit and were coming in to land, Charles said, 'I don't want you to use your landing lights to start with. I want you to learn how to read the perspective of the flare path and understand from that when you should flare out for the landing.'

After Georgia had done a few circuits and bumps she had got the hang of landing at night with the aid of the flare path giving her direction and perspective, and Charles was pleased with her progress.

'Tonight, we have a number of people on the threshold of the runway who will be keeping a lookout for any animals—stray dogs or cats or any other animal that might be wandering around, and they'll chase them away,' Charles said. 'But if there was no one there it would be important to fly over the runway with your landing lights on before landing to check it's clear.'

Georgia wished her session could have been longer as she had really enjoyed flying at night, but there were other students waiting, so reluctantly she vacated the aeroplane and went to join the crowd at the end of the runway to allow the next person to have a turn.

'Did you enjoy your first night session?' Amar asked Georgia as she went to sit by him on the grass.

'Yes, it's sort of really different at night. Everything seems more intense somehow, but it's not difficult—not on a beautiful night like this. It's funny, when you're quite high you can actually see the outline of the runway in the moonlight. But as soon as you get lower down it disappears into gloomy darkness and you really need the flare path to give you the direction of the runway.'

'How was it being instructed by Charles?'

'Well, you should know—you've had several lessons with him, haven't you?'

'Yes, I have, but because I know you have an aversion for the man, I've never liked to say what a good instructor he is!'

'All right, I have to agree he's an okay instructor,' said Georgia grudgingly.

'Would you like a drink?' Amar inquired. 'I'm going to ask everyone if they want something and I'll go and bring it from the bar.'

'That's kind of you, Amar; I'll come with you to help you carry it all.'

When they got back and everyone had their drinks, Georgia lay on her back and stared at the night sky. It was so beautiful with the brilliant moon and millions of sparkling stars. It gave her a feeling of peace, and the burble of voices and laughter near her seemed to recede as sleep almost overcame her. She was brought back to full consciousness by the return of the two aeroplanes and then everyone seemed to drift back to the clubhouse.

'Where's Georgia?' Charles asked after he had debriefed the pilots who had partaken in the night flying exercise. Georgia had not been among them.

'I saw her heading for the airstrip in her Land Rover,' said Clive. 'I think she was going to bring in the lamps we were using for the flare path.'

'So why is she doing it alone?' asked Charles. 'All of you took part in the night flying exercises, so surely you should be helping her to bring in the lamps!'

The little group looked at each other guiltily. None of them had even thought to give her a hand, they had all been so keen to have a beer in the clubhouse and talk about their experience of flying at night.

Georgia was surprised when Charles emerged out of the dark when she parked her Land Rover and had started to take the lamps back to the store room.

'Thanks for bringing in the lamps, Georgia,' he said. 'I'll give you a hand to put them away.'

'Thank you,' Georgia said when they had stored the lamps safely in a cupboard. 'I'm going for a shower now and then to bed. I feel completely knackered!'

Chapter 6

Cordelia and Fleur

When Charles got home that night, he lay thinking about Georgia before he fell asleep. If he was honest with himself, he knew they had got off to a bad start partly because she had reminded him of someone from his past whom he had disliked. But now that he knew her better he knew that she was nothing like Fleur Digby. Georgia was a kind and helpful person who didn't mind working hard for what she wanted to achieve. Charles had no idea why she had fallen out with her family—or even if she had, in fact, fallen out with her family—he had only assumed that. But since moving into the club she had donated a huge amount of her time and energy to improve things there, to the extent that people were now taking her for granted. No one would have ever taken Fleur for granted—or Cordelia for that matter! His mind drifted back into the past to a time when he had been working in Dorset.

'Have you noticed our latest groupie?' Brent asked Charles as he helped him push the Supercub that they had been using to tow gliders back into the hanger.

'No, not really, why do you ask?'

Charles was a keen gliding enthusiast and he was also one of the pilots that launched the gliders using the Supercub to tow them up to height. On the days when the weather was suitable for gliding, he and the other enthusiasts would gather for a few hours of excitement and fun wheeling about the bright skies in their gliders. Usually, he was kept very busy towing up the gliders when he wasn't actually flying a glider himself, and he didn't take much notice of the crowd that always gathered to watch them. Mostly, they tended to be partners or friends of those participating in the sport, but there was almost always a contingent of glamourous girls who were more interested in the men flying the gliders than the sport itself. He and Brent referred to them as groupies.

'God, you must have blinkers on, Charles, or maybe you're just plain blind,' said Brent. 'This woman is absolutely gorgeous, the sort of girl every man would wish to have on his arm! Her face, well, unbelievable, and her body—boy of boy!' In an expansive gesture Brent's hands drew an imaginary outline of the woman's body in the air.

'Well, all our followers are glamourous, aren't they?' Charles said disinterestedly. He would have preferred it if only those who were really interested in gliding followed them around.

'But this one is really special, mate. I mean really special—a real catch.'

'Well, does she have a name?'

'Yes, I have found that out. Her name is Miss Cordelia Digby!'

'Cordelia? What sort of name is that?'

'It's a beautiful name for a beautiful woman,' said Brent. He was really smitten.

Having been made aware of the fact there was a woman among the groupies about whom everyone was talking, Charles looked for her when he went back to the club house to have a beer. He saw her almost at once. She was within a group of glamourous women, but as Brent had indicated, she stood out from them all. She was tall for a woman and everything about her was perfect, from her curvy figure to her flawless complexion and classical beauty. Her ash blond hair cascaded to her shoulders looking like spun silk and she had intense violet eyes—which Charles suddenly realised were looking straight at him.

When she saw she had his attention, Cordelia left the group of women and came over to him.

'You were one of the pilots who was towing the gliders up,' she said without preamble. 'I'm Cordelia Digby.'

'Er, how do you do?' said Charles feeling rather flustered. 'Charles Lenten. Pleased to meet you.'

Cordelia ran her tongue over her lips and placed her empty glass onto the bar.

'Would you like another?' Charles enquired, taking the hint.

'Yes please. It's a gin and tonic.'

For the rest of the evening Cordelia monopolised Charles and he was aware of the envious looks he was getting from many of the other men—not least from Brent! However, he was enjoying himself too much to worry about anyone else. He found Cordelia to be an amusing and endearing person with whom to socialise, and by the end of the evening they had swapped phone numbers.

Thus began an exciting and steamy relationship between the two of them. It didn't matter to Charles that Cordelia was a few years older than him; he was completely swept away by her sparkling personality and utter dismissal of convention. Charles had spent much of his young life growing up in a foster home. His foster parents were good, God-fearing people who tried to instil in their many foster children the morals and values in which they believed, and Charles had taken on board all their instruction and now lived his life accordingly.

Since Charles had left his foster home and ventured out into the world on his own, he had tried to live his life in harmony with the accepted principles that had been instilled in him and he was surprised when Cordelia declared him to be old fashioned and boring.

'Life is for living, you silly boy,' she chided him. 'You're only given one life and it's up to you to make sure you enjoy it to the full.'

'But I do enjoy my life of flying,' objected Charles.

'Flying, yes; but what about the other times in your life when you're not flying? You're like a staid old man with a hearing aid and a walking stick carefully pottering up the pavement and being careful not to fall off the curb!'

'I am *not!*'

'Yes you are! Let me take you by the hand and show you how to live a little.'

Charles was quite besotted and willingly let Cordelia show him how to live a little! It almost blew his mind at the way she flouted convention and made up the rules to suit herself as she bounced through life. There was never a dull moment and he had to agree that he had never had so much fun, even though he was, at times, afraid her escapades would land them in big trouble.

'Forget the rule-book,' Cordelia told him. 'Just indulge in your passions and desires and enjoy your life!'

It felt to Charles as if he had unexpectedly moved into the fast lane. Life seemed to suddenly be painted in brighter colours as it whooshed by in an exhilarating series of exciting activities, and he had never felt more alive or happy. There was only one thing that puzzled Charles and that was why Cordelia had chosen him when, with her looks and charisma, she could have had the pick of the bunch. He was aware he earned a modest salary as a flying instructor and from towing gliders into the air, and he couldn't give her the expensive gifts he felt she deserved. He also knew he wasn't the most handsome man in the club, but Cordelia had seemed attracted to him as soon as they met. His only worry was that it was too good to last.

As the days went past his infatuation turned to love, and he worried all the more that Cordelia would tire with his company and move on. However, she claimed to love him as well, so he just pushed his insecurities to the back of his mind and enjoyed the moment. His friends seemed surprised that the two of them, with their completely different personalities and interests, had hit it off so well.

'You do know you're punching way above your weight?' he was asked several times. And although he denied it, he secretly agreed with them. But overall, his friends were pleased for him; it was only his best friend Wayne who remained sceptical.

'She's bad news, mate,' Wayne warned Charles. 'I get feelings about people you know and trust me; I'm getting a very bad feeling about Cordelia!'

Charles though his friend was perhaps a bit jealous and ignored his warning. He was having a great time with Cordelia and although they didn't have a lot of common interests, that really didn't seem to matter. Cordelia worked in a beauty salon and wasn't at all interested in flying or aeroplanes. She freely admitted to Charles that she had only come to watch the gliders because she was looking for a boyfriend! Consequently, Charles spent considerably less time at the club so he could do things with Cordelia that she enjoyed, and he knew Wayne disapproved of that as well.

After a while Charles decided that it would be the right time to propose to Cordelia. He knew he was head over heels in love with her and although he had only known her for a few weeks he knew he wanted to make her his own. But just before he did Cordelia dropped her bombshell.

'It's the end of the summer school holiday next week, Charles, and there's someone very special that I would like you to meet at the weekend.'

'Oh, yes?' Charles wondered who it could be.

'It's my daughter, Fleur,' continued Cordelia calmly. 'She's been staying with her grandparents in Ireland for the summer holidays, but is coming home for the start of the school term.'

To say Charles was astonished would have been an understatement. Cordelia had never mentioned she had a daughter and, as far as he had been aware, Cordelia had never been married. Now he stared at her in surprise. She appeared to be totally unconcerned as she walked alongside him and this rather shocked him as well because, if he was right and she had never married, having a child out of wedlock in the 1960's was considered a shameful thing.

'Why're you looking at me like that?' Cordelia asked.

'I . . . er, I never realised you'd been married,' stuttered Charles, not wanting to insult her.

'I haven't,' said Cordelia laughing. 'I had an affair when I was very young with a much older man and Fleur was the outcome. I refused to give her up for adoption, so my parents have helped me to raise her.'

Cordelia didn't appear to think what she had done was a disgrace and she looked challengingly at Charles. 'Is Fleur going to be a problem in our relationship?' she asked.

'No . . . it's just a bit of a surprise that you have a daughter, that's all. You haven't mentioned her up until now. How old is she anyway?'

'She'll be thirteen in a couple of weeks.'

'Thirteen? My God, Cordelia, you must have been about ten when you had her!'

'No, I was fourteen. I told you I was very young when I had the relationship.'

'So, what about her father? Does he still feature in your lives?'

Cordelia laughed. 'No, Cillian was an Irish gypsy lad who I fell in lust with. He had already gone by the time I discovered I was pregnant.'

'Why didn't you tell me about all this before now?'

'Because I wanted to get to know you better first. I know we've become serious about each other over the last few weeks, but if our relationship had not developed, having a daughter would have been immaterial and there would have been no necessity for me to tell you about Fleur.'

Reading between the lines, Charles realised that Cordelia had not wanted to risk being judged as a loose woman. Since the pill had been approved as a contraceptive in 1960, couples had indulged in sex with wild abandon; but if a woman was caught out and fell pregnant it carried a lot of stigma. Charles had been one of those people who considered a baby born out of wedlock was a shameful thing, but now he was confronted by the fact that his girlfriend had a child he had to accept that he was actually a hypocrite, because he had been enjoying sex with Cordelia for the past few weeks and in no way thought of her as a slut.

'You having a daughter changes nothing between us,' Charles reassured Cordelia. 'I'm looking forward to meeting her.'

Charles felt ashamed when he thought about his immediate reaction when he heard his girlfriend had had a child out of wedlock. He hoped he had hidden his feelings from Cordelia and she didn't suspect that at first, he had felt repelled by her announcement, but she was very perceptive and he wasn't sure if she hadn't realised how he had felt when she told him about Fleur. He decided to make amends by proposing straight away to show her that he wasn't fazed in any way, and she immediately agreed to become his wife.

Charles imagined Fleur would be a little girl who looked like her mother, so he had a big surprise when he met her. She was almost as tall as Fleur and had a very well-developed body. Her unblemished skin was naturally touched with colour and she had shoulder length jet black hair. But it was her face that riveted Charles. Yes, it was undeniably beautiful, with straight black eyebrows, dark flashing eyes, a small nose and full lips, but the expression on it could only be described as one of malevolence.

'Pleased to meet you,' Charles said warmly when Cordelia introduced him to her daughter.

When Fleur shook his hand, her own hand was as cold as her expression. 'You must have loads of money,' she said disdainfully. 'Mother only likes men who are loaded or are stunningly handsome and, well . . . it's got to be money with you!'

These rude words rendered Charles completely speechless, but Cordelia burst out laughing. 'You are a little minx, Fleur! But I can guarantee you will soon love Charles as much as I do.'

So began an uneasy start to Charles's relationship to Cordelia's daughter and as time went past it didn't get any easier. It seemed to Charles that Fleur had an inherent evilness that he assumed she had inherited from her father. She was malicious and spiteful and tried to put Charles down at every opportunity. She also flaunted her rapidly developing body and wore the most outrageous clothes. However, Cordelia could see no wrong in her daughter and continually made excuses for her bad behaviour.

'She's just at an age when she's starting to find her feet,' Cordelia said to Charles when he had had yet another fallout with Fleur and she had screamed insults at him, and then left with her dark eyes flashing with anger and her lips in a pout. 'Don't you remember when you were thirteen going on fourteen? The hormones were raging through your body making you feel confused; you felt anyone over eighteen was an old fuddy-duddy and you definitely felt superior to your parents in every respect!'

'The trouble with Fleur is that she's actually thirteen going on twenty-five and she has no respect for anyone,' said Charles wearily. 'She's always so rude to me, to you as well half the time, but you let her get away with it!'

'She's just going through a stage,' said Cordelia indulgently. 'Just give her a break.'

Charles did give her a break for Cordelia's sake. He really didn't want to lose the woman he adored, and when Fleur began to feel she had defeated Charles in the battle of wills with which they had been engaged since she had first met him, she became more amenable. Thereafter followed a more peaceable period of time and Charles felt that a truce had been made with Fleur, and he could indulge in his relationship with her mother without causing discord between the three of them.

When Fleur heard that Charles and Cordelia were engaged to be married, she had not received the news with delight. She didn't like the thought of anyone else competing for her mother's affections and it took Cordelia a while to talk her round to the idea. After that, Fleur seemed to accept the situation, although Charles wasn't quite sure if she only did so because she was to be their bridesmaid and would have the chance to dress up and be admired. Fleur loved her clothes, and although Charles secretly thought she looked like a prostitute when she left the house in a micro-mini skirt, fishnet tights and a blouse that exposed far more of her cleavage than was acceptable, he never made a comment.

The wedding plans were going well and although they were having to pay for everything themselves, because Cordelia said her family was too poor to contribute and Charles's parents had passed away. They, or rather Cordelia and Fleur, wanted it to be a spectacular occasion with no expense spared. Charles couldn't help wincing when the bills started to come in, but when he saw how happy Cordelia and Fleur were, he forced himself to be quiet while the two girls bantered about who was going to look the best.

'I know you're going to be the bride, Mother, and the focal point of the wedding, but I bet I'll outshine you in the dress I've chosen and every eye will be on me!'

'Don't bet on it, my darling,' responded Cordelia. 'There's no doubt you will look absolutely stunning, but you'll be but a poor reflection of your mother in her fine gown!'

Charles had had to buy a new suite for the occasion and Wayne, whom he had persuaded to be his best man, also had to be suitably attired. They went together to buy their suits.

'Mate, do you really have to purchase the most expensive suite in the shop?' Wayne asked in disbelief, when Charles has selected the one he wanted.

'I need to look good when I'm with my two glittering girls,' Charles responded. 'Anyway, Cordelia would kill me if I bought anything cheaper!'

'Well, so long as you don't expect me to buy one as expensive as that,' said Wayne looking disapproving.

It was only three weeks to their wedding day when Charles went shopping for a gift for the bridesmaid as it was tradition for the groom to do so. After selecting a pretty wrist watch, he set off back home and decided to take a shortcut he knew down a quiet lane that was flanked by a number of magnificent oak trees. It was a favourite haunt for young lovers who had nowhere more private to go, and on previous occasions when he had used the lane, he had seen a few couples skulking among the trees as they indulged in their passion.

He was about half way along the lane when he noticed two lovers half hidden behind one of the trees, totally engrossed in a passionate kiss. As he got closer, he felt quite disgusted to see the boy had pushed up the girl's very short skirt on one side and slipped his hand into her panties. Charles didn't think there was any harm in a kiss, but public caressing of intimate parts offended him. He lengthened his stride in an attempt to get past them as quickly as possible and then he suddenly recognised the clothes in which the girl was dressed. It was Fleur!

'Get your hands off that girl at once,' Charles commanded the boy loudly.

The boy jumped back in alarm at the rough tone of Charles's voice. He had greasy, shoulder length, red hair and when he turned to see who had shouted at him, Charles saw he had pale watery eyes and a crop of red pimples across his forehead. He opened his mouth to say something but Fleur beat him to it.

'How dare you interrupt us, Charles?' she demanded. 'This is none of your bloody business!'

'It certainly is my business! You're about to become my step-daughter and I will not have you behaving like a strumpet!'

'A strumpet? What century do you come from? Anyway, I don't have to listen to you—not now and not when you marry my mother! My life is my life and I won't have anyone telling me what to do!'

'You will come home with me right now and explain to your mother what you were doing when I found you,' said Charles. 'I don't think she'll be any more impressed than I am at your actions.'

'No, I'm not coming home. Gavin and I are going to carry on from where we left off, and you can trot along!'

But when Gavin saw Charles's face turning a dark shade of puce, he turned to Fleur hastily and said, 'Better cool it for now, babe, we'll catch up another time, hey?' And with that he walked off.

'See what you've done now,' said Fleur furiously. 'You're a flaming idiot, Charles, and from now it it's going to be war!' Then she turned a flounced off as well.

Much to Charles's chagrin, Cordelia didn't seem unduly perturbed when she was told what her daughter had been doing with Gavin in public.

'All girls of her age like to experiment a bit with their boyfriends,' Cordelia said. 'It was unfortunate that you saw them kissing, but they were just having a bit of fun. Don't be such a prude, Charles.'

'I'm not a prude,' Charles objected. 'I don't mind if she just kisses a boy, but I really don't like to see my step-daughter-to-be having her private parts caressed by a boy in public—and surely you should feel as outraged as I do!'

They ended up having a flaming row and when at last Charles stormed out of Cordelia's flat, he was incensed to find Fleur behind the door listening to every word that was said.

'I told you it would be war,' she spat at him maliciously, 'and I have Mother on my side!

During the days leading up their wedding day Charles and Cordelia called a truce, but Fleur was as mean and spiky to Charles as she could be, and Charles felt the uncomfortable atmosphere was causing Cordelia to withhold her affections to a certain degree. However, he decided they would be able to sort everything out when they went on their honeymoon and Fleur was not around to stir up emotions. Since they had spent so much on the actual wedding they had decided to go down to Cornwall for their honeymoon, because it was cheaper than going to France as Cordelia had originally planned.

'Cornwall will be lovely,' Charles assured Cordelia. 'And when we've had a chance to earn a bit more money and fill up the coffers, we'll definitely have a trip to France—it'll be something to look forward to after all the excitement is over.'

On the day of the wedding, Charles was standing nervously in the church with Wayne at his side. Every seat in the church had been taken and some guests found they had to stand at the back as there was nowhere left to sit. The organ was playing softly and there was an air of expectation as everyone waited for the bride and her entourage to arrive. Charles kept looking around; his stomach was in knots, longing for the ceremony to be over.

'Relax, mate,' said Wayne. 'You're sweating like a pig!'

Charles tried to relax, but when Cordelia didn't arrive on time he started to sweat even more.

'It's okay,' Wayne reassured him. 'It's the bride's prerogative to be late, she'll be here soon.'

But time ticked away and still there was no sign of the bride.

'Something's wrong,' said Charles to Wayne. 'They must have had an accident on the way here or something.'

Charles could tell from the rustlings coming from the guests that they were getting impatient and the vicar who was to perform the ceremony was looking worried. Eventually, he whispered to Charles that he had to officiate at another wedding immediately after this one, and if the bride didn't appear in the next couple of minutes, he would have to ask them to leave the church.

Charles didn't know what to do. He was convinced that the bridal car must have been involved in an accident and he felt sick with worry. Eventually, after the vicar had another word with them, Wayne took charge of the situation and turned to speak to the guests.

'I'm sorry, there seems to have been a problem,' he said. 'We'll all have to vacate the church now because another wedding is due to be conducted here shortly. Perhaps we can just all wait outside until things have been clarified.'

Everyone rose and filed outside. They stood in the church garden in groups under the shade of the trees talking quietly to each other. Everyone was wondering why the bride hadn't arrived.

'I need to drive along the route they were going to take to get here and see what's happened,' said Charles worriedly.

'Okay, we'll go in my car and I'll drive,' Wayne decided. He didn't think Charles was in any state to drive anywhere.

They were just making their way to where Wayne had parked his car when they heard someone say, 'Isn't that Fleur coming?'

Charles looked along the road, half expecting to see Fleur bloodied and bruised in her bridesmaid outfit, coming to tell them in a distraught manner that there had been a dreadful accident. But instead, he saw Fleur was on a bicycle and was wearing a pair of very short shorts and a tight T-shirt. She had a triumphant expression on her face and she shouted loudly to Charles as she came to a skidding stop in front of the church garden.

'Mother sent me to tell you the wedding's off,' she told him loudly, to ensure that all the guests could hear as well. An expression of vindictive jubilation was plain to see on her face. 'She's met someone else and doesn't want to marry you now!' Fleur passed a sealed envelope to Charles. 'She's explained it all in this letter,' she said. Then turning to everyone in general she continued. 'Oh, and since the reception has been paid for, she suggests you all go and have a good old party to celebrate Charles's non-wedding!' She turned back to Charles, 'And you can go and enjoy a little holiday by yourself in Cornwall,' she sneered. 'Andreas will be taking Mother to Monte Carlo!'

Fleur turned to go and then remembered something else. 'Oh yes, I almost forgot,' she said, feeling for something in her shorts pocket. 'Mother wants you to have this back.' She produced the diamond engagement ring Charles had beggared himself to buy for Cordelia and gave it to him. 'Andreas is going to buy her another one that you don't need a magnifying glass to see the diamond!' With that she jumped on her bicycle gleefully and rode off leaving the guests and Charles completely speechless.

Charles had to sit down on the low church wall because his head was spinning. He couldn't believe this was happening. The guests started to melt away, some of them passing a word of condolence to Charles or touching him compassionately before leaving. Soon he was left with only Wayne at his side.

'Come on, mate, let's get you home,' Wayne said gently. 'The guests for the next wedding are starting to arrive now, so it's time we left.'

When he got Charles back to his flat, Wayne made him a cup of tea and asked his friend if he'd like him to stay.

'No, I'll be okay,' said Charles.

'Look, although it doesn't seem so now, it's probably better that you haven't married Cordelia. It wouldn't have worked, mate, because after all the excitement had passed you would have realised the two of you were completely incompatible. You would also have had the additional problem of Fleur, a step-daughter from hell—and I can only see her getting worse as she gets older. The marriage would ultimately have ended in divorce so, believe it or not, you've had a lucky escape.'

But right then Charles couldn't think like that. He felt deeply hurt and humiliated—how could Cordelia have sent her daughter to say the marriage was off? It seemed so cruel, and although Cordelia was a lot of things, he had never though she would be capable of cruelty. After Wayne had left, he sat fingering the letter that Fleur had given him. He had felt, in the last couple of weeks that things hadn't been right between Cordelia and himself, but he thought it was because of the blow-up they had had over Fleur and her boyfriend. But now he realised it must have been because she'd met this Andreas, who was seemingly more wealthy that he. Eventually he ripped open the envelope and unfolded the letter.

Dearest Charles,

I'm so sorry, I really am. I know I should have come and told you in person that the wedding is off. I admit I am a coward to send Fleur instead, but I just couldn't bear to see the pain and hurt in your face when you were told the wedding was no longer going to happen. Because, believe it or not, I do care about you and I hate to think how hurt you must be feeling reading this letter, but I really don't think that our marriage would have worked.

As you know, Fleur will always be my priority and I know you question my methods of bringing her up. As she gets older things are going to get even more difficult—I know because I was just like her as a teenager. I put my parents through the wringer and because they tried to force me to conform, I did the complete opposite to what they wanted and ended up pregnant. So, I don't want to make that mistake with Fleur, I want to take an easier line and hope she will respond to that. But with your conservative ideas, you would never be comfortable with that method, you and I would always be arguing about her—like we did last week. So, I really think it's best that we don't get married now. It would only make all three of us miserable, and life is too short to be miserable!

Take care,

Cordelia.

Cordelia made no mention of another man in her life called Andreas and Charles wondered if Fleur had just made that up to humiliate him in front of all the wedding guests. However, in the following days Wayne did discover that Cordelia was going out with an Italian called Andreas. When he found this out Charles felt even more bitter and miserable. He dreaded bumping into them or Fleur and when he got the opportunity to leave the country and go and work in Kenya, he was greatly relieved.

Now as he lay in his bed, he wondered again why Georgia had reminded him of Fleur. Physically she didn't resemble her in the slightest, apart from having full lips. But on reflection, Georgia's lips were usually smiling while Fleur's were pouting. Maybe it was because he had felt Georgia had defied him when he had first arrived and she flew off to her uncle's farm before he had checked her out. Whatever the reason, it was invalid now that he had got to know Georgia a bit better and he knew he must make an effort to improve his relationship with her.

Chapter 7

The Fly-in

On the Friday morning before the weekend of the fly-in there seemed to be an air of expectancy in and around the flying club. The first of the visitors was expected to arrive on Friday afternoon and everything had been made ready for the big weekend. Charles helped where he could, but he was busy instructing students, so it was Georgia who was rushing around making sure everything was organised and ready. She was like a little dynamo as she raced from one thing to another, inspecting the bedrooms, checking on the kitchen and making sure that they had sufficient supplies for the weekend.

'Are you sure we've got enough food and drink in?' she enquired of Sam and Solomon.

'We have enough food,' Solomon reassured her. 'Tonight and Sunday night, I will cook for anyone who wants to order, tomorrow night we are having a barbeque; all the meat is in our fridge and salads and bread will be served with the meat. We have enough eggs, bacon, cereal, bread and fruit for the breakfasts, and I will be serving sandwiches, quiche, baguettes, pizza and sausage rolls at lunch time.'

'Good. What about tea and coffee—have we got plenty?'

'Yes, we have more than enough. Many of the ladies have also donated puddings and cakes and biscuits, so I can promise you,

Miss Georgia, everything is ready!'

'Mr Howard has ordered in plenty of alcohol,' Sam reassured Georgia when she turned to him.

'What about soft drinks? Coke and orange juice, that sort of thing; if it's hot people will be drinking a lot of soft drinks.'

'Yes, we have enough. Our store is full of all the drinks the people will want to have.'

'And the extra staff that have been laid on, have they arrived and are you happy with them?'

'Yes,' both men said in unison.

'They are people we know and have recommended to Mr Howard,' Sam said. 'So, we are sure that they will be okay.'

Having satisfied herself that everything in the kitchen and bar was organised, Georgia poked her nose into the bedrooms. She felt gratified that they looked so nice now with carpets on the floor and matching bedspreads and curtains. After that she went to check on the garden. It certainly made the little clubhouse look more permanent and inviting. Before, it had almost seemed as though it had been incidentally dropped onto the apron by a mistake, but now it reposed within its fence with a brilliant green lawn growing all around and pretty flowers and shrubs along the borders. Howard had managed to acquire a number of little tables and chairs and they had been set up outside on the veranda and on the lawn, so people could sit and enjoy a drink and something to eat while they watched the events of the day.

Inside the clubhouse everything was spic and span since the cleaners had given it an extra good going over. It now looked inviting with the freshly decorated walls, the new wooden barstools and the pictures that had been donated and hung. Georgia had even managed to acquire some new chair covers for the easy chairs and a rug to go in front of the fireplace.

'Have we been able to sort out accommodation for all those who have asked for it?' Charles asked Georgia when he was grabbing a coffee in between teaching students.

'Yes, both rooms are booked and we've also made bookings for people in the hotels. Lots of members have offered their spare rooms for our guests as well, and most of those have been taken.'

'What about the inevitable last-minute pleas for accommodation by people who haven't asked for it as yet?'

'Well, there're still a few rooms on offer from our members; I'm sure we'll be able to house them all. How about you—do you have a spare room we could use if someone needs one?'

'Yes, I do. I'll get Emmanuel to get it ready in case it's needed.'

Not long after midday people started to fly in and soon the apron had a long line of aeroplanes parked along the border. Hans was in charge of the parking and he greeted each person who arrived and told them where to park. When they walked to the clubhouse Georgia was there to receive them. She checked to make sure each person had accommodation and asked if they would need transport to get to their lodgings later in the evening.

'How are we doing?' Charles asked, coming in with the student he had been instructing.

'Everything's going well,' Georgia told him. 'No hiccups yet!'

'Good. Thanks for all you're doing, Georgia. I've got one more student this afternoon and then I'll be free to come and give you a hand.' He noted with mild surprise that Georgia was not wearing her normal shorts, tee-shirt and flip-flops, but had changed into some grey jeans and had a buttoned-up blouse and boots with heels on her feet, which made her look a little taller. She had also applied a touch of makeup and the overall effect made her look more mature.

That evening the club hummed with life. The pilots, who had come from far and wide, alone or with their families, mingled and caught up with friends and acquaintances they hadn't seen for a while. The social members were also there in force, many of them were accommodating visitors in their spare rooms. In the little groups of people that had formed, the conversation was mainly all about flying—someone's latest adventure when airborne, the various attributes of different aircraft, the excitement of gliding or skydiving, the new strips that had been opened recently and their suitability for various aircraft.

'Old Jack Suthers has built a strip on his land almost on the summit of Dundori,' one of the pilots was saying. 'I hope to God no one tries to land there in anything less than a 180. They'd get in okay, but at that altitude the strip would be far too short for, say, a Cessna 150 to take off from.'

Charles went home to shower and change for the evening and asked Emmanuel to get the spare room ready in case it was needed. When he got back to the club Georgia was waiting to speak to him.

'Charles, I have a couple, George and Jasmine Pearce, who need accommodation. They fly into Lanet occasionally from their farm and usually take one of the club rooms for the night. They had no idea we were having a fly-in this weekend, so they arrived to find the rooms taken and accommodation in the hotels in Nakuru also booked up.'

'Yes, of course they can stay with me,' said Charles. 'You'd better introduce them to me so I can invite them to use my spare room.'

'Thanks Charles, you're a life saver,' said Georgia, leading him to the couple, but she didn't quite meet his eyes when she said it and Charles wondered why.

When Georgia introduced Charles to the couple, he found that Jasmine was considerably younger than her husband. She was a big boned woman with a homely face, but she was pleasant and friendly. George was bald and had a pencil line moustache. He had developed a small paunch and his stomach strained against the buttons of his shirt.

'Very kind of you to offer us accommodation, what!' George said, looking delighted that they had got a room in the chief flying instructor's house. He immediately engaged Charles in conversation, but Charles found him rather obsequious and was not enjoying the man's ingratiating conversation.

'I have to go and circulate,' Charles said as soon as he felt he could get away without causing offence. 'But I'll catch up with you later and dive you back to mine.'

Later that evening Howard said to Charles, 'I hear you've drawn the short straw and have the Pearces staying with you tonight!'

'Why the short straw?' Charles enquired suspiciously.

'Well, George has a bit of a reputation—I thought you would have heard the gossip about him by now—and consequently no one is keen to offer him accommodation.'

'What sort of reputation?' Charles asked. 'What's he done?'

'I couldn't possibly say, not with the man standing right in this room!'

'Yes, you must! He can't hear you above all this chatter and I'm not going to put up someone who may be a chainsaw murderer, for all I know!'

'Calm down man! George isn't a chainsaw murdered, but some of the things he's done in the past are somewhat abhorrent to say the least. He originates from England and I think he was in the army. But he immigrated to Zambia where he opened a transport business. Every year he'd hire white men to be the drivers of his lorries, since he said they were more reliable than black drivers and he engaged them on a year's contract. However, he would only pay them a pittance of a salary, but with a promise of a big bonus corresponding with the profits he made during the year that they worked for him. On paper this seemed to be a very good deal as his business was very profitable. But a couple of weeks before he was due to give his driver a bonus, George would think up a bogus reason to sack him, so the poor fellow would have worked for him for a year for virtually nothing!'

'What a mean trick!' Charles exclaimed, shooting a disgusted look in George's direction.

'He got away with it for a few years,' Howard continued. 'Then the last driver he employed in Zambia committed suicide when he found he wasn't to receive his bonus. He put a gun in his mouth and shot himself in front of his wife and two little girls.'

'Oh my God!'

'Yes, well, when others in the transport business heard about this, they started warning anyone who might be thinking about signing up with George that they could be making a big mistake. Soon George could not get drivers, neither white nor black, because his reputation had been ruined, so he moved to Kenya and he's got a farm in the Nyeri area now.'

'Does he still persist in conducting his business in a disreputable way?'

'No, I don't think so. He married Jasmine shortly after arriving in Kenya; she's a local girl and not a bad lass. I think she was . . . um, well, left on the shelf, as they say, and she married him without really knowing what he was capable of doing, but they seem to have made a go of the marriage and she appears to keep him on the straight and narrow now.'

Charles didn't really want to play host to such a despicable man, but he could hardly withdraw his invitation now so he decided he would just have to go along with it.

The evening went well, everyone seemed to have a great time catching up with old friends and Sam was kept very busy behind the bar. Solomon and the kitchen staff were also very active in the kitchen and plate after plate of delicious smelling food was produced and served. Before everyone made an exodus for their sleeping accommodation later that night, Charles managed to corner Georgia.

'Thanks a bunch for setting me up with the most reviled man in the country,' he said.

'Sorry Charles, but no one else would have been willing to have him and you agreed readily enough when I asked you; I didn't have to twist your arm.'

'That was before I knew what he'd done!'

'Well, I didn't know that, did I?' She smiled at him sweetly.

'You might have warned me.'

'I know, I probably should have warned you, but then you might have said no and I really wanted to find them a place to stay, because although George is such a monster, Jasmine is a really sweet person and it was for her sake that I tricked you into having them.'

Charles dutifully collected his guests before he went home and offered them a coffee when they arrived at the house.

'Damn good of you to put us up, what,' said George.

'Yes, it really is,' Jasmine added. 'We had no idea that there was anything special on at Lanet this weekend, so we really would have been stuck for accommodation had you not kindly offered us your spare room.'

'Do you often fly into Lanet?' Charles asked. He didn't remember seeing them flying in since he had been there.

'No, we don't tend to leave the farm much,' said George. 'But very occasionally we fly into Lanet and we usually get a taxi to Nakuru and see a film, or go to the Stags Head Hotel for a meal. Sometimes we even stay there for the night because the rooms at the club are somewhat austere.'

'They've actually been done up and are quite nice now,' Charles told them.

'Yes, we noticed how much work has been done in and around the clubhouse,' said Jasmine. 'It's looking really good now.'

To Charles's relief he found that entertaining the couple was not as wearisome as he had feared it would be. George lost his ingratiating manner when he started talking about his time in the army and he had some interesting and sometimes hilarious stories to tell.

'I should have stayed in the army,' George said. 'I was very young when I went in, but I found I was made for the army and the army was made for me. However, after the war they didn't need us all and I was tempted to go out and sample the delights of the world outside the constraints of the army. It wasn't a wise decision; I found I struggled to go it alone and I've made some big mistakes. Lucky for me, I found Jasmine as well and that was my saving grace.' He gave his wife an adoring look.

Jasmine was a quiet person, but as Georgia had said, she was very nice and Charles had to agree with George that he was lucky to find her. They obviously loved each other and Charles felt slightly envious of their close relationship.

The next morning, they were all up bright and early and Emmanuel served them a full English breakfast before they headed for the airfield.

'So, what have we got to look forward to today?' George asked Charles as they drove the short distance to the club.

'Well, we're expecting more people to fly in today and we're going to have some competitions—bomb dropping, forced landings and the old favourite with the toilet rolls.'

'Toilet rolls?'

'Yes, you know, the pilot takes up a toilet roll and drops it out of the window so that it unravels, then he has to do a steep turn and cut the roll with the propeller, then turn again and cut it once more and so on. The pilot who cuts his toilet roll the most times is the winner. It's more difficult than it sounds. Many a pilot chucks out the roll, but can't even see it when he's turned around!'

'You should be good at the bomb dropping,' Jasmine said to her husband. 'Being in the forces would have trained you well for something like that!'

'I was in army, my sweet, not the air force! But what jolly good fun!'

When they got to the airfield the glider was already being pulled out and the skydivers had arrived from Nairobi in force.

'Are you going to drive the car that launches the gliders?' Charles asked Georgia when he saw her.

'No. I was, but Kenny Yates is going to drive it now because there's been a change of plan. The skydiver's pilot couldn't make it at the last minute. He was due to fly in this morning from Nairobi in the aeroplane that they were going to use to take them up, so they had a bit of a problem when he let them know he wasn't coming. I resolved that for them by asking Kenny to launch the gliders as I know he's quite capable of doing that, and then I was able to offer to take the skydivers up in our 182. William has already removed the passenger seats and taken the door off and the skydivers are ready to roll now, so, I'll see you later.'

'Okay, but listen Georgia, the skydivers will encourage you to fly up to the altitude they want to jump from as fast as possible, and then tell you to get back to the ground as quickly as you can. The shorter the period of time you spend in the air the better it is for them because it saves them money. But keep your eye on the temperature gauge; be careful not to overheat the engine going up and then over cool it on your descent.'

'Right, I'll bear that in mind,' said Georgia. 'I'll need to keep a good lookout for other aircraft as well, because there's going to be a lot of activity around here today. The skydivers have also warned me not to fly into their people descending on their parachutes!'

The first three skydivers that Georgia took up were all experienced and had done many jumps. Phil, Jeff and Panos were laughing and joking as they got ready for their jump; each one was checking and re-checking the straps and equipment on themselves and also on their friends.

'You better go and get your coat on, doll,' said Jeff to Georgia. 'It's going to be bloody cold with the door off when we get to altitude.'

Since it was very warm on the ground, Georgia hadn't thought of that and she hurried to get her anorak. The men were ready for her when she came back.

'We're all veteran skydivers,' Panos told Georgia. 'But today it will be a new experience for us because we've never been taken up by a child before!' They all roared with laughter and Georgia joined in. She could see there was no malice in the remark.

The men scramble into the Cessna 182 and sat awkwardly on the floor with their parachutes strapped to their backs. Georgia was amused to see that they had brought some Playboy magazines to read while she flew them up to altitude.

'Try and get us up to altitude as quickly as you can,' said Phil. 'Then don't dawdle on the way down.' Georgia nodded, but she knew she had to bear in mind what Charles had told her.

It was extremely noisy flying with the door off and the wind rushed in adding to the noise. Georgia was glad she had her anorak on. She wondered if the guys were enjoying the magazines as she climbed to the required height. When they were ready to make an exit, she gave a call on the radio to warn anyone flying in the area that skydivers would be dropping, and she pulled back the throttle and reduced the airspeed while she tried to keep the aeroplane as steady as she could as they approached the drop zone. One after the other the men dived headfirst out of the Cessna, whooping as they did.

'See you on the ground, my lovely,' yelled Phil as he made his exit.

Georgia banked around as she started her descent and strained her eyes to see the skydivers. Eventually, when she was beginning to worry that something bad had happened, she saw the three parachutes blossom and she heaved a sigh of relief.

When Georgia had landed, she gathered up the Playboy magazines and took them back to the skydivers. 'Thanks, doll,' said Jeff. 'I'm coming up with you again now, but this time we have two other people who are very inexperienced. Tim has done five jumps on the static line and this will be his first freefall jump where he'll have to pull the ripcord himself, and Jess has just completed her ground training, so this'll be her first jump ever on the static line.

Georgia looked at Tim and Jess. Tim was wearing a blue jumpsuit and he was looking very serious as he checked Jess's straps and equipment. Jess was dressed in a bright yellow jumpsuit and in contrast to Tim's serious face, hers was creased in lines of laughter as she giggled at something he had said. Georgia detected a note of hysteria in the giggles and rightly discerned that Jess's laughter was brought on by nerves.

Jeff went to check over both of their equipment and straps.

'Don't forget you're not going to be on the static line this time,' he said to Tim. 'You have to pull your own ripcord.'

'I'm seriously not going to forget that!' Tim said emphatically.

'Now Jess, you're going to be on the static line,' said Jeff. 'All you have to remember is to put yourself in a banana shape when you jump and keep yourself stable so that your limbs don't get tangled up in the lines as your chute opens, okay?'

'Yes,' said Jess with another giggle.

'Now listen, Georgia,' said Jeff. 'As experienced skydivers, Phil, Panos and I just dived out of the open door of the aeroplane when we were over the jump zone, but because these guys are beginners the format is a bit different. When we're getting close to the jump zone, I'll ask Tim to get into position. He'll them clamber out of the door and put one foot on the footstep and the other on the wheel of the aircraft while he hangs onto the wing strut. As you can imagine, it will be a rather precarious position for him to be in with the wind rushing by etc., so you will need to throttle back to reduce the airflow and also try and keep the aeroplane as level and stable as you can. Oh yes, and don't forget to put the hand brake on before he puts his foot on the wheel! He'll hang on until I'm happy he's in the right place to drop and then I'll tap him on the shoulder and, hopefully, he'll jump backwards and fall away from the aeroplane. As soon as you see him go could you please bank steeply to the right so that I can keep an eye on him as he goes down. Got that?'

'Yes.'

'Good. Then as soon as I tell you, you can go around again so that we can line up for Jess's drop and the same applies again. But remember, this is her first drop so she may be a bit awkward getting out of the aeroplane. If she bottles it and doesn't jump when I tap her on the shoulder, I'll get her back inside and we'll go around again for a second try, that's unless she's sure she doesn't want to try again. In that case, I'll jump out and she can come back to earth with you!'

The atmosphere in the aeroplane was completely different to what it had been on the previous trip. Then, the guys had laughed and joked as they ogled the nudes in the Playboy magazine, filling the cockpit with their excitement and delight to be going up for another jump. Now, an air of tension and anxiety seemed to swirl around the four people in the aeroplane as they all sat in silence during the ascent.

As they came in for their first run over the drop zone, Tim got ready to make his exit. As soon as Georgia throttled back, he clambered out and got into position with his feet firmly on the foot step and wheel and his hands clinging tightly onto the wing strut. Georgia noticed that his mouth was set in a straight firm line and he looked ahead as he waited for the tap. As soon as Jeff touched his arm he jumped backwards and disappeared from sight. Georgia immediately pushed the throttle open and banked to the right while Jeff stuck his head out of the door and craned his neck to watch Tim's progress.

'Perfect!' Jeff shouted after a few moments. 'Now it's your turn Jess.'

Georgia got them into position again and with a lot of shuffling, Jess managed to climb out of the door and hung precariously on the wing strut with her feet teetering on the wheel and footstep. Georgia did her utmost to keep the aeroplane stable as she watched Jess waiting for the tap on her arm that would indicate she should commence her drop. The girl's yellow jumpsuit was pressed hard against her body with the force of the wind and rippled at the back, while long tendrils of fair hair flew out from beneath her helmet. Jess was looking into the cockpit through her goggles and her big blue eyes were huge with fear. Georgia could only imagine the trepidation Jess was feeling as she waited for the tap.

When Jeff gave her the signal to go, Jess didn't hesitate and she disappeared from view. Georgia immediately banked around so Jeff could check the girl's progress. After a minute he pulled back from the door laughing.

'Did she do all right?' Georgia enquired.

'Yeah, she was a bit unstable as she didn't get her banana shape quite right, but not bad for a first jump. Now all she has to do is remember how to land without hurting herself.'

As they went around again so that Jeff could jump out over the drop zone he shouted to Georgia, 'You should think about having a jump yourself sometime, it's a great adrenaline rush!' She just laughed and put up her thumbs, but she wasn't sure it was something she wanted to do.

There was plenty of activity in and around the Lanet area that morning and everyone had to be constantly aware that there were gliders and skydivers as well as a large number of aeroplanes in the sky. Looking down as she dropped her skydivers, Georgia could see the action on the ground as well. The skydivers who had already jumped had started the process of repacking their chutes and had them stretched out on the grass. The brightly coloured silk fluttered in the breeze, as they carefully started the process of folding and packing them so that they would open without malfunctioning.

Those in charge of the gliding had a good number of people eager to try the sport and at intervals the Chevy would roar along the runway as it launched a glider. Apart from the clubs T21 glider, there were two other gliders that were privately owned. They were also taking up passengers and judging by the crowd it was proving to be popular.

The competitions were also in full swing and Georgia saw more than one roll of toilet paper floating down uncut. Obviously, the pilots who had thrown them out had lost sight of them and they would eventually fall to the earth like a huge string of spaghetti.

The spectators thronged around the clubhouse with cameras and drinks in their hands, and Georgia could see the bar staff busily collecting up the dirty glasses and serving the food that had been ordered. It all looked very positive to her, but it wasn't until they broke for lunch that she could ask how things were going.

'It's turning out to be a huge success,' said Howard, beaming with delight when she asked him. 'Charles has been very busy with his taster secessions and we've had several people sign up to learn to fly already. The competitions have been a triumph and everyone taking part have enjoyed themselves immensely; even those who didn't get anywhere near the target! I believe your friend, Amar, won the forced landing competition. Also, the bar and kitchen are doing a roaring trade and the spectators are having a wonderful time.'

It was a very busy day for all involved and in the evening the kitchen staff lit the barbeques and put up trestle tables on which to place the food. When Georgia made her way to her bedroom after she had dropped the last lot of skydivers, she saw that the people who had been employed to run the disco were setting everything up in the clubhouse. They had taken most of the furniture out of the main room and stacked it in the lecture room, so there would be plenty of room for dancing, and now they were setting up all their equipment—their sound systems and various lights.

Now that the activities on the airfield had ceased, people started to drift away and drive home so that they could shower and change for the disco. Howard had told Georgia that he expected a number of people who weren't even interested in flying to turn up for the evening as the disco had been widely advertised, so they were anticipating a huge crowd.

Charles took his guests home so that they could freshen up and change for the evening. When they returned to the club people were already arriving in anticipation of a barbeque and an evening of dancing.

The bar had been set up outside at one end of the veranda so that there would be more room inside to dance, and Charles and the Pearces were sitting there having a drink when Georgia made an appearance. Charles stared at her in amazement.

'My God, girl!' George exclaimed. 'You scrub up well!'

'You look lovely, darling,' said Jasmine smiling at Georgia. 'Come and have a drink with us.'

Georgia was wearing a white trouser suit and very high heels that boosted her height. Her freshly shampooed hair hung in a shiny curtain around her shoulders and she had applied makeup which made her greenish eyes appear huge and luminous, while her full lips were tinted pink and looked sensuous and sexy. Up until then, Georgia had always appeared to Charles as a rather precocious little girl, but now, for the first time, he saw her through Randy's eyes—a sensual and attractive woman.

Georgia didn't sit with them for long as she was called away on some errand, but as she disappeared into the clubhouse, Charles found himself hoping that he would have the opportunity to have a dance with her later that evening.

Chapter 8

The Discotheque

As Charles and the others sat sipping their drinks there suddenly came from inside the clubhouse an eruption of loud Beatles music that boomed out and made normal conversation almost impossible. Coloured disco light that had been activated reflected out onto the veranda and danced across the ground as they rotated around. It was a call for the people to come and dance and many couples made their way inside and started to twist and shout with the Beatles. The coloured disco lights suddenly went out and were immediately replaced by a brilliantly bright white light that was flashing rapidly.

'Oh my goodness!' Jasmine exclaimed. 'That's really weird! What's going on?'

'It's just the strobe light,' Charles explained. 'Look through the door, Jasmine, and you'll see all the dancing people will appear to be dancing in jerks as the light catches them.'

All three of them peered through the door at the crowded dance floor. The dancers that were gyrating to the loud music did indeed appear to be jerking and twitching in the flashing light. Those who were wearing white were shown up in sharp relief as their clothes became dazzling in the brightness of the beams. Charles caught sight of Georgia immediately in her white trouser suit, she was dancing with wild abandon and in the flashes Charles could see she was smiling at her dance partner while her hair flew out in all directions.

'It's all a bit overpowering, what?' said George. 'Let's have another drink before we venture into the fray.'

After they got their drinks they went to sit at one of the tables in the garden where it wasn't so noisy. It was a beautiful night with millions of twinkling stars and a half moon shining in the sky above them. Inside, the strobe light stopped as abruptly as it had started and the revellers were suddenly bathed in an ultra violet light that made all those in pale clothes glow like fireflies.

'Come on darling, let's go and dance,' Jasmine urged her husband. She jumped up and taking him by the hand led him into the clubhouse. Charles was left sitting on his own, but at that moment two men arrived and zoned in on him.

'Charlie, me boy—all alone?' Randy boomed. 'Klaus, go and get us all a drink, there's a good fellow. Charlie looks as though he need cheering up!'

Neither Randy nor Klaus had taken offense when Charles had reported their bad flying practices to their boss and now they flew back to the Lanet airstrip in a more conventional manner. Charles had grown to like the brash American. Klaus was more of an enigma, but he seemed a pleasant enough bloke.

'I'm hoping to get a dance with the elusive Georgia,' said Randy as he sipped his drink. 'Trouble is, she's so damn popular— everyone wants to dance with her. I thought maybe I could get her drunk and persuade her to come flying with me, if you know what I mean!' He winked at Charles.

'Well, she only drinks Coke as far as I know,' said Charles. 'So that plan certainly won't work!'

'You're right. And she only drinks it through a straw, so I couldn't even slip something into her drink to make her more amenable!' Randy saw Charles's disapproving expression and laughed. 'I'm only kidding, man! She's the most alluring woman I've ever met, but I'd never take advantage of her unless she was agreeable.' Turning to Klaus he said, 'What do you think?'

'About what, my friend?'

'About Georgia, you silly old goat; don't you ever listen to what's been said?'

'Georgia is a good girl—not for you! You too old to be her boyfriend, anyway! You like father or uncle.'

'A *father or an uncle?*' Randy sounded outraged. 'I'm in the prime of life, as you very well know, and I'm virile and sexy— women just can't get enough of me!'

'Not Georgia!'

'No, well, she ain't the only fish in the sea and I'm a goin' fishing tonight to catch me a nice fat fish!' With that, Randy got up and walked into the clubhouse.

Klaus wasn't the most scintillating company, so Charles soon followed Randy and found that there were plenty of women willing to dance with the chief flying instructor! Because the music was so loud there was little chance of making conversation, but the beat of the rhythm and the flashing of the lights soon got into Charles's head and he was twisting, jerking and gyrating with the best of them. Often his eyes strayed towards Georgia and she never seemed to be off the dance floor. As Randy had mentioned, as well as every man from the club wanting to dance with her, the men from the gliders club and the skydivers group also wanted to partner her on the dance floor, as she was a helpful and popular person. Charles noticed she danced with great energy, but in a sinuous, graceful and exceedingly sexy way. He hoped she would be free to dance with him at some stage, but didn't have high hopes.

It was almost midnight and Charles was dancing with a rather rotund girl who was the daughter of one of the farmers in the area. Margaret was a jolly girl who was throwing herself into dancing the rock and roll, almost pulling Charles off his feet as she did so. She wasn't very pleased when their dance was suddenly interrupted by Jeff who was accompanied by Georgia.

'Sorry to interrupt,' said Georgia to them both. 'Jeff has a request to make to you, Charles.'

'It's a beautiful nigh outside,' said Jeff. 'The stars are twinkling and the moon is shining. The gang and I thought it would be a wonderful night to do a skydive and Georgia has agreed to take us up—with your approval of course.' He looked at Charles appealingly.

'Whoa, hang on a minute,' said Charles. 'You guys have all been drinking!'

'I haven't,' interjected Georgia. 'I've drunk nothing but Coca Cola all evening.'

'I know, but the skydivers haven't stuck to the soft stuff!'

'Some of us have,' objected Jeff. 'And all those who want to jump have had no more than one or two drinks. I wouldn't even consider a night jump if we'd been drinking excessively.'

'Oh, come on Charles,' urged Georgia sensing Charles was about to refuse them his permission. 'The guys have brought meteor flares and it will be a spectacular sight for the revellers to see them falling like meteors from the sky.'

'Well. . .' Charles didn't know what rule, if any, applied to drinking and skydiving, and he had no jurisdiction over them anyway. But he did know for sure that Georgia hadn't touched a drop of alcohol all night and she had a valid night rating; also, he could trust her to take the 182 up and bring it safely back again. 'Okay,' he said at last. 'But you're responsible for the skydivers, Jeff, and I'm trusting you not to let anyone who has consumed a large amount of alcohol go up in one of our aeroplanes. Also, you must assist Georgia to put out the flare path and, more importantly, help her to bring back the lamps when you've finished.'

'Good man!' said Jeff. 'I agree to all your conditions. Come on, Georgia, let's get organised.' Charles could see by Georgia's bouncy body language that she was delighted to be able to fly the skydivers at night.

It was very cold as Georgia piloted the three skydivers up to altitude and she shivered as the wind howled in through the open door. But she always enjoyed flying at night because the dark star encrusted sky seemed so immense and beautiful, and the world with all its problems lay forgotten in the inky blackness below.

When they reached the required height and she had got them over the jump zone that they had marked with lamps on the ground, the three men dived out and Georgia banked around and watched as they descended, looking like meteorites because of the magnesium flares they had attached to their legs. Then she made a leisurely descent and joined the circuit. She would have preferred to stay up for a longer period, but knew she mustn't linger as it would cost the skydivers extra if she took her time.

On the ground the revellers had been alerted to the fact that there was to be a night skydive and they had all abandoned the dance floor to watch the skydivers' descent. It was a wonderful bit of unexpected entertainment that was hugely enjoyed, and the crowd all clapped appreciatively as the three men landed without incident on the marked-out area. Most of the people had returned to the dance floor before Georgia had touched down and returned to the apron, but a small knot of people had stayed to watch her come down. When she climbed out of the Cessna, they all spontaneously applauded.

'Why did people clap me when I landed?' Georgia asked Jeff as he helped her to bring in the flare path. 'I didn't do anything special!'

'Well, they certainly thought you did! You look so young, Georgia, and there aren't that many woman pilots in this country yet, so that gives you kudos.'

The next morning as Charles drove his guests back to the club-house, he could see that George looked a bit under the weather and guessed he was suffering with a hangover. Jasmine, however, was in high spirits and she asked Charles what was in store for them that day.

'Well, we've arranged for several flying displays to be performed for the enjoyment of the crowd. Dave Hill is going to fly in from Nairobi in his Chipmunk and do a couple of low altitude aerobatic displays, and that's very thrilling to watch. Klaus and Randy are going to give a crop-spraying demonstration on the land in-between the two runways in front of the clubhouse, and there're going to be more displays from the skydivers and gliders. It should be a good day. Mark Fleming will be back giving joyrides in his Dragon Rapide as well, and I'll still be doing taster secessions in the 150.'

It was another beautiful day and the crowds soon came streaming in with their cameras in their hands. Soon the air was filled with action and entertainment as the events got underway. Georgia took the skydivers up again, but on this day only the experienced were participating because they were putting on displays for the crowd. They all had their meteor flares strapped to their legs so that they could be seen from the ground as they dropped trailing the smoke behind them. They would then join together in the air before breaking apart and opening their chutes in preparation for landing. Since they wanted more than three people in the sky at once, Zail agreed to take three more skydivers up in his aeroplane so that there would be sufficient numbers to give a good performance. After taking off, Zail tucked his aeroplane under Georgia's wing and they flew in formation up until they had dropped their skydivers. A little later, when Georgia and Zail had landed and parked on the apron, Zail walked to the clubhouse with Georgia.

'Did you know Amar won the forced landing competition yesterday?' Zail asked her proudly. 'He won a silver beer mug and is very pleased with himself!'

'Yes, I did, and good for him! I haven't seen him to congratulate him yet, but when I do, I'm going to tell him that since he's proved he's now a proficient pilot, he really must sign up for his PPL flying test again.'

'I know. I've been telling him to do that but he still hesitates.'

'Well, he kind of lost his confidence after the last time he took the test, but he has no excuse now. I've been flying with him for a while and I know he's quite capable of passing, all he needs to do is to keep his nerves under control.'

'Please encourage him to take the test again,' Zail begged Georgia.

The gruff throaty roar of the two bright yellow Ag Cats approaching prevented them from speaking further, and they both turned to watch the crop spraying pilots put their aeroplanes through their paces. Klaus and Randy started at opposite ends of the designated area on which they were to demonstrate their profession. As they flew over the land at a very low level they deployed the spray, which in this case was just water, and then at the end of the area they pulled up sharply and did a low-level steep turn to bring them back to the area on which they were spraying. The spectacle of the two robust bi-planes being thrown around at such low level, the terrific noise of the Pratt and Whitney 600hp engines, and the precision of the falling spray were impressive, and the crowd was soon completely immersed in the drama of the action as they filmed the display. They gasped when the two aeroplanes met in the middle of the field, but Klaus and Randy expertly avoided colliding and continued to the opposite ends of the area. When they at last landed and the terrific noise of the engines died away, the crowd clapped enthusiastically.

'Well, that's me finished flying for the day, so I'm going to order me a big fat Bourbon,' said Randy as he and Klaus walked to the clubhouse amid the clapping people. 'Georgia,' he said, suddenly spying her. 'How did I do?'

'You both were pretty impressive,' said Georgia smiling at them.

'How about you come up with me later? I could teach you a thing or two!'

'I'm sure you could,' said Georgia giggling. 'But I think we've had this conversation before—and anyway, you want to have a Bourbon.'

'It's not the only thing I want,' muttered Randy.

After the crop spraying there was a display put on by Bruce Little in his Blue Bird glider. After getting up to a suitable height he put the sleek elegant glider into a series of beautiful aerobatic manoeuvres that were both graceful and silent, contrasting greatly to the Ag Cats displays of noisy raw power. The club's T21 sat on the end of the runway like a lumpy old lady who had to watch a younger and infinitely more beautiful version of herself take centre stage.

When Dave Hill burst upon the scene in his Chipmunk, he lost no time in wowing the crowd. Flying low along the runway he suddenly pulled up into a low-level loop, making everyone gasp in astonishment. Thereafter, he performed an extraordinary variety of aerobatics, all at low level in front of the crowd, causing them to exclaim in wonder that he didn't crash into the ground as he came out of the manoeuvres.

'I can hardly watch him doing that stuff,' said Howard to Georgia. 'The man must have nerves of steel to perform aerobatics at that low altitude!'

'Oh Howard, I'd love to be able to do that,' said Georgia, turning her shining eyes on him for a moment. 'Flying is always thrilling, but to be able to perform precise manoeuvres like that would be exhilarating beyond measure!'

'Well,' said Howard thoughtfully, 'the next thing on my shopping list for the club is another aeroplane, so perhaps we should think about getting one that is capable of performing aerobatics.'

'That would be wonderful! How long do you think it will take before we can afford one?'

'I'd have to look into the figures to answer that,' said Howard. 'But this weekend has been an unmitigated success in every way, and financially we should have a good few pennies to put towards a new aeroplane.'

No one could have contradicted Howard about the success of the fly-in and as the last of the visitors took off for home and the weary crowd straggled to their cars, Jasmine sought out Charles.

'Charles, this is a bit of an imposition, but we were wondering if we could stay with you for another night? We have business to do in Nakuru tomorrow, you see.'

'Yes, that's absolutely fine,' said Charles. He had not found their presence in his house as irksome as he had feared. In fact, he found he really liked Jasmine and he'd had a good few laughs with George, so he didn't have any objections to them staying another night.

They decided to eat at the club before going back to Charles's house and as they waited for their food they relaxed with a drink. The past three days had been very busy and Charles was aching with tiredness, but in a good way because of the success of the weekend. Georgia had also ordered some food, but had gone to have a shower while it was being prepared.

The radio suddenly crackled and a voice announced that they would be landing in approximately five minutes. 'Hello,' said George. 'Someone has left it a bit late to come to the fly-in, what!'

Charles glanced out of the window; the short African dusk was quickly dissolving into darkness so he went to the radio and enquired if the approaching aeroplane would like car headlights shining down the runway to give them direction.

'Negative,' came back the reply. 'I have the runway visual.'

Charles watched anxiously as the small aeroplane joined the circuit and came into land. The last thing he wanted was for someone to prang their aeroplane on the runway and spoil the end of a wonderful weekend, but the aircraft landed safely and Charles saw it was a Piper Super Cub when it taxied onto the apron. He waited on the veranda to greet the pilot.

Two men alighted from the aeroplane. The older of the two was a lean sinewy man who was bald and deeply tanned. He moved with feline grace and when he got to the veranda Charles saw that his pale eyes were inscrutable and rather cold. The other man was much younger and was heavy set. He had a shock of dark hair and his handsome face was marred by a long scar that ran along his hairline and down his temple. His intense green eyes were shadowed and held an enigmatic quality that Charles found unsettling as he stepped forward to meet the pair.

'Good evening. I'm Charles Lenten, chief flying instructor. Welcome to our club. I'm sorry you've just missed our fly-in.'

'Yes, we heard something was going on this weekend,' said the bald man. 'Cade Heston,' he added, shaking Charles's hand. 'And this is my son, Benedict. We just swung by to see Georgia—is she here?'

'Yes, she's just gone to have a shower, but I expect she'll be here in a minute. Why don't you come and have a drink while you wait for her?' Charles couldn't help wondering why these two rather dubious looking characters wanted to see Georgia.

The men were just taking the first sip of their drinks when Georgia appeared.

'Cade, Ben, good to see you,' Georgia greeted them, but Charles couldn't help noticing that she looked a bit apprehensive.

'Let me get you a drink,' Benedict said to Georgia. 'Is it the usual Coke?'

'Yes, with a straw rather than a glass, please.'

When she had got her Coke, Georgia and the two men retreated to a table where they could talk in private. Charles watched her covertly as he and the Pearces tucked into their meal. Everything looked very intense as Cade spoke quietly to her and when Georgia was served, her food it lay congealing and untouched on the plate. Charles felt very curious as to what was going on.

'Do you know Cade and Benedict Heston?' Charles asked George when they got back to his house.

'Only by reputation,' said George. 'This is the first time I've met them, but they're well known around here.'

'For what reason?'

'Well, Cade, who originates from South West Africa, apparently worked as a spy for the British in Europe during the war. I guess he was useful to them because he could speak German fluently. But it was later that he became legendary, during the years of the Mau-Mau rebellion. He came to this country after the war and bought a farm, but during the years of the Mau-Mau uprising the farmers were getting hammered and there was a period during that time when things were going very badly for all the settlers. The police and army just didn't seem to be able to get a handle on things, so some of the local whites decided to set up their own commando groups and Cade was one of the people who was really successful. He winkled out and dispatched a great number of the Mau-Mau, if the rumours I've heard are true and he became one of the Mau-Mau's most feared and hated rivals. They came after him in the end, but he wasn't at home when they struck. His wife was murdered and they left his infant son for dead, but Benedict lived. It made Cade even more bitter and he threw the rule book out of the window and really went after the insurgents with murderous intent after that.'

'So, what does he do now that the emergency is over?'

'He's still got his farm near Ol Joro Orok, but he spends a lot of his time hunting game. However, it's well known that he has empathetically stated on several occasions that the only sort of hunting that gives him real satisfaction is man hunting!'

Charles wondered again what business Georgia could be conducting with a man like that.

Chapter 9

Disturbing revelations

Monday was Charles's official day off, but on the Monday after the fly-in he headed for the airfield once again in the early morning where he had arranged to meet Bruce Little. Bruce had agreed to let Charles take up his Blue Bird glider when he realised that Charles was an experienced glider pilot, and Charles was looking forward to a few relaxing hours of soaring quietly on the strong thermals above Kenya's beautiful countryside. Over the weekend their taster flights had been very popular and the result had been a good number of eager people signing up to do their PPL, so this was to be a day of relaxation and enjoyment for Charles before he threw himself into the fray again the next day, where he knew they had end to end bookings.

Although Charles and Bruce had arrived at the club before seven in the morning, Georgia was not there. Since the only other person to be found was Sam, they enlisted him to help with the launch as they would need someone to run with the wing at the start of the take-off. Bruce would be driving the tow car, of course.

'When I've launched you, I'll take Sam back to the clubhouse and then put the Chevy back in the hanger,' Bruce told Charles in his booming voice. 'Then I'm heading for Nairobi to meet my daughter who's flying in from London. Take as much time as you like in the air with the Blue Bird and when you do come down, I'm sure you'll find some kind soul in the club willing to help you tow her back to the hanger where you can put her to bed.'

Once in the air, Charles caught a thermal and spiralled up into the clear blue sky. He knew that Kenya and the Nakuru area in particular, was considered one of the world's best places to glide due to the strong thermals that formed above the countryside, so he knew he could stay up for as long as he liked. To start with, he kept within the area of the airfield and watched with interest the activity below. Hans was working because his designated day off was Friday, so from his lofty position in the sky, Charles watched him take off with his first student for the day. Then he saw Amar and Georgia fly off in Zail's 182 and assumed that they were going to deliver meat to one of the butcheries. He wondered how many hours Georgia had logged since passing her PPL, it must be a fair number he decided, because she was always at the club and was willing to fly anyone or anything anywhere, at the drop of a hat, and people were aware of this and often took advantage of the fact there was a competent pilot who was willing to work for nothing.

Charles wasn't quite sure when Hans was quitting his job as assistant instructor, but with the boost the fly-in had given the club, Charles knew he wouldn't be able to cope without help, with the number of students who wanted to learn to fly. He decided he must ask Georgia if she had logged the required 200 hours flight time with 150 of them as pilot in charge, that was necessary before training to be an assistant instructor, and if she had, he would encourage her to do the training if she wanted to work at the club in that capacity. The thought of her working alongside him no longer dismayed him. She was obviously passionate about flying and he admired her for her persistence and determination to gain experience. She also had a magnetic property about her persona to which people involuntarily responded, but it wasn't just that, it was the fact that she was always there to help others when they needed help and that endeared her to all those who knew her.

As Charles enjoyed spiralling up on the thermals among the clouds he thought about Georgia. He had avoided her to start with because they had got off to a bad start and she had reminded him somehow of Fleur, so consequently she was a bit of an enigma to him now. Why was it she was living in the club with her cat when she had admitted to him that she did have a home, Charles wondered. Was he right to assume it was because she had fallen out with her parents? How did she manage for money? Although she seemed to work hard every day everything she did was on a voluntary basis, but she still had to pay for her room and food, so who was paying for that? She had loads of friends, but apart from the uncle that she still visited in the Thomson's Falls area, she didn't talk about any of her relatives. And the strange thing was, in a club where many of the members would gossip freely about each other, no one ever talked about Georgia or her circumstances. Charles decided that he would ask the girl if she wanted to do her assistant instructors rating, and at the same time try and find out a bit more about her.

When Charles landed the Blue Bird, he let it run to the side of the airstrip so that there was space for incoming and outgoing aircraft to land or take off, and then he walked to the club house to find someone to help him tow the glider to the hanger. To his surprise there was no one there. Hans was still airborne with one of his students and Sam was busy doing something out the back. Charles decided he would wait until the barman had finished whatever he was doing and then ask him to come and walk with the wing of the Blue Bird while he towed it back to the hangar. Alternatively, if anyone else suitable turned up before then, he would enlist their help.

Charles was sitting in one of the armchairs reading a 'Wings Over Africa' magazine when Amar and Georgia landed on their return trip from delivering meat.

'Ah ha, just the two people I wanted to see,' said Charles as they walked in. 'Georgia, I was wondering if you'd give me a hand to get the Blue Bird back into the hangar?'

'Of course,' Georgia said without hesitation. 'Do you want to do it now?'

'No, have a drink first, you both look hot and thirsty,' said Charles, seeing Sam suddenly appearing behind the bar. 'We'll do it after you've rehydrated yourself. Meanwhile, I want to talk to Amar.'

Charles noticed, with some surprise, that Georgia didn't look her normal chirpy self and she had dark circles under her eyes. He wondered if she was tired from the activities over the weekend, or if she was felling unwell for another reason.

'How can I help you?' said Amar when he was sipping an orange juice.

'I wanted to talk to you about re-sitting your PPL flying test,' said Charles. 'You're perfectly capable of passing it now and I don't see any reason for hesitating any longer.'

'Well. . .' said Amar looking uncertain.

'Of course, you must do it,' interjected Georgia. 'I've been telling him for ages that he's ready. Surely winning the forced landing competition proves that you are, Amar?'

'I've got a couple of other chaps ready to do their flight test and I'd like to put you forward as well, Amar,' said Charles. 'We'll make sure it's a different examiner this time, so he'll be completely impartial and there's absolutely no reason for you to fail if you just fly like you have been for the past couple of months.'

'Okay,' Amar looked resigned. 'My father has also been on at me to have another go at it and I know I must, but the butterflies in my stomach turn into huge fluttering crows when I think of doing another flight test!'

'You'll be absolutely fine,' Georgia assured him with conviction.

'Of course, you will,' agreed Charles. 'I wouldn't put you up for your test if I wasn't sure you were unquestionably ready.'

After Amar left to tell his father that he had signed up for another flight test, Georgia drove Charles back to the Blue Bird in her Land Rover. Once the glider was attached to her vehicle with a tow rope, she pulled it at snail's pace to the hanger while Charles kept the glider level as walked with the wing. Once they had got it safely housed, they drove back to the club house.

Charles glanced at Georgia as she drove them back. There was something inscrutable about her expression and she definitely looked under the weather.

'You must be exhausted after the weekend's activities,' he commented.

'No, not really, it was great fun, wasn't it?' She smiled at him wanly.

'Yes, and we made a lot of money—which was our main

objective. But you do look a bit tired today, Georgia.'

'It's nothing to do with the fly-in,' she said. 'It's, well, something else,' she bit her lip.

They had now reached the clubhouse and as they walked in Charles said, 'It's probably none of my business, but if I can help in any way. . . ?'

'No, I don't think you can . . . it's about my parents, you see.'

'Your parents?'

'You haven't been told, have you? I asked everyone not to talk or gossip about it, but I'm surprised that some of the consummate gossipers have been able to hold their tongues!'

'No one has told me anything about your parents,' Charles assured her, wondering what was coming.

'Well, they were murdered on our farm about eighteen months ago,' said Georgia shortly.

'Oh, my goodness, I'm so sorry—I had no idea,' Charles felt shocked. 'I thought maybe that you'd fallen out with them and decided to branch out by yourself, but how awful for you that they were murdered. Did they apprehend who did it?'

'No. The police thought it was a just a plain robbery that went wrong, even though nothing was taken. They said that when I turned up at the crucial moment the thieves probably took fright and ran away, but I don't think that's right.'

'You disturbed the murderers?'

'Personally, I don't think I did. I went out to a party on that night and I didn't get back until dawn was breaking. I was using my Vespa scooter at the time, so if they had still been there, they could have easily killed me as well.

'I knew something was wrong even as I drove up to the homestead because none of the dogs came to greet me as they usually did, and the askari didn't appear either. I called to the dogs when I stopped, but they didn't come because the bastards had poisoned them and they were dead! Three of our four cats also ate the poisoned meat and died, it was only Beano who didn't.'

Georgia stopped, she looked really distressed. She bit her lip and sniffed before going on.

'I didn't know the dogs and cats were dead at that stage, but I sensed something was very wrong and as soon as I went into the house, I heard a strange moaning sound and found Maina, our askari, sitting in the passage holding his head. I yelled to my parents, but there was no reply so I went to their room and. . . and it was ransacked and there was blood everywhere.' A tear rolled down Georgia's cheek. 'My parents were already dead and I couldn't do anything for them, but the worst thing was they hadn't just been killed, they had been tortured.' A silent shudder shook the girl's body and Charles put him arm around her.

'I'm so sorry,' he said. 'What a dreadful thing for you to have seen.'

'The police were pretty damn useless, they just kept saying it was thieves looking for money, but if that were true why didn't they just kill my parents, why waste time by torturing them? Maina told them it was two white men who had killed my parents, but because white people don't normally attack their own kind in this country, the police wouldn't believe him. They said he was involved in the attack and was just trying to make a cover story for himself. I didn't believe he was involved, but they arrested him anyway. Later, he was released because of lack of evidence.'

'What an absolutely horrible situation for you,' said Charles. 'No wonder you told me that you didn't have a home you wanted to return to!'

'No, it would be impossible for me to ever go back there permanently after witnessing what I did,' said Georgia sadly. 'I'm an only child and I inherited the farm after my parents' death. It was my father's wish that I'd eventually marry a farmer who would carry on the good work he had started on our farm, but even if I do marry a farmer that's not going to happen because I can't go back. I lease the farm to my uncle, Mum's brother, who lives on his farm near Thomson's Falls, and he and his son Euan run it between them. We have a profit-sharing agreement which benefits us all.'

'So did you come and live here at the club straight after all that happened?'

'No. I went to live with my uncle and aunt to start with. But I had already started to learn how to fly here at Lanet, so it seemed sensible to come and live here after a while. I was able to bring Beano with me because they had a mice problem here and were looking for a cat.'

'This is a terrible thing for you to have to come to terms with,' said Charles, feeling quite distressed for Georgia.

'Yes, it's not something you can ever get over,' agreed Georgia. 'But what I really wanted was for the perpetrators of the crime to be punished. The police have been so bloody useless—they just say it must have been common criminals and they can't find any evidence to charge anyone. So, I decided to ask Cade and Benedict to help me. Cade knew my father during the war—they were both working for the British as spies—and later Cade became well known when he and his commandoes were so successful in tracking down and eliminating Mau-Mau insurgents. I thought if anyone could find out who had murdered my parents it would be him.'

'He came to see you yesterday evening, didn't he?' prompted Charles.

'Yes; and what he told me was quite disturbing. He said he didn't think my parents had died at the hands of common criminals. Apparently, according to their post-mortem results which I have never been privy to, my mother had been tortured to death. My father had also been tortured but his cause of death was a heart attack. Cade thinks that whoever attacked them was trying to get information out of my father. He thinks my father either couldn't or wouldn't give them the information they wanted, so they started on my mother to try and loosen his tongue and that's when he had a heart attack. Cade then assumed they ransacked the room to look for the information they required and would have ransacked the whole house had they not been disturbed by our askari. Cade doesn't think Maina had anything to do with the attack.'

'Do you know what they could have been looking for?' Charles asked.

'No, but Cade says he thinks it could have been something that Dad found out about when he was working as a spy during the war. That makes sense, because I know he moved to Kenya because he didn't feel safe living in Britain after the war.'

'Does Cade have any idea who it could be who murdered your parents?'

'He hinted that whoever murdered them could be someone

from Europe, but he said he wasn't sure yet and would have to do some more investigations.'

'So, what happens now?'

'Well, Cade will continue with his investigations and he'll let me know if he finds out anything else. Meanwhile, I'll continue living here, so long as no one objects. It was hard meeting with Cade and Benedict last night and having all the wounds ripped open again, but I've managed to build a life for myself here. I have a career path that I intend to follow and most of the people in the club are like family to me now. My parents wouldn't have wanted me to mope around and do nothing—I think they would be pleased with what I've achieved.'

'I'm sure they would,' agreed Charles. 'I'm so sorry, Georgia, I had no idea what you've gone through. I think that you've done really well. Actually, I wanted to talk to you about doing your assistant flying instructors rating. Maybe now is not a good time since you're feeling a bit low, but. . .'

'No, now *is* a good time,' Georgia interrupted him. 'I need other things to focus on and I've almost amassed the number of required hours, so let's talk about me doing my assistant flying instructor's course.'

Chapter 10

Elyie Springs

Charles found he missed Georgia when she went to Nairobi for a few weeks to prepare for and sit her assistant instructors rating exams. He had got used to seeing her diminutive figure rushing about the club, checking everything was running smoothly and helping out whenever required. He found he had a huge amount of respect for her now—it couldn't have been easy for her to pick herself up after the brutal murder of her parents and plan for her future. She obviously had a very strong character and she didn't focus on herself, but tried to be kind and helpful to everyone.

It was a Tuesday evening when the telephone in the clubhouse office rang and Charles answered it.

'This is your new assistant flying instructor speaking,' Georgia sounded ecstatic. 'I passed Charles! I'm now qualified and can come home!'

'Good for you, girl!' Charles said, feeling very pleased for her. 'We've all been missing you and everyone will be delighted to hear your news. When're you coming back?'

'Tomorrow. I've already filled up the Landy and checked the oil, so I'll be on my way early and see you all before lunch.'

'Great. I'll tell Beano that you'll be coming home. I've been keeping an eye on him like you asked me to, but I think he's been missing you a bit.'

'Can't wait to get back and see him—and you all,' Georgia sounded joyful.

'Oh yes, I've got another bit of good news for you,' said Charles before he rang off. 'Amar has just passed his flying test! You can't imagine how happy and relieved he was when he heard he'd passed!'

'Congratulations to him! I'm so pleased for him. Please tell him "well done" from me.'

Everyone was pleased to see Georgia when she arrived back.

'When is she going to start instructing?' Howard asked Charles that evening when he and Mary came to the club for a meal.

'Tomorrow,' said Charles. 'Since we had the fly-in, Hans and I have had more students than we can comfortably handle, so she'll be a very welcome additional member of the team.

For the next three months the three instructors worked flat out. At first, some of the students were a bit dubious when they were told they would be instructed by a woman who appeared to be little more than a girl. But very soon Georgia became recognised as an excellent instructor and the students were happy to fly with her, because she was confident and very efficient. Having a female instructor also inspired other women to learn to fly and the club ceased to be such a male dominated establishment.

'We've had six batches of students in three months doing their flight tests and they've all passed,' Charles told Georgia and Hans with satisfaction, as they sat at the bar celebrating with the latest batch of students that had just passed their flying tests.

'That's good going,' agreed Hans. 'But at what cost, Charles? I don't think we've had a full day off between us in those three months!'

'Well, I've enjoyed every minute of it,' said Georgia as she sucked up her Coca Cola through a straw.

'Yes, but Hans has got a point,' said Charles. 'I think we should all have a weekend off and fly somewhere different for a couple of days of rest and relief.'

'Good idea,' said Howard, joining into the conversation. 'Why don't you gather a bunch of friends and fly up to Eliye Springs for a weekend? I'd be happy to give you "mate's rates" on the accommodation and you could relax by the lake, swim, go fishing or do a bit of mini-sailing. I'm sure you'd all have a great time!'

Somehow, that idea was very appealing and in no time at all a weekend fly-in to Eliye Springs had been organised. All the club's aeroplanes were booked and Howard and a number of other members who had aeroplanes also said they would be coming. Any vacant seats were offered to those needing transport and they were quickly snapped up!

On the day of departure, Georgia and Charles were to fly the club's Cessna182 to Eliye with Klaus and Randy as passengers. When they had all stowed their bags in the luggage compartment Randy asked, 'Who's going to pilot this aeroplane, Charles or Georgia?'

'I am,' said Charles and Georgia in unison.

'No, I am,' Charles repeated emphatically. 'I'm the senior pilot here, so I get to fly the aeroplane.'

'But you've never flown to Lake Rodolph before,' objected Georgia. 'I've done the trip dozens of times since I almost always do the vegetable run to the lodge, so I should be the one in the left-hand seat!'

'Ah ha, a dispute,' said Randy in delight. 'Who will win—the *senior* pilot, who always does everything properly, by the book no less, or the feisty *junior* pilot who throws caution to the wind and flies like a maniac?'

His remark brought howls of protest from both Georgia and Charles, causing Randy to howl with laughter. He just loved to instigate dissention!

'We vill have a vote,' said Klaus decisively. He was tired of standing around and just wanted to get on with things.

'Good idea,' Randy said. 'Raise your hands all those who want Georgia to be the pilot.' Georgia, Klaus and Randy all put their hands up. 'Sorry, old boy,' Randy put on an atrocious British accent. 'Looks like Georgia will be flying us to Elyie Springs.'

Charles threw his hands up in defeat. 'I don't know why you guys aren't flying up in your Ag Cats, anyway,' he said.

'I think you know very vell that the Ag Cats cannot carry fuel enough for long distances,' said Klaus testily. 'Come on, are we going to go?'

Charles didn't really mind that Georgia was flying, he would have preferred to be the pilot himself, but at least he could relax and enjoy the scenery. But a short while into the flight his brow furrowed and he turned to Georgia. 'Aren't you going to fly up the Kerio Valley?' he asked.

'No, I never do that. I just fly in a straight line to Elyie, it's quicker that way.'

'But. . . Howard and some of the others have told me it's safer to fly up the Kerio Valley because you have to fly over the Loriu Range when you go in a straight line, and should you have an engine failure there would be absolutely no chance of surviving a forced landing.'

'Relax, Charles. We're not going to have an engine failure or a forced landing; stop being so paranoid!'

'I'm *not* being paranoid, I'm just being sensible,' Charles objected. 'You never know when you might have an engine failure and it pays to be careful. I think you should fly up the Kerio Valley.'

'Well, I'm the pilot and I don't think that's necessary!'

'Another disagreement,' said Randy with delight. 'Perhaps we should have a vote on this as well. 'Klaus, what do you think?'

'I think we go the quickest way. I'm tired of all this—what you say? Yes, tittle tattle,' said Klaus testily.

'I think we should go in a straight line as well,' said Randy. 'So, you're out voted again, Charlie boy!'

'Well, I was just trying to keep us all safe,' said Charles resignedly. 'And I'll remind you all of this conversation when we crash!'

'No, you won't, because we'll all be dead,' said Randy, and he roared with laughter again. 'Tell me, Charles, are all British people so fearful?' he asked when he stopped laughing. 'You do know that Elyie Springs is a very remote location and there're many dangers lurking around Lake Rudolph? There're millions of venomous snakes and scorpions that exist in the volcanic rocks that surround the lake, there're hippos living in the area that can chop a man in half with one chomp of their fearsome jaws, and the lake itself is a breeding ground for the Nile crocodiles. These crocs are the second largest in the world; they can grow up to six meters—six meters, Charles, and are smaller only than the saltwater crocs! They're considered to be one of the most dangerous and deadliest predators and they're capable of taking down any animal that comes close to the water in which they live. At the last count it was estimated that there were 14,000 of these brutes living in Lake Rudolph!'

'Shut up, Randy,' said Georgia. 'It's not worth thinking about all the dangers you might meet in this world, and you'll spoil Charles's weekend if you keep harping on about the perils that you might encounter. If anyone gets chopped by a hippo or eaten by a croc it'll probably be you, anyway!'

'No, it's more likely to be Klaus,' said Randy, jabbing Klaus in the ribs with his elbow. 'They like nothing better than a bit of prime German flesh!'

'No, better they eat you,' said Klaus. 'Then they have meat and alcohol together with one gulp!'

Randy burst into delighted laughter. 'You're right, I intend filling my body with alcohol from the moment I step into to bar!'

'You know what? You're all completely mad,' said Charles laughing. 'It must be living at high altitude for so long that's affected your brains and caused you to throw caution to the wind—there can be no other explanation!'

'Well, if you stay in Kenya for long enough, you'll also be infected with altitude madness,' said Georgia with a giggle.

'More likely I'll be infected with madness after living with you lot for the weekend!' Charles commented wryly.

'As a matter of fact, Charles, you're lucky to be flying to Lake Rodolph,' said Randy. 'If we had to drive to the lake, it would take two or three days, if we were lucky, because the road is so bad. We could bog down in the sand, get stuck in mud or have a mechanical failure and be stranded on the road for days without food and water.'

'God forbid I ever get into a situation like that with you three for company,' said Charles with feeling. 'No doubt you'd be catching scorpions to roast and eat—and telling me to drink my own pee!'

❖

Howard and Mary had taken off after Georgia and her passengers and they had Bruce Little and William Reese with them. Bruce had toyed with the idea of trying to fly his glider all the way to

Eliye Springs, but had discounted it as impractical in the end. Although he was sure he would make it, he was unsure how he would be able to launch his glider for the return trip, so he accepted a lift with Howard. Willian was happy to set aside his spanners for a couple of days and was pleased he had managed to get a lift with one of the older pilots who wasn't likely to do anything stupid. The conversation in their aeroplane was also about Lake Rudolph, but differed considerably to the banter that was going on in the club's182.

'Does anyone know why the lake was named Lake Rudolph?' Bruce enquired.

'Yes,' said Howard. 'The first Europeans to have recorded visiting the lake were a Hungarian and an Austrian in 1888. They named the lake in honour of Crown Prince Rudolf of Austria. But it's also known as the Jade Sea, this is because when you approach the lake from ground level through the arid countryside, the algae in the lake that rises to the surface when the weather is calm gives the water a turquoise colour.'

'Is there a lot of game in the area?' William enquired.

'There is game, but not in huge amounts,' said Howard. 'The lake itself has a huge number of Nile crocodile in it, and there's hippo as well as a variety of fish. There's also a great assortment of birds that live around the lake—sandpipers, African skimmers, cormorants, bustards, even flamingos.'

One after another the aeroplanes that had flown from Lanet landed at the airstrip and parked in a line near the shed that supplied the fuel. Transport in the form of a long-wheel-base Land Rover arrived to shuttle the guests to the lodge.

'Come on Georgia, climb on before you get left behind,' said Randy when he and Klaus and Charles had clambered onto the back of the open Land Rover.

'No, I'm just going to refuel the 182 before I go to the lodge,' said Georgia. 'I'll catch a lift on the next shuttle. It'll just save time when we're ready to fly home.'

'Do you want a hand?' Charles asked.

'No, you carry on,' Georgia waved them away. 'I can easily manage; I've done it so many times and John does all the pumping, anyway.'

John was pleased to see her because she was a frequent visitor to the strip, since she had continued to do the vegetable run for Eliye Springs even after qualifying as an assistant instructor, and she always brought him something when she came. Usually, it was chocolate or a fizzy drink, but today she had some T-shirts that she no longer wore which she gave him for his children. He appeared clad in a dirty pair of shorts and nothing else and accepted her gift with delight.

'Now my children will be very smart and modern,' he remarked in glee.

Very soon he had the drum out and was busy pumping the fuel into the wing tanks of the Cessna 182.

'It's so hot,' he said. 'And now so many aeroplanes to refuel!'

'Never mind,' Georgia consoled him. 'At least you won't be bored for a couple of days and you should earn a few nice tips.'

John was running with sweat when they had finished refuelling the 182. It ran down his naked torso and face in rivulets. Although Georgia had done none of the pumping, she was also drenched with perspiration by the time they were finished. She gave John a generous tip in addition to the T-shirts before taxying the 182 to the parking area, thinking that he deserved it since he had to work in these temperatures every day.

When Georgia eventually got to the lodge, she found the others had already started to relax. Many had changed into cooler clothing and nearly everyone had a glass in their hand. Randy was propping up the bar as usual and Klaus was sitting outside in the shade with a mug of beer.

'Georgia, can I buy you a drink?' Charles appeared at her side. He had put on a pair of shorts and the first three buttons of his shirt were open.

'I just need to find out where I'm sleeping so that I can put my backpack away, and then I'd love a drink,' said Georgia.

'Hello, I'm Tim Bailey, the manager,' said a man coming up to her as she drifted away to find out where her accommodation would be. 'And you're the elusive Georgia who flies all our groceries to the Eliye strip and then disappears back to civilization without dropping by!'

Tim was in his mid-twenties and had flyaway fine blond hair.

His dark blue eyes studied Georgia as he spoke and his teeth looked very white against his deeply tanned face. His muscular body was clad in a green vest and a pair of shorts and he exuded virile masculinity.

'I know, I always seem to be in such a hurry,' said Georgia looking at him with appreciation. 'But if I'd realised what a nice place this is, I'd have definitely come and seen you.'

It was lovely at the lodge. The rustic palm thatched buildings were built close to the top of the lake's beach and nestled among the Doum palms trees. It was like an oasis in the arid desert, but the view in front of the buildings was of the beautiful unspoiled beach and the cool jade green lake.

'Well, the next time you deliver the groceries, come in and have some lunch before you rush off,' said Tim. 'The various people that Howard has, in the past, sent to deliver our groceries have always done that and lunch will be on the house.'

'Thanks Tim, I'll definitely come from now on.'

'Good. Now let me show you where you'll be sleeping this weekend.'

Tim would normally have got one of his staff to show a guest their accommodation, but he was fascinated by this tiny girl of whom Howard spoke so highly. On first glance she appeared little more than a child, but on further inspection he could see she was a woman in every sense of the word and she exuded a sexuality that excited him. He left her to get settled in and unpacked and wondered if his reaction to her had been because he lived a life of celibacy for the most part, stuck up in this remote northern part of Kenya. He hadn't managed to find a woman who would be prepared to stay here permanently, so far away from civilization, the shops, and everything else that went with living closer to a town or city.

When Georgia came back to claim her drink, she had changed out of her shorts and T-shirt and was wearing her bikini, over which she had put a short beach dress. She had also piled her hair on to the top of her head and secured it there, because she found it very hot when it was hanging around her neck. Tim was on the lookout for her and as soon as she appeared he rushed to ask her what she would like to drink. He thought she looked sexier than ever with her hair up.

'Can I have a Coke, please?'

'Just a Coke? Nothing stronger?' Tim sounded surprised.

'Yes, just a Coke—and could I have a straw rather than a glass, please?'

'Coming up.'

Charles saw her through the crowd at the bar just as Tim came up with her Coke.

'Oh, I see you've ordered,' said Charles. 'I'll pay for your drink.'

'No, this one's on the house,' said Tim. 'Special treatment for a special lady who flies all our groceries in from Nakuru.'

Charles noticed how Tim looked at Georgia and for some reason it annoyed him. He was glad when the manager was called away by one of his staff.

'What're you going to do after lunch?' Charles asked Georgia.

'I'm going to ask Tim if he can set up some water-skiing for us,' said Georgia, sucking at her straw. 'Gosh this Coke tastes good—I was really parched with thirst!' She had another slurp before she went on. 'I love water-skiing and it's calm today, so I think we should take the opportunity to do it. Tomorrow the wind will probably be blowing and it may be a bit rough for water-skiing. Can you water-ski, Charles?'

'Yes, I can, but what about the crocks?' Charles said, looking uneasily at the beautiful lake that glittered invitingly before them.'

'Oh Charles, you can't come for a weekend to a place like this and not go in the lake! Tim says it's safe enough here at Eliye. The local Africans go in the lake around here and they always know where it's safe. You'll die of heatstroke if you don't go in the water, Charles!'

Just then Tim appeared; he announced to everyone that lunch was being served.

'Could you set up some water-skiing for us after lunch?' Georgia asked him.

'Yes of course. You go and enjoy your lunch and I'll get the boat and equipment ready,' said Tim grinning at her. He was looking forward to seeing her in her bikini. 'The mini-sails are all ready for use as well, if anyone's interested.'

After they had digested their lunch a group of people who

enjoyed water-skiing walked to where Tim had the boat and skies ready. Charles was among them; he walked down in his swimming trunks with his towel slung around his neck. Georgia noticed that his body looked hard and toned and although he didn't have the dark tan that Tim had picked up living in Elyie, he was lightly tanned to a golden brown and looked fit. Although she had known Charles for months now, she had never really thought of him as anything more than an instructor from England—and a bit of a prat! But now she noticed he was actually an attractive man with his curly, longish hair, deep blue eyes and good physique. She wondered why he didn't have a girlfriend. He'd certainly had a lot of attention from the younger single females who frequented the club, but although he had been courteous and kind to them all, he had never formed a relationship with anyone. The thought that he could be gay flitted through her head, but she discounted it almost immediately. There was nothing gay about Charles, so his lack of interest when it came to women must be due to something else.

Georgia was proficient when it came to water-skiing because her father had enjoyed the sport and introduced his daughter to it when she was still very young. Now she chose to use only one ski and manoeuvred it with skill, zigzagging behind the boat and jumping over the wake. Her hair had come loose and now blew around her head as she zipped along. "Small but perfectly formed" came into Charles's mind as he watched her. When she was dressed in her normal shorts and T-shirt she looked like a little girl, but now that she was clad in nothing more than a bikini, he could see that although everything was in miniature, she had all the curves of a woman and he realised with a jolt that she was incredibly attractive and sexy. For the first time he realised why Randy had been so keen to get his hands on her!

Randy was suddenly at Charles's side; he had a glass of Bourbon in his hand and a camera hanging around his neck. 'My God, what a beautiful sight,' he murmured, putting his drink down and getting his camera ready to take some pictures of Georgia skimming over the water. Charles found himself wishing he could stop Randy. He could just imagine the American drooling over the photos once they had been developed, and he hated the thought of that.

'Are you going to have a go at water-skiing, Charlie boy?' Randy asked.

'Yes, I'm up next,' said Charles.

'Good. I'll take some photos of you as well—hopefully going arse over tip and falling into the gaping jaws of a Nile crock!' Randy roared with laughter.

Charles grinned weakly, 'How about you, are you going to have a go?'

'No way,' Randy laughed. 'I've never done it and never want to! What I'm going to do is sit in the shallow water to keep cool and watch everyone else make a fool of themselves.'

When it was Charles's turn, he chose to use two skis and he had a bit of a wobble when he got up but managed to steady himself. He didn't want to give Randy the opportunity to photograph him in a compromising situation, but more than that, he didn't want to fall in because he was secretly worried about the crocodiles that lurked under the surface of the beautiful lake.

'You looked good,' said Georgia when he got back without mishap.

'I'm a bit rusty, but I really enjoyed that,' said Charles grinning at her.

'Come on, let's bag ourselves a mini-sail,' said Georgia. 'There're too many people wanting to water-ski and we'd have to wait for ages for our turns to come round again.' She was never one to sit around idly, and Charles found himself being dragged away from what he perceived as the safest water sport in which to indulge at Lake Rudolph.

'Do you know how to sail one of these things?' Charles asked when they got their mini-sail.

'Yes, I did a bit of sailing with Dad, so I know the basics although I'm no expert. Come on, it's a lot of fun.'

It was a lot of fun although they continually capsized, causing the adrenaline to rush through Charles's veins when he thought of the crocodiles watching their floundering bodies in the water and thinking of a meal.

'We're getting the hang of this,' said Georgia at last when they managed to stay upright for a while.

'Yes, it's amazing how quickly one learns when the alternative could be disastrous!' Charles pulled a face and made Georgia giggle.

'Well, this has been such fun, but I guess we should go in now and let someone else have a turn,' Georgia eventually said rather reluctantly.

Charles wished that they could spend more time on the mini-sail; he was enjoying Georgia's company and didn't really want to share her with anyone else. He felt quite reluctant to relinquish the mini-sail, but as soon as they sailed back to the shore of the lake there was someone else waiting for a turn.

'Come on, I'll buy you a drink,' said Charles as he retrieved his towel. 'That was great, Georgia—this is going to be a good weekend!'

Chapter 11

Love Blossoms

That evening Tim had organised a dance for his guests. He didn't have any disco lights or any fancy equipment, but the lodge did have a good sound-system and a selection of records with popular music from the last few years. Soon the dancing area was crowded with people as they jiggled and gyrated to the beat of the music.

Charles had managed to have a couple of dances with Georgia before she was whisked away by one of her many admirers, and his hopes of monopolising her for the evening were soon dissolving. He did keep an eye on her though so he noticed that when she was dancing with Glen, one of the glider pilots, while *Get Off My Cloud* by the Rolling Stones played on the stereo system, she looked upset. He wondered why.

The next record to play was *Yesterday* by the Beatles and as Charles watched Georgia, her face crumpled. With a quick word to Glen, she suddenly excused herself and hastily left the dance floor. Glen looked mildly surprised, but he let her go and wandered up to the bar to get himself another drink. Charles followed Georgia at a distance wondering what had upset her. He trailed her as she made her way to the beach where she sank down and sat in the sand. Charles kept out of sight, not wanting to disturb her if she just wanted to have a moment to herself, but when he heard her sobbing, he went right up to her and sat down beside her.

'Whatever's the matter?' Charles asked.

'Oh, don't worry about me,' said Georgia hastily wiping her eyes on the back of her hand. 'I'm okay.'

But Charles could feel her shaking and it was obvious that she wasn't okay. He put a comforting arm around her shoulders.

'But clearly you aren't!' he said. 'Something's upset you—was it Glen?'

'No, it's nothing to do with Glen. It was the music that was being played. Dad and Mum loved to dance, but Dad had a habit of singing while they danced when he'd had a few beers and it embarrassed Mum. She used to try and shush him up, but he just sang all the louder. *Get Off My Cloud* was one of his favourite songs and he used to sing really loudly when it came on, so when it played tonight, I could almost hear him singing along. It made me feel emotional; then when the next song to play was *Yesterday*. The lyrics reminded me that—*yesterday,* (when my parents were still alive), *all my troubles seemed so far away, but now it looks as though they're here to stay.* I know, I'm being silly, but it suddenly all got to me.'

'You're not being silly at all,' Charles comforted her. 'Getting over your parents' murder is a hell of a thing and it's not going to be easy or happen quickly. You've done wonderfully well so far and I'm sure they'd be proud of you, but you're entitled to have a wobble from time to time.'

'I just miss them so much,' said Georgia, her eyes filling with tears again. 'We were such a close family and Dad was different to anyone else I knew. He was quite fearless and always up for trying something new. His motto was "carpe diem"—seize the day. He was never still and was always rushing around trying to do different things or make things better. When I said I wanted to learn how to fly, he was delighted and encouraged me to follow my dream. Both my parents were so supportive and sometimes I just can't imagine how I'm going to go forward without their support.'

'From what you've told me about your father, you're a real chip off the old block!' said Charles. 'And of course you are managing perfectly to go forward without their support—look at what you've achieved already! It's what your father would expect, isn't it?'

'Yes, I suppose so. He always tried to make me be independent and stand on my own feet. I just wish it didn't hurt so much that they're not here anymore. And I don't even have the satisfaction of knowing that their murderers have been brought to justice.'

'Has Cade not come up with any answers, then?'

'No, not yet, but he will. He's the type who won't let it go until he's found answers. But even when he does, it won't bring Dad and Mum back, will it? I just wish I didn't feel so alone all the time.'

'Don't you have any other relatives in this country? What about your uncle and his family?'

'Yes, of course I do have Uncle Oliver and Aunt Fiona. Oliver is my mother's brother and they've been very good to me. I think I told you before that Uncle Oliver and Euan, his son, run my father's farm now. But Oliver isn't anything like my father; he's a good solid farmer who was the son of a farmer, and although he and Euan do a great job, they seem dull and unadventurous to me. Oliver certainly doesn't like the profession that I've chosen, he still thinks that girls should marry and spend their lives having children and looking after their husbands! I lived with them for a while after Mum and Dad were murdered, but although they were really kind to me, I felt suffocated, and that's one of the reasons why I moved into the club.'

'Well, you've already started to rebuild your life and made a pretty good job of it. Everyone likes you and thinks you're a really great girl; look how popular you are on the dance floor. I only had one or two measly dances with you before you were whipped away!'

Georgia laughed and Charles felt glad that he had managed to cheer her up a bit.

'What about you, Charles?' Georgia asked. 'I've been selfishly prattling on about myself, but I'd love to know what brought you out to Africa.'

'It's a long and rather sordid and sorry tale,' Charles admitted.

'Well, we've got all night. It's nice sitting here in the moonlight, so if you want to talk about it I'm willing to listen.'

Charles still had his arm around Georgia and it felt good to be close to her. He didn't want anything to change yet, so he told her about his disastrous love affair with Cordelia and the consequences.

'People can be so horrible sometimes,' Georgia commiserated after he had finished his tale. 'I can understand that sometimes people can fall out of love, but it doesn't give them the right to treat someone badly and have no compassion when they know they're going to break a heart.'

'Yes, but sometimes that's the way of the world,' said Charles. 'And I thought that getting away from England and starting afresh in Kenya would be a good plan.'

'So, we're both trying to rebuild our lives,' murmured Georgia.

She was looking at him and he could just make out her features in the moonlight while her hair fluttered in the strengthening breeze. Her face appeared to be pale and ethereal and her features were finely sculptured in the beams of the moon. Her long eyelashes seemed to interlace above her eyes which looked huge and compassionate. He could see there was a sheen of moonlight on her full lips and they were slightly parted. Suddenly, without thought, he bent forward and brushed her lips with his. She seemed to hesitate for a second, but then she responded and Charles tightened his arm around her and drew her towards him. Soon the kisses became more passionate.

It was the strong wind that blew up that drove them off the beach in the end, and they reluctantly went back to the dance. By this time the music being played was much slower so that the dancers could smooch around the dancing area in each other's arms. Frank Sinatra was singing *Strangers in the Night* as they arrived and Charles immediately took Georgia in his arms and led her around the dance floor.

'No one is going to dance with you this evening except me,' he whispered.

Later when he went to buy them both a drink he found Randy, who was propping up the bar, gazing at him speculatively out of half-shut bloodshot eyes. The man had positioned himself where he could keep an eye on the dancers and he was obviously very drunk, but he smiled at Charles and said without slurring, 'Took you a while, Charlie boy, but you got there in the end. Take very good care of her.'

❖

It was obvious to everyone the next morning that Charles and Georgia were in the first flush of romance and they were pleased for the couple.

'Come on you two love birds, we're going fishing,' Randy shouted to them. 'I've reserved you places in the boat I'm going on.' Charles was astonished that Randy seemed to be showing no ill effects from the copious amount of alcohol that he had consumed the previous evening. He looked as fresh as a daisy and was clad in his swimming trunks and a brightly coloured shirt.

'Now where's Klaus got to?' Randy asked looking around. 'I told him he had to come fishing today and he said he'd be here.' But Klaus must have had other ideas and when he appeared on the horizon, he just waved them away. 'Silly old fool,' muttered Randy. 'I guess he just wants to sit drinking at the bar all day! Never mind, we're going to catch us a heap of fish, Klaus or no Klaus!'

Apart from Randy, Charles and Georgia, there was Hans and his pretty girlfriend Suzie Appleton in the boat, and at the last-minute William rushed up to take Klaus's place.

'Boat is full now,' said Aaron, the African boat driver. 'We go.'

The wind that had blown strongly all night had now dropped and it was hot and calm out on the lake. They hadn't gone far before the first Nile Perch was caught and soon they were being hooked one after the other.

'Fishing has never been so easy,' said Charles, as he landed yet another fish.

'The lake has many fish,' Aaron told them. 'It is full of Nile Perch and the crocodiles feast on them. That is why it is safe to swim in the lake—the crocodiles do not want to eat people when there are so many fish to eat.'

'Now, I bet hearing that has made you feel relieved, Charlie boy,' said Randy. 'You don't have worry about the crocs because they're busy eating the fish!'

After a bit it got very hot and the novelty of catching Nile Perch had worn thin.

'Take us to Central Island, Aaron,' said Randy. 'It'll be

interesting to have a look around it.

'There are three lakes on the island,' Aaron told them. 'Crocodile Lake, Flamingo Crater Lake and Tilapia Crater Lake. Where we land, Crocodile Lake will close, but I must advise there are many, many crocodiles there! It is there that they breed and Nile crocodile mothers bury their eggs on the beach to stop the Monitor lizards from finding and eating them. Yes, you can hear squeak, squeak, from the babies in the eggs under the sand and their mummies stand guard and they become very, very kali if they think there is danger to their babies, so you must be aware!'

When they got to the island, they all got out and scrambled up the hill so that they could look down on Crocodile Lake.

'Phew, it's hot enough, isn't it?' Charles wiped his perspiring forehead.

'Yes, but worth the climb and hot conditions,' said Georgia. 'Look at those crocodiles on the beach down there—there're masses of them!'

Charles felt quite glad the crocs were a fair distance from where they stood on the hill, and he was amazed when Randy said he was going to walk down to Crocodile Lake.

'Whatever would you want to do that for?' Charles asked. 'Can't you see all the crocodiles? They're probably guarding the eggs they've buried and will be aggressive as hell!'

'I'm goin' to get me a baby crocodile,' said Randy. 'Why do you think I carried this bucket all the way up here?' He brandished the red bucket he had brought from the boat. 'It's to put my baby croc in!'

'Is the man drunk or has he gone mad?' Charles asked.

'Both!' Hans gave a little laugh.

'Seriously, I don't think it's a good idea for you to walk down to that beach where there're so many crocodiles, Randy,' Georgia look at him in concern.

'At last! The lady cares about me!' Randy laughed loudly. 'Have no fear, sweetheart, I'm indestructible!' With that he lolloped down the hill swinging his bucket above his head as he went.

The others watched him as he ran onto the beach. Several of the large crocodiles were alarmed by his sudden approach and scuttled swiftly into the water. This gave Randy the confidence to chase up the beach and look for a baby crocodile. The others saw him stop abruptly and bend down with his back to them and then they heard him exclaim in pain and then bellow out a swear word. A movement to his left suddenly caught their attention; a huge crocodile had raised herself up and was coming at speed towards him.

'Randy, *run!*' shouted Charles. The others joined him in encouraging Randy to make a swift departure, because the crocodile's intent was obvious.

They watched in an agony of suspense as Randy twirled around and, with one glance at the approaching croc, sprinted away from it. They could see the crocodile was easily gaining on Randy and the drama being played out in front of them seemed to be heading for one conclusion, but after about ten meters when the snout of the crocodile was virtually on Randy's heels, she slowed and stopped for a moment as though to catch her breath. Randy was full of adrenaline and powered on up the hill towards the others, leaving the crocodile lying disconsolately at the bottom.

'I got one!' Randy panted as he sprinted up to the others. He had a big grin on his face and looked immensely pleased with himself. 'It gave me a nasty nip, but I got it anyway!'

'You stupid bastard!' said Hans angrily. 'You were nearly eaten by a f-ing croc and we would have had to watch!'

'Sorry you had to miss such engaging entertainment,' said Randy laughing. 'But I was in no danger really.'

'You were, Randy,' said Suzie. 'That croc was within an inch of your feet before she stopped.'

'Probably got a whiff of his feet and had to sit down for a moment,' suggested William wryly.

'What you ignorant folk don't know is that a crocodile can only run fast for about ten meters and then has to stop or slow down,' said Randy. 'I knew that in my peak physical fitness, I could easily outrun the thing.'

'Physically fit, you? How could you be fit when you put away so much alcohol every day?' Charles laughed at Randy.

'Just shows what a super-human I am,' said Randy glibly. 'Anyway, look what I got!' Up until then the others had been so distracted that they hadn't seen that Randy really did have a baby crocodile in the bucket. 'It may be small, but the vicious little bastard bit the hell out of my fingers when I picked it up!' Randy held up his bloodied fingers.

'Serve you right. Now you're going to have to go down the hill again and put it back on the beach,' said Suzie.

'You've got to be joking!' Randy laughed. 'I risked my life and nearly had a finger severed to get this little fellow. I'm certainly not going to put him back!'

'What're you going to do with it, Randy?' Georgia asked.

'I'll look after it until it's grown big and then I'll make handbags and purses out of its hide. You can make a fortune out of crocodile skin bags and things in America.'

'Ugh, it all sounds rather sordid to me,' said Georgia. 'Is it even legal to remove it from its environment to another location without consent from the Wildlife Department?'

'Who cares? No one will even know that I've snitched a croc from Central Island!'

The little croc glared at the group of people gazing down at him. His protruding round eyes glittered with malevolence and his jaws gaped slightly, as though daring one of the onlookers to put their fingers too near him.

'Well, rather you than me,' said Charles. 'He looks like a damn unfriendly animal to me and I wouldn't want to have him for a pet!'

'Come on,' said William. 'Let's get back to the boat and home to Eliye. I'm absolutely parched and if we stand here in the glaring hot sun for much longer, we'll all become desiccated!'

They returned to the boat and at first Aaron was speechless when he saw the baby crocodile in the bucket. But when he did find his tongue, he had quite a bit to say about it.

'You did a very bad and dangerous thing taking that baby,' he chastised Randy. 'What if you had been caught by its mother? You would have been killed in front of your friends and I would probably be sacked for letting you do such an irresponsible thing!'

'Relax, my friend,' said Randy. 'I'm alive as you can see, and no-one had to witness a death or be fired on my account. Anyway, those watching would probably have been pleased to see my demise—all except Georgia—because you love me, don't you darlin'?'

'I certainly wouldn't like to see you being eaten by a croc,' said Georgia with a shudder.

As the boat made its way across the glittering water heading for Eliye, the passengers fell silent and there was none of the banter that had filled the boat on their outward trip. The intense heat coupled with the gentle motion of their passage made them drowsy and only Aaron, who still had a disapproving expression on his face, was alert. William decided to stretch out his legs as he was getting cramp in them, and he accidently upset the bucket in which the baby crocodile resided. In a flash, the little creature scuttled among the feet of those on the boat looking to avenge himself of the indignity of being put in a bucket. All hell broke loose as the tiny jaws with their razor-sharp teeth snapped at bare toes and ankles!

'For God's sake, get the little bugger back in the bucket,' said Charles, drawing his feet up just in time.

'I will,' gasped Randy, trying to catch the croc without being bitten. 'Come here you little bastard—oh no you don't, don't even try and bite me!' But the feisty crocodile was feeling agitated and pugnacious and was bent on doing as much damage as possible while he had the chance.

The boat rocked dangerously as the mayhem continued and Aaron shouted at them all to sit down. Georgia and Suzie couldn't stop giggling—they had both tucked their legs up out of harm's way and they found the sight of such a small creature causing so much chaos hilarious. Hans and Charles were attempting to herd the little creature back into the bucket which lay on its side, while Randy lunged at the croc while trying to avoid being bitten. William was doing his best to keep out of its way and when it suddenly ran in his direction, he whipped off his hat and waved it at the creature, making Georgia and Suzi laugh even more hysterically. The croc suddenly latched on to the brim of the hat, snatching it out of William's hand. In a flash, Randy grabbed the other side of the hat and lifted it up with the croc still hanging on to it for dear life. Charles quickly righted the bucket and pushed it to Randy so that he could drop the hat and the croc into it.

'Got you, you little bastard!' said Randy in satisfaction.

'Can I have my hat back?' William asked as he felt the full heat of the sun's rays on his bald pate.

'Not unless you want to put your hand into the bucket with the crocodile,' said Randy. 'And please, William, if you want to kick the bucket, don't do it in this boat!'

Everyone laughed, but it was more from relief than anything else.

Georgia dug a scarf out of her bag and tied it on William's head so that he looked like a pirate. 'It's probably not as protective as your hat, but it's better than nothing,' she said.

When they got back to the lodge, they all headed for the bar because they were parched with thirst.

'Well, that was jolly good fun as you Brits say,' said Randy. He had managed to steal a spoonful of beer out of Klaus's tankard and was trying to feed it to the crocodile. 'Hopefully, a drop of alcohol will help to give this little chap a more friendly disposition.'

'Or it will poison the poor creature,' said Georgia. 'Come on Charles, drink up your Cola, then we can go mini-sailing again.'

Will I ever be able to keep up with this little dynamo? Charles thought as he followed Georgia out of the bar. They had already caught masses of fish, been complicit in the abduction of a baby crocodile, escaped its gnashing jaws when it escaped in the boat, and then nearly died of thirst before they had returned to Elyie. Surely that should have been enough excitement for one day? But there she was, raring to go again!

However, it was nice to be alone with her out on the water. They had bettered their co-ordination when it came to sailing the little craft and it was a pleasure to see the joy in Georgia's eyes as they sailed over the beautiful Jade Sea. Later, when they returned to land, the sun was setting, a great iridescent orange orb on the horizon that reflected its sparkling colour over the lake and turned it to liquid gold. When they had pulled the boat up the beach, Charles took Georgia in his arms and looked into her eyes. He could see the setting sun reflected there and the last of the sun's rays spilled over them causing them both to glow in the pleasing bronze light. The feel of her lithe wet body pressed against his felt sublime as he kissed her passionately.

'What a weekend this has been,' Charles said after a bit.

'I thought it would be a good laugh and a nice break to have a weekend in Elyie with a bunch of friends, but I never imagined how wonderful it was all going to turn out.'

Chapter 12

Life goes on

The next morning after breakfast the group of friends prepared to return to Lanet. Tim had a new crowd of visitors arriving later that morning, so he asked them to vacate their rooms as soon as possible so that the staff could clean them and make them ready for the next lot of people.

Klaus arrived at the breakfast table looking rather dishevelled and grumpy. His face was creased in angry lines and he definitely needed a shave. Georgia was surprised to see him in that state, because normally he turned himself out immaculately and although he could be dour, he never usually appeared to be irritable or petulant.

'What's up with Klaus?' she asked Randy when the German had gone to get himself some breakfast cereal.

'Well, as you know he was sharing a room with me and this morning when he got up for a shave, he found Herb in the basin.'

'Herb?'

'Yup, Herb, my baby crocodile. I thought that was a good place to keep him overnight. Anyway, I had scrounged some raw meat and fish from the kitchen to feed the little beggar, and, well, he's a bit of a messy eater—and then to compound things he had a crap! So, when Klaus wanted to use the basin for his morning ablutions, he found not only a crocodile in situ but also a huge mess and he wasn't amused!' He wanted me to get Herb out and clean the basin so he could use it, but I didn't want to move Herb before he had to be put in his bucket for transportation, so we had a bit of a fall out!'

Later, when they were taken to the airstrip in the Land Rover, Klaus was still in a bad mood and things didn't get any better when he realised that Randy intended to keep the crocodile in its bucket on the floor at his feet during the flight back to Lanet.

'Put it in the luggage compartment,' Klaus demanded.

'No, the bucket might fall over and then the little bastard would be free to cause all sorts of chaos,' said Randy.

'I will not. . . I refuse, I absolutely refuse to sit next to that creature!' Klaus was infuriated at the idea of having the crocodile in the cabin.

'Well, if you really don't want to, the alternative is that you start walking! Herb stays with me so that I can keep him safe!'

The two crop sprayers glared at each other, neither willing to back down.

'Look, I'll sit in the back with Randy and the crocodile,' suggested Georgia, thinking it was the best way to defuse the situation.

'No,' Charles cut in quickly. He didn't like the idea of Georgia sitting close to Randy's wandering hands for two hours! 'You need the flying hours, Georgia, so you fly and I'll sit in the back with Randy. Does that suite you guys?'

'I'd rather sit with Georgia,' said Randy.

'Yes, I am happy with that arrangement,' said Klaus. 'You vill do as you're told, Randy,' he added. 'You've caused enough trouble as it is.'

'*I've* caused trouble?' Randy sounded outraged.

'Come on then, let's get going.' Georgia didn't want more arguments to start and further delay them. She was glad she had already refuelled and they could leave immediately. As they taxied to the top of the airstrip for take-off, she waved to John, who was already looking aggrieved at all the pumping he was faced with that day.

No-one argued about which route to take on the return trip. All of them wanted to get home as quickly as possible and after two hours of flying they were glad to touch down at Lanet without incident.

Amar Singh had landed seconds before them. He had just returned from delivering meat to one of their butcheries, and he walked over to welcome them as they all tumbled out of the 182.

'Well done, sweetie,' said Charles to Georgia, dropping a kiss on her head. 'You got us home in record time. I don't think I could have stood a minute more in that aeroplane with two grumpy crop sprayers and a vicious, irritable crocodile!' He went to remove their bags from the luggage compartment and nodding to Amar, he carried their bags to the clubhouse.

'Hi Georgia,' said Amar, coming up. He had a startled look on his face.

'Hi Amar, have you just come back from delivering meat?'

'Yes, but now I think there is something wrong with my eyesight!'

'What?'

'Yes, first I thought I saw Charles kissing you— *Charles* kissing *you*? Then I passed Randy and he appeared to have a *crocodile* in the bucket he was carrying? My God, I must be going blind—or maybe mad!'

'No, you're not! Randy caught that baby crocodile while we were at Lake Rudolph and insisted on bringing it back. And Charles and me—well, it just kind of happened!'

'Charles and *you*? No! How can that be?'

'I know. I can hardly believe it myself! I guess we just got off on the wrong foot to start with because he's actually a very nice guy and I just didn't see it at first.'

'Well yes, I've always thought he was okay,' said Amar. 'But what a turn-around for you! Do you love him?'

'It's just too soon to know what I really feel about him,' said Georgia honestly. 'I guess time will tell.'

During the next few weeks, the instructors at Lanet were once again kept busy by a stream of keen students who wanted to learn to fly. Hans delayed his departure because he said he didn't want to leave the other two in the lurch, but in reality, he and Suzi had fallen deeply in love and he wanted more time to persuade his girlfriend to become his wife. Suzi confided in Georgia that she absolutely adored Hanse, but wasn't sure she wanted to leave Kenya for Germany. However, Hanse prevailed upon Suzi and eventually she capitulated and agreed to marry him.

'I don't have any doubts about our relationship,' Suzi assured Georgia. 'But I've been brought up on a farm in Kenya like you Georgia, and I worry that being an airline pilot's wife in Germany will be very unlike what I'm used to. I'll have to learn German for starters and the way of life will be completely different.'

However, on her wedding day Suzi looked absolutely radiant. She floated up the aisle on the arm of her father, Godfrey Appleton, a vision in white lace studded with shining pearls. Hans's sister, Freda, followed behind her as maid of honour and trailing behind were two cute little flower girls, Hilda, who was the youngest sister of Hans, and Suzie's little sister, Josie. Suzi's face was full of joy as Godfrey steered her into position beside Hans. The whole of the flying club had been invited to the wedding and the church bulged at the seams with all the people.

Georgia and Charles sat together on one of the pews, their fingers entwined. Their love affair had grown from strength to strength during the previous weeks and they were now inseparable. Although Suzi was a vision of beauty, Charles only had eyes for Georgia. She wore a figure-hugging dress of green, a colour that particularly suited her, and her hair hung in shining curls around her shoulders. She had applied make up, making her eyes look huge and luminous and her lips soft, pink and inviting. She wore very high heels to boost her height and Charles thought she looked every inch a woman. He was so proud to be the man at her side.

Georgia was also pleased to be with Charles. He looked so handsome in his suite with his white shirt freshly laundered and pressed to perfection by Emmanuel. He had brought a new dimension into her life and loving him had eased the pain of losing her parents. She and Charles were very different in character; Charles being a steady person who liked to obey rules and keep his life on a very even keel, while Georgia was more adventurous and tended to push the boundaries from time to time, if she thought she could do so without causing harm to herself or anyone else. But as they say, opposites attract and they couldn't have been more happy together.

When the church service was over and everyone drove to Godfrey's farm where the reception was being held, the song "*Red Balloon*" was playing over the sound system:

"In and out of the red balloon, marry the farmer's daughter. . ."

'The farmer's daughter is going to miss all this,' Georgia remarked, looking round appreciatively at the beautiful spacious garden in which the reception was being held.

Soon Champaign was being handed out so that they could toast the bride and groom.

'Would you like me to get you a straw?' Charles joked.

'Gosh no! Doesn't drinking alcohol through a straw make you get drunk more quickly?' Georgia asked. Her nose wrinkled as she sipped a little of her Champaign.

'I don't know. Does it? It doesn't look like you're enjoying your drink!' Charles remarked.

'Well, I'm not really. I'd prefer a Coke any day—with a straw of course—but I wouldn't insult the lovely couple by toasting them with Cola!'

Soon the reception was in full swing and everyone looked relaxed and happy. Even Mr Schmidt, Hans's father, looked more comfortable. He, apparently, couldn't speak any English and had appeared uneasy at the wedding ceremony, but now he was chatting away to Klaus. Having found a fellow German had made it easier and Georgia felt happy for him as he laughed with the crop sprayer. Mrs Schmidt spoke English quite well, and she seemed to be getting on well with Howard and Mary.

'Gosh, look at those two little flower girls,' said Georgia as the two little girls ran past giggling. 'Neither of them can speak nor understand the other's language, but they're having a whale of a time together!'

'Kids are like that,' Charles said. 'Unlike adults, they don't let the boundaries of language limit them.'

Eventually, it was time for the married couple to depart on their honeymoon and Suzi changed out of her wedding gown and appeared in a smart little blue outfit. There was much banter as they ran to their car, but eventually they departed, trailing cans and long streamers of toilet paper behind them. Someone had scrawled "Just Married" in lipstick on the back window of their car.

'They're heading for the Stags Head Hotel tonight,' Georgia told Charles. 'Tomorrow they're driving down to the coast. Don't tell anyone where they'll be tonight though; Suzi doesn't want anyone to go and play a prank on them there!'

'Why aren't they flying to the coast?' Charles wanted to know.

'Well, I suppose it's because they'll need a car when they get there. But talking of the coast, Charles, some months ago—long before we, um, got close, I agreed to go to the coast with Oliver and Fiona and Euan and Diana and the boys for Christmas. I'd actually much rather spend Christmas with you, but I just don't think I can get out of going without offending my family—and I don't want to do that because they've been so kind and supportive since Mum and Dad died.'

'Oh hell,' said Charles looking disappointed. 'I was looking forward to spending Christmas with you.'

'I know; it's a complete bummer. But I was thinking if I just spent Christmas with them, I could then make an excuse to come back for the New Year. That way, I wouldn't be offending them and we could have some fun time together during the festive season. I always think Christmas is for kids anyway, with Father Christmas and presents etcetera, but New Year is for adults because it's celebrated with parties and dances that are normally good fun.'

'Yes, that would be really great,' said Charles brightening up. 'I could fly down to the coast and collect you and we can have a ball together during the New Year celebrations.'

'But what'll you do at Christmas?'

'Well, Mary and Howard have invited me to have Christmas with them, they said you'd be welcome as well, but I sort of stalled them because I didn't know what you wanted to do.'

'Oh good, you go to them and then you won't be alone. I hate the thought of us being apart, but Christmas isn't for ages, is it?'

'It's over two months away, but people like to get organised, don't they?'

Hans and Suzi were flying back to Germany as soon as they got back from their honeymoon and everyone was sad to see them go. Georgia was especially sorry to say goodbye to Suzi as they had known each other for most of their lives. However, the work load increased with Hans's departure, so she didn't have time to think too much about her loss. In the little amount of spare time that she and Charles had, they were completely inseparable and they tried to get away from the club together when they snatched a few hours for themselves.

'It's lovely here,' said Charles to Georgia one afternoon when they had escaped from the club for the afternoon and had driven to Lake Naivasha. They were relaxing on the grass on a rug and Charles was gazing across the beautiful water of the lake through half shut eyes, while he held Georgia close to his side.

The lake was hugged by grassy banks and forests of olive trees, and acacias also grew around providing a wonderful habitat for the many birds and wild life that resided there. They had already seen giraffe wandering among the acacia and Colobus monkeys swinging in the branches.

'It's another little piece of paradise,' Georgia agreed. 'It all looks so calm and beautiful, but the lake can change very quickly and get extremely rough, Charles, some people have been caught out in little boats and capsized. Some have even been drowned because there's a lot of water weed that can entangle your legs.'

'It's hard to imagine it rough on a day like this.'

'Yes, but sudden storms often blow up and change things in an instant. The Masia's name for the lake is Nai'posha and it means rough water.'

'It would be nice to have a house here, wouldn't it?'

'Yes, perhaps we should buy the Djin Palace and live there together,' Georgia joked.

'The Djin Palace? Howard mentioned that place to me when I first arrived in the country, and I sort of understood from what he said that things had gone on there that he didn't approve of.'

'Gosh yes, you're right. Howard certainly wouldn't approve of what went on there in the past! It was built by Major Ramsay in the 1920s, I think. He decided to build a Moorish style mansion for his wife and incorporated a spectacular inner court yard with fountains etcetera, and there was also a squash court and swimming pool. I think he even managed to create a polo field on the property grounds. Then he invited all the rich and famous 'blue bloods' who had moved out to Kenya after the first war, to visit them. Most of them lived in the Wanjohi Valley area and they were known as the Happy Valley Set because they all threw orgies and wife swapping parties, all spiced up by taking drugs! Major Ramsay's parties were notorious for their immorality and wantonness, according to my father.'

'Goodness, it does sound rather decadent!' Charles was intrigued to hear about this bit of Kenya's spicy history.

'Yes, that's why Howard couldn't possibly approve! My father used to talk about the Happy Valley crowd sometimes and deride them as people who had too much money and the morals of a tomcat! But he also said that some of the Happy Valley Set had farms, and because they could afford to bring in good cattle stock from Europe, the quality of cattle in Kenya overall was greatly enhanced.'

'So, all was not lost, then. Are these people still around?'

'No—well, yes, some of them are and their descendants are still around—the Cholmodeleys and the Delamers—but the parties have stopped. I think the height of the Happy Valley Set was in the late 1920s, but in the 1940s they were still at it and then Lord Errol was murdered. Perhaps that's when the decline set in.'

'Who murdered him, and why?'

'He was a womaniser and I think it's generally thought that Sir Jock Delves Broughton shot him, although he was never convicted for the crime. Lord Errol was having an affair with Sir Jock's wife, Diana, you see.'

'It all sounds a bit sordid.'

'Yes, I agree. Although Sir Jock was never convicted, he did commit suicide about a year later and that kind of makes me think he was guilty. His wife Diana went on to marry Lord Delamer and they're still alive. I don't know where they live now, but I think it could be at the coast.'

'So, who lives in the Djinn Palace now?'

'I really don't know. Sometimes when I fly back from Nairobi, I drop down low over Lake Naivasha and have a look at the place as

I fly past it, but it always seems deserted; no parties are held there now, as far as I know.'

'It's interesting to learn about the history of this area—whoever would have thought that a place like this would have such a colourful past,' Charles said, lying back and pulling Georgia with him. 'What else do you know about Lake Naivasha?'

'Well, from the 1930s until the 1950s, the lake was used as a landing place for flying boats. The Imperial Airways passenger and mail route from Southampton in Britain to South Africa passed more or less over Lake Naivasha I think, so it was a good place to stop off. I believe it was Kenya's first international airport.'

'Really? Well, I guess it was convenient for the Happy Valley Set if they wanted to come and go between Europe and Kenya!'

'Yes. Well, as far as I know the Flying Boat Service, as it was known, lasted until aviation technology allowed large planes to land on dry earth, and then Embakasi Airport was built close to Nairobi in about 1958. The flying boats are just part of Naivasha's history now, but if you were able to afford to fly in those days it must have been a nice way to travel. My father told me that it took a week for a flying boat to travel from Britain to Naivasha and another ten days to Cape Town, so there must have been many stops on the way and the passengers would probably have seen quite a few different areas in the world. I guess the actual trip would have been an important part of your holiday in those days.'

'Yes, it's so different now, isn't it?' You're packed into the airliners like sardines and transported across the world at high speed.'

The two of them lay on the grass enjoying each other's company and the pleasant surroundings. The sun was warm and great cumulous clouds floated overhead. They could hear the chittering of a flock of Guinea Foul and in the distance they heard the cry of a fish eagle. Two Ibis flew overhead and skimmed the water before landing in the shallows.

'This place is a real haven for birds, isn't it?' Charles remarked. 'It's so perfect, but being Africa, you're going to tell me that there're dangers lurking!'

'No, not really; there are hippo and you always have to be careful around hippo, but there aren't any crocodiles!'

'Well, thank goodness for small blessings!'

'Next time we come here we must hire a boat and go out on the lake,' said Georgia.

'Yes, that would be nice,' agreed Charles. But secretly he was glad to just sit still with the woman he loved for a while. Georgia was always so restless and he loved doing things with her, but sometimes he wished she would just calm down a bit. 'Tell me about your family,' he invited.

'Well, you know a lot about them already.'

'No, I don't. I know they were murdered but you haven't told me much else about your parents, or any of your other relatives.'

'Well, my grandfather, Dad's father, fought in the first war, but when it ended, he had to remain in Germany for some time after it finished. I'm not sure why, but while he was there, he fell in love with a German girl of Jewish origin and married her. They had a son, my father, and they lived in Germany for about ten years. Then my grandmother died of breast cancer and my grandfather was heartbroken. He decided to return to England with his son. He bought a farm in Devon and eventually remarried an English woman. Dad grew up on the farm and always intended to stay farming in Devon. But then the Second World War broke out and because he could speak fluent German he was recruited as a spy. Dad said he saw terrible things and learned stuff that he thought would endanger his life even after the war ended. He would never talk of what he had seen and heard, because I guess it was so upsetting. By the end of the war both his father and step-mother had died, so he decided to sell the farm and move far away to another continent. Before he left England, he met and fell in love with the woman who was to become my mother, so as soon as he was established in Kenya, she followed him here and they were married. I was born nine months later!'

'Do you think he would ever have gone back to England?'

'No, he loved it here and so did Mum. They were here to stay and I feel dreadfully sad that their lives were cut short when they were so happy.'

'Yes, I guess we should always enjoy every day as it comes, because no one knows what the future holds.'

They were both silent for a few minutes and then Charles said,

'Did your father ever teach you to speak German?'

'Yes—well, he tried! Actually, I do understand spoken German quite well, but I'm rubbish at speaking it myself!'

'You speak Swahili well though, don't you?'

'I learned Swahili from my ayah. She didn't really speak English, so it was natural for her to talk to me in Swahili and I just picked it up from her. Anyway, it's your turn now; tell me about your parents and family.'

'My parents died in a road accident when I was about seven years old. I don't remember them very well; all my memories of my time with them are very fuzzy and indistinct. I ended up in a foster home. A couple called Veronica and Hamish Goodrick fostered me, together with a whole lot of other children. They were good solid citizens and they taught us to be moral and upright. They were never overly harsh or too soft with us, we never lacked food or a warm bed to sleep in, but I always felt there was something missing and I think it was the love that comes with being in a real family. I think I've become a bit pedantic about keeping to the rules and regulations, because that's what Veronica and Hamish always drummed into us.'

'I'm so sorry that you had to grow up like that.'

'No, it was okay. It would have been better with my own mum and dad of course, but the Goodricks were good folk and I think I'm a fairly upright citizen due to them instilling good morals and principles into me as I grew up. Maybe I'm a bit too much of a stickler; maybe that's why I couldn't get on with Fleur—I probably expected too much of her.'

'Well, from what you've told me about her, I think she totally lacked morals and principles and was a horrible little madam! You could have done her a world of good if her mother had backed you up!'

'Well, it's all water under the bridge and I'm glad now that things didn't work out between me and Cordelia. I would never have met you had things been different.' Charles smiled at Georgia fondly.

'We didn't get off to a very good start though, did we?' Georgia said thoughtfully.

'No, but that was because all the stuff I'd experienced with

Cordelia and Fleur was still filling my head when I first arrived in Kenya, and it was blinding me to the wonderful person you are!'

'I thought you were a bit of a prat at first,' admitted Georgia. 'You seemed so uptight!'

'I probably was, but what about now?'

'You're totally different now. You're still a stickler for the rules, but you've adapted to the more relaxed way of thinking here and stopped being so prattish!'

'Thank you. . . I think!' Charles grinned at her. 'Everything is so different here; there're so many different characters and personalities and it's a great leveller because when you see all their different takes on life, it makes you think. It somehow changes your perception on how things should be—to a certain extent anyway.'

'Well, when you first arrived, I wished Howard had chosen someone else,' Georgia admitted. 'But now I'm really glad it's you—and that we've found each other!'

Chapter 13

Exciting news as Christmas approaches

'**K**eep your eyes on the ground and ease back on the control column. Feel the aeroplane sinking towards the ground, feel the amount of lift left in the wings, keep it steady. . . steady, keep easing back—not too hard or you'll balloon—keep going straight down the runway, be careful not to drift off centre. . . hold it off, let her sink naturally. . . there you go!'

The wheels of the aeroplane touched the ground gently and the huge man in the left-hand seat turned and gave Georgia a grin.

'I'm getting the hang of it,' he said jubilantly. 'At last!'

Georgia smiled back at him. Hector was rugby player and his position in the pack was fullback. His large muscular body overflowed his seat and his big meaty hands looked huge on the control column. Despite his size, he had a gentle touch on the controls and Georgia was pleased with his progress. She knew that he was going to learn to fly and get his PPL without too much difficulty, unlike some of the others she had taught in the past few months. Some of them were torturously slow to pick up the basics, and sometimes she wondered how the little Cessna 150s withstood the abuse to their undercarriages when the students banged them down onto the runway.

'Do you want to book your next lesson, Heck?' Georgia asked the student when they returned to the club.

'I think I'll have to wait until after Christmas now,' he replied. 'It's an expensive time of the year, isn't it? Presents to buy, parties to attend, girlfriend to please,' he spread out his hands and grinned ruefully at Georgia.

'Well, don't leave it too long; you really need to keep the continuity up or you'll start to regress. If you're serious about a career in flying, you might find you need to make some sacrifices.'

'Okay, I'll book my next lesson and try and cut down on the socialising,' Hector said, looking a bit rueful.

After Hector had left Georgia went to the bar and ordered a coffee. Charles was sitting at one of the tables with a young man of Dutch origin who had received flying instruction earlier that morning. The lad was very young and his fair hair fell over his eyes as he listened intently to what Charles was saying.

'You tend to be rather rough when you're handling the controls,' Charles told him. 'You need to handle them sensitively. An aeroplane is designed to fly and that's what it wants to do. You just have to help it by operating the controls in a delicate and sympathetic manner.'

'I try to do that,' said the boy looking worried, 'but it seems I'm failing.'

'Look, you need to handle an aeroplane gently, like you would a woman,' Charles was trying to find a good analogy to describe how the boy should be handling the controls.

'But. . . I've never handled a woman,' the boy admitted, looking puzzled.

Charles glanced imploringly at Georgia who was trying to supress a giggle. She decided to come to his aid, so she picked up her coffee and joined them at their table.

'Look, Johan, your father trains racehorses, doesn't he? And you help him,' said Georgia.

'Yes, that is correct.'

'Well, I'm sure you wouldn't treat one of your horses roughly, would you? You train them to respond to the slightest touch—and that's how an aeroplane is as well. You just need to think of it as one of your racehorses.'

Johan's frown disappeared as comprehension dawned in his face and he smiled at Georgia. 'Yes, I can see now what you're saying,' he said.

'Good. Now, have you booked your next lesson?'

'Yes, I'm coming again tomorrow morning.'

'Fair enough.'

'Why are you so intent on getting everyone to book their next lesson?' Charles asked Georgia when Johan had left and they were alone.

'Well, Christmas is coming and everyone seems to be easing off,' said Georgia. 'We can't have that!'

'Why not? We've been flat out for months. Surely, it's nice to have a bit more time to catch our breaths?'

'Yes. . . but Howard told me the other evening that the club's been doing so well financially, we'll soon be able to buy another aeroplane. He's promised to get one that's capable of doing aerobatics and I just can't wait to learn!'

'So, you crack the whip and slave-drive us all just so you can learn how to do aerobatics?' Charles joked.

'Yes. What better reason?' Georgia laughed. 'You've already learned how to do aerobatics, haven't you?'

'Yes, I learned on an old Tiger Moth. It has an open cockpit, so you had to make sure you strapped yourself in tightly! I'll teach you to do aerobatics when we get the new aeroplane.'

'Well, that makes me all the more determined to keep everyone's nose to the grindstone, so we can get the aeroplane sooner rather than later!'

Later that evening when Howard unexpectedly came in for a drink, Georgia cornered him and asked him how close they were to being able to buy an aerobatic aeroplane for the club.

'That's why I'm here tonight,' said Howard, his eyes twinkling. 'You've both been working incredibly hard and now, at last, we have enough in the kitty to get another aeroplane as planned. I've been doing some homework and I think I've found us a good aeroplane that's capable of doing aerobatics for a reasonable price. It's called a Citabria and basically, it's a rehashed 7 AC Champ that's been modified for aerobatics. From what I read it's considered a good little aeroplane, and if we got one, we could also tow gliders with it as it's more than capable of doing that. It is a taildragger, which is no bad thing because it will enable people who have only flown aeroplanes with nose wheels to get experience with a tail wheel.'

'It sounds ideal,' said Georgia, her eyes shining.

'I've got some of the information about it in my car,' said Howard. 'Let me go and get it.'

While he went to his car, Georgia called Charles so that he could be there when Howard came back. Together, they looked over the information that Howard had compiled on the aeroplane. It was a fabric covered tandem two-seater, with the pilot flying from the front seat and the passenger seated directly behind him.

'I see it has heel brakes,' said Charles. 'You'll need to change your normal footwear, Georgia, because you'd certainly have a problem applying the brakes if you were wearing flip-flops!'

'You've been longing to get me out of my flip-flops ever since we met,' said Georgia with a laugh. 'Seems you've at last found a way to get them off my feet!'

Just then Randy walked in and came to see what they were looking at.

'A Citabria!' Randy exclaimed. 'Did you know the name Citabria is the word "airbatic" spelled backwards? I've done quite a bit of flying in one of these myself, they're nice little aeroplanes to fly. Can be a bit twitchy on landing, but nothing that can't be handled.'

'Have you done any aerobatics in a Citabria?' Georgia asked him.

'Sure have. They're not a Chipmunk or a Pitts, but yes, they do aerobatics. They don't really have the structural beef to do outside loops safely, but they will do all the inside manoeuvres and the 150hp does a fairly good job of holding altitude. You have work hard, mind, when you're doing aerobatics in a Citabria!'

'What about inverted flying?' Georgia wanted to know.

'Yes, the Citabria has an inverted system that allows you to fly upside down for about two minutes before the engine starts to splutter. But the flat bottom wing only wants to lift in one direction, so when you're flying inverted, you'll find you have to push the stick almost out of sight under the panel!'

'Two minutes doesn't sound very long,' said Georgia sounding rather disappointed.

'Trust me, two minutes of flying upside down seems a very

long time when you're actually doing it!' Charles assured her.

'Well, what do you all think? Should we get a Citabria for the club?' Howard asked.

The affirmative was unanimous and Howard smiled at the animated faces around him. 'Well, we should have one delivered here before Christmas, if all goes well!'

'Before Christmas? Oh, my goodness, that's fantastic!' Georgia exclaimed.

'Let me buy you all a drink to celebrate,' said Randy. 'Georgia, you need to order a proper adult drink now that you're in an adult relationship and considering learning how to do aerobatics, so what will you have?'

'I'll have a bottle of Coke with a straw, please Randy,' said Georgia sweetly.

'You'll never grow hairs on your chest and be able to do aerobatics if you keep on drinking that insipid drink,' said Randy disapprovingly.

'Trust me, I will learn how to do aerobatics,' said Georgia laughing. 'But as for the hairs on my chest—well, I think I'll pass on those!'

The little group sat talking animatedly about the new aerobatic aeroplane that they were going to acquire. Then when Howard had left to talk to someone else, Randy said, 'I'm afraid I had to get rid of Herbie.'

'Who?' Charles looked mystified.

'The baby crocodile,' Georgia reminded him. 'The one Randy picked up when we had that weekend at Lake Rudolph.

'Oh yes,' said Charles remembering. 'Why did you have to get rid of it, Randy? I thought you were going to let it grow big and then make it into handbags or something.'

'That was the plan,' Randy agreed. 'But the little beggar was ruining my love life!'

'How so?'

'Well, you know women—they seem to keep needing to wash and bath—so when they discovered the bathroom was also the residence of a grumpy crocodile and he was an ornery, smelly, messy creature, they weren't very impressed!'

'I should think not!' Georgia exclaimed. 'Why didn't you build

Herbie a pool outside? I'm sure he didn't like living in your bathroom!'

'I was going to, but then I discovered that crocodiles only grow about 12.6 centimetres a year, so I'd have to keep him for about forty years before he was big enough to be made into handbags—perhaps even longer! Hell, I probably won't even be in this country in forty years—I may not even be alive!' So, I had no motivation to build Herbie a pool and since I didn't know what to do with him, I kept him in the bath. I thought he might at least grow to like me, but he never did. He was a cantankerous, ill-tempered little bastard and he always wanted to bite me. Talk about biting the hand that feeds you!'

'Well, he was obviously unhappy living in your bathroom,' said Georgia. 'If you had got off your bum and built him a nice place to live in, he might have become more amenable.'

'I doubt it,' said Randy. 'He was born with a snappy disposition and wasn't about to change!'

'So, what have you done with him?' Charles wanted to know.

'I released him in Lake Naivasha,' said Randy, taking a swallow of his drink.

'What?' Charles looked absolutely appalled. 'There're no crocodiles in Lake Naivasha and now you've gone and put one there? Are you completely out of your mind?'

'Well, after the way he behaved while he was with me, I don't really care if he's lonely. He's the cause of all my girlfriends deserting me, now he can get a taste of his own medicine,' Randy declared.

'But Randy. . . a crocodile in Lake Naivasha,' said Charles. 'It could become a real danger to people, especially as they'll be unaware that there is a crocodile there.'

'He's only little and won't hurt anyone very much even if he does bite them.'

'But. . . he's not going to stay little, is he? And what then?'

'Well, people have to dodge the hippos, so they'll have to dodge Herbie as well. It's no big deal.'

'I can't believe you're saying this, Randy! Surly you can see it was highly inappropriate and irresponsible putting a crocodile into a lake which is crocodile free?' Charles was really disgusted.

'My God, Georgia, I thought this man wasn't quite so uptight since you've been going out with him, but it seems you've still got a lot of work to do on him, girl! I'm off now, got a hot date and no Herbie in the bathroom to worry about!' Randy swallowed the last of his drink and then marched out of the clubhouse.

'Georgia, why didn't you back me up?' Charles demanded. He was still looking appalled and was shocked when he suddenly noticed his girlfriend was laughing.

'Oh Charles, Randy was winding you up. I'm quite sure he didn't put Herbie in Lake Naivasha!'

'But. . . then why did he say he did?'

'Well, you know how Randy likes to cause dissention; he's hoping you'll tell everyone else that he's put a croc in Lake Naivasha and there'll be a big hoo-ha and everyone will get riled and, well, who knows where it would lead! He absolutely loves situations like that. But I know Randy well, and I know he wouldn't be as stupid as to put a crocodile into Lake Naivasha.'

'So where has he put it?'

'I don't know. Maybe he's knocked it on the head or something—but look, there's Klaus coming in, maybe he will know.'

Klaus clicked his heels and bowed to Georgia when she called him over.

'Come and have a drink with us,' she said. 'We've got something to ask you.'

When they asked Klaus if he knew what had happened to Randy's crocodile, he shook his head and laughed.

'Randy is a very funny man,' he said. 'Very soon after stealing that crocodile he begins to hate it. He tells me it is ruining his life, so I told him to get rid of it—shoot it—but he wouldn't. He eventually borrowed an aeroplane from a friend and took the creature back to Lake Rudolph. He even took it back to Central Island where it came from, so that it can again be with its family!'

'He's just told us that he had released it in Lake Naivasha,' said Charles, who still looked annoyed.

'That man likes to cause controversy,' said Klaus laughing. 'But maybe we forgive him, yes? Because his heart is good.'

During the following days, Charles and Georgia were less busy because most people were thinking about Christmas and preparing for it. Howard told them that everyone seemed to dissipate over Christmas, because they went on holiday or spent time visiting friends. But he decided that before everyone disappeared, they should have a dance at the club to celebrate the fruition of all their hard work and the success it had brought for the club.

'We'll hold it on one of our normal social evenings, but we'll make it a bit more special with dancing and a slap-up meal of turkey and Christmas pudding. How does that sound?' Howard suggested.

Howard was able to borrow a good sound system for the evening and Georgia persuaded everyone to bring in their own favourite dance records.

'Just make sure you mark them clearly with your names so you get them back after the dance,' she said.

'Who's going to be the disc-jockey?' Charles wanted to know.

'William has volunteered to do that,' said Georgia. 'He fancies himself as a disc-jockey and he assures me that he can really get a party going with good music.'

Everyone was keen to contribute to the forthcoming party and offers of Christmas pudding, mince pies and homemade sweets came rolling in. Zail Singh said he would donate the turkeys and Geoffrey Appleton offered to provide the potatoes and vegetables. Georgia was kept busy helping Howard and Mary to organise everything. Despite her encouraging every student to continue with their flight instruction, most of them were slacking off and getting into the Christmas spirit, so she found she had more free time in which to help. Charles also assisted where he could, but as he said, his talents didn't really extend to domestic organisation!

'You really love organising social gatherings, don't you?' Charles said fondly to Georgia.

'I just like to be kept busy,' said Georgia smiling at him. 'And something like this is fun to organise, isn't it?'

'You seem to have been born with ants in your pants; I'd never met a person who always had to be doing something, until I met you!'

'Well, I've got something for you to do now, lazybones. I want to decorate the club and so you can start by putting up all these paper chains. Then there's about a hundred balloons to blow up.'

'Okay, I think I might manage to do that without making a hash of it. What about a Christmas tree? Are we having one?'

'Yes, Howard is bringing one this evening and Mary says she has a box of decorations that we can use. We can decorate the tree together later on, if you like.'

They waited until the usual evening crowd had left before starting on the tree. Mary had provided everything they needed to make it look good. There were strings of lights, tinsel and dozens of different coloured baubles.

'It looks lovely now, doesn't it?' Georgia stepped back to inspect their work when they had finished.'

'Yes, it just needs a fairy on the top.'

But there was no fairy in the box of decorations. Suddenly, Charles grabbed Georgia and hoisted her onto his shoulder.

'You can be the fairy, sweetie,' he said. 'You'll look absolutely lovely sitting up on top of the tree!'

Georgia giggled, she wiggled down from his shoulder and wrapped her legs around his body so that her face was opposite his, and then she kissed him.

'Last year I felt so sad at Christmas,' she admitted. 'I missed not having Mum and Dad so much, but this Christmas I've got you and it's so special! I love you, Charles.'

Chapter 14

The Christmas Party and the Citabria

On the night of the party, the clubhouse was bursting at the seams. It was the 15th of December and everyone was in the Christmas spirit and wanted to let their hair down and have a good time. Unlike the fly-in, the majority of the people attending were club members who lived within travelling distance to Lanet. The only people who flew in were George and Jasmine Pearce and they had booked a room for the night.

William surprised everyone by arriving dressed as Santa Clause. Now, he presided over the sound system and selected the records that he thought would be good to get the party going.

'Where did he get his Santa suit?' Georgia asked Howard.

'I've got no idea,' admitted Howard. 'But he's also got Santa hats for the kitchen and bar staff.'

Georgia saw that Sam was wearing his hat at a jaunty angle and he was looking extremely pleased with his head attire. Everyone had dressed up for the occasion and while Georgia was admiring Sam's hat, Howard was admiring her. Georgia looked so different when she dressed nicely, he thought. Her normal attire of shorts and a T-shirt made her look like a child, but tonight, dressed in a blue satin trouser suite, with makeup and her fair hair swept up and cascading down in curls, she looked every inch a woman. He noticed she was wearing high heels which boosted her height, but he knew that once the dancing started, they would be discarded.

'Howard, any news of the Citabria?' Georgia asked him hopefully.

'Well, I was hoping it would arrive before Christmas,' said Howard. 'But I haven't heard yet when it's going to be delivered.'

'I'm driving down to the coast with my uncle and family the day after tomorrow,' said Georgia. 'I was really hoping that it would be here before I left.'

'Look, I'm sure it will be here by the time you get back,' Howard reassured Georgia with a kind smile. 'It'll be something to look forward to after all the hype of Christmas!'

William was as good as his word and soon had the party rocking with his disc-jockey skills. He had a huge selection of records that everyone had lent for the occasion, and he had sorted them out so that he could dictate the mood of the dance through his choice of music. Now the clubhouse throbbed to the loud beat of the music and the dance floor was soon full of enthusiastic dancers. Charles left no one in any doubt that he was going to monopolise Georgia for the greater part of the evening, but at times he was ready to relinquish her to another dance partner so that he could rest and have a drink. He was amazed at the energy his girlfriend possessed, she threw herself into the dances with such enthusiasm and her verve and vigour seemed to be powered by some internal dynamo because she never seemed to tire!

Randy had arrived for the dance with a handsome black lady on his arm. She was almost as tall as him, but she was slim and looked beautiful in a very short white dress.

'Georgia, Charles, may I present Victoria to you?' said Randy giving Georgia a challenging look. He hoped that he would see a little bit of jealously in her eyes.

'Vicky,' Georgia squeaked. 'I haven't seen you for ages—how are you?' The two women embraced.

'You two know each other, then?' Randy said, looking a bit disappointed.

'We used to go to the same school,' said Georgia. 'It's so good to see you again Vicky, what have you been up to since I last saw you? And how did you fall into the clutches of this terrible man?'

While Georgia introduced her old school friend to Charles,

Randy went to the bar to buy some drinks. When he got back, he found the two girls chatting away animatedly.

'G and T for you, my dear,' he said, handing a glass that chinked with ice and had a slice of lemon floating in it to Vicky. 'And for my little uninitiated friend, a bottle of Coke with a straw!'

'You haven't changed then,' said Vicky to Georgia. 'Still drinking Coke through a straw!' They both laughed.

'Where's Charles? I've got a beer for him.'

'He's just gone to have a word with Zail,' said Georgia. 'Oh, here he is now. Come on everyone, let's dance!'

'At least give us a chance to have a drink,' complained Randy. 'Was this girl as annoying at school as she is now, Victoria? I've never met anyone so annoying in all my life!' He glowered at Georgia, making both her and Vickie giggle.

Soon they were all on the dance floor; in fact, it seemed that with William's careful selection of records it made everyone in the room want to dance. Georgia noticed with amusement that even Klaus, who normally would just prop up the bar and watch things, was now jumping up and down on the dance floor in a rather staccato way, while his partner jiggled and jumped with him.

When the food was ready it was served on the veranda as there was no space for the tables inside the club house while the dance was in progress. It was a beautiful warm night and the tables had been charmingly decorated with a Christmas theme. Everyone tucked into the delicious meal with relish and there was much banter and laughter.

During the meal Howard tapped on his glass to get everyone's attention and then he stood up to thank everyone for coming to the dance.

'I also have to thank everyone who has helped to make this occasion such a success,' Howard said. 'There are too many to thank individually, but collectively you've done a magnificent job and I think everyone here is grateful to you for putting in the work to make this such a glorious achievement.' He stopped for a moment while everyone clapped and then he went on. 'I would, however, like to mention two people who have not only worked hard to make this party a triumph, but have also worked tirelessly throughout the year to make our flying club so successful. Please could everyone raise their glasses to our instructors, Charles and Georgia.' Everyone clapped and cheered while Charles and Georgia looked rather embarrassed.

When everyone was satiated, they drifted back to the bar to buy another drink and the dancing started once more. But Georgia and Charles remained outside for a while after everyone else went in, they moved into the garden where they had a lingering kiss in the shadow of one of the bushes.

'It's such a beautiful night,' said Georgia, looking at the clear star-studded sky. She was about to say something else, but Charles cut her off.

'Don't even *think* about it!' he said.

'What?'

'I know what you were going to suggest, and no, we're certainly not going to go night-flying tonight!'

'Oh, my goodness, you can read my mind!'

'Yes, my precious darling, I can read you like a book now!'

'Well, it *is* the *perfect* night for. . .'

'No, tonight we're going to dance—no flying tonight—I absolutely forbid it!'

'Oh, well, let's just go back and dance then,' said Georgia laughing.

'Yes, but there's something I want to ask you first before we go back, Georgia. I thought I'd never be able to trust another woman enough to love her, but I've found with you that I can and I'm absolutely head over heels in love with you. I can't imagine living without you now, so I was hoping that you might agree to become my wife?'

'Oh Charles,' Georgia sounded breathless because this was the last thing she had been expecting. 'I'd. . . I'd love to become your wife, but you've rather taken me by surprise!'

'So, is that a yes then?'

'Of course it is! I love you too and. . .' Charles cut off her next words as he bent to give her a passionate kiss.'

'I know I haven't done a very good job of this proposal' Charles admitted when he stopped kissing Georgia. 'I should have had a ring and got down on one knee, but it just seemed the perfect time to ask you. . . and I'm so glad you said yes!'

'Of course, I said yes,' said Georgia laughing. 'It doesn't matter how you asked—or that you didn't have a ring; all that matters is that you want to marry me.'

'We can fly to Nairobi and buy a ring for you,' said Charles. 'You can choose one that you like.'

'Oh Charles, I can't wait! But let's keep our engagement a secret until after Christmas and New Year. I'd like to make a big announcement and with all the hype of the festive season that wouldn't be possible right now. So, let's get the ring in the New Year and then announce our engagement—we could even have an engagement party!'

After a little more time by themselves in the garden, Georgia and Charles made their way back into the clubhouse, and had not everyone been having such a good time they might have noticed the happy glow radiating from the couple.

As the night went on and more and more alcohol was consumed, the dancing got more vigorous and many people added their voices to music that was being played. At one stage, William put on some Scottish music and those who knew the steps formed an Eightsome Reel, while the others stood on the side-line clapping or doing their own versions of the Highland Fling and the Sword Dance! All of them whooped enthusiastically at the appropriate moments and nearly brought the roof down.

After that, everyone formed a Conga and swirled around the clubhouse before going out into the garden and onto the apron to weave around the parked aircraft. When they eventually got back and the Conga line broke up, everyone was exhausted so William played slow music to enable everybody to dance less vigorously and catch their breath.

'This is more like it,' said Charles as he guided Georgia around the dance floor while he held her in his arms. Now I can savour the feel of your sweet body against mine and not have to watch you leaping about like a demented frog!'

Oh Charles, this evening has been so much fun,' said Georgia. 'A few months ago, I could not even imagine that I would ever be happy again—and here I am, happier than I've ever been in my life! I have you, and also so much to look forward to. Sometimes,

I just wonder if all this happiness can last.'

'Of course it can. With you and me together, we can make our own happiness, can't we?'

The party went on until the stars started to fade and the dark sky began to lighten. As dawn broke, the revellers started to drift away and make their way home. Eventually, the only people remaining were Georgia, Charles, Howard, Mary and George and Jasmine Pearce. All the kitchen and bar staff that had helped to make the dance so successful were sent home to sleep for the day. Everything seemed very quiet after the noise of the party as they sat together sipping cups of tea on the veranda as they watched the sun rising.

'Who's feeling hungry?' Georgia suddenly asked. 'I'm volunteering to make everyone a bacon and egg breakfast!'

'My goodness, what on earth is that girl on?' Howard asked when Georgia had dragged Charles into the kitchen to help her prepare the breakfast. 'Talk about a live-wire!'

'It must be all the Coca Cola she drinks,' suggested Jasmine. 'She must have drunk gallons last night, and now all that sugar is coming out in the form of energy!'

The six of them had just finished the breakfast that Georgia and Charles had prepared when the radio crackled and an incoming aeroplane announced its approach.

'Who could be flying in at eight o'clock on a Sunday morning?' Howard wondered.

They all stood on the veranda and watched as a little aeroplane joined the circuit and then approached for landing. As it touched down, they could see it was a gaily painted red and white taildragger.

'Oh, my goodness!' Georgia suddenly exclaimed as the little aeroplane turned off the runway and headed for the apron. 'It's the Citabria!'

'Good gracious! I think you're right!' Howard said in surprise. 'No-one told me that it was going to be delivered today!'

They all crowded out to see the aeroplane as it came to a stop. Georgia thought it looked like a cheeky little thing, with its nose stuck up in the air like it didn't give a fig about what anyone thought. The young man who scrambled out grinned at them.

'This is a great little aeroplane,' he said to them. 'A real cracker!' He introduced himself to them as Ken Neal and explained he was just the delivery boy.

'I wasn't actually told this aeroplane was going to be delivered today,' said Howard.

'No? Well, I was lucky to be greeted by a reception party, then,' said Ken. 'I did wonder if anyone would be here at this time on a Sunday morning.'

Ken was amused when he learned that they were the remnants of a Christmas party that had taken place the previous evening. 'It must have been a hell of a party,' he said with a grin as he looked around at debris that was now being cleaned up by the cleaning staff. 'I should have got here yesterday so I could have joined in!'

It transpired that Ken was hoping that someone would be able to fly him back to Nairobi that morning.

'I'll do it,' said Georgia immediately. 'I'm the only one who hasn't been drinking, so it has to be me!' She looked smug.

'Are you sure you're not too tired?' Howard asked.

'I'm not tired at all,' she reassured him. 'I'll fly Ken to Nairobi in the 182 and be back in a couple of hours. But first, perhaps, you'd like some breakfast and a cup of tea or coffee, Ken?'

Ken settled for a cup of coffee without the breakfast and while he was drinking it Georgia had a shower and changed into her normal shorts and T-shirt. She could see Ken was looking at her a bit apprehensively when she returned, so she quickly reassured him, 'I'm older than I look and I'm actually the assistant flying instructor in this club,' she said. 'I promise I'll get you back to Nairobi in one piece!'

Charles went with her to do the pre-flight checks on the Cessna 182. 'Are you sure you're not too tired?' He looked worried.

'Do I look tired?' Georgia replied.

Charles looked into her clear sparkling eyes and laughed. 'No, anything but,' he admitted. 'How do you do it? You must have expended a huge amount of energy just organising the party—and then all that dancing you did last night! You *must* be tired!'

'Well, I'm not! My head is too full of love for you and excitement about the Citabria to have any tiredness in it!'

'Well, just be careful. I'll be here when you get back and

perhaps this evening, we can go up in the Citabria.'

'Can't wait,' said Georgia, kissing him on the nose.

When Georgia got back from Nairobi, she found Charles asleep on the sofa in the clubhouse with Beano curled up on his chest. The cleaning staff had put everything back to normal, but now they had left and Charles was the only one there. George and Jasmine had obviously flown out earlier. Georgia could see that Charles must have been home to shower and change, and she stood looking at his face in repose as he slept. She had thought him such a prat when he had first arrived, but now she could see the firm uncompromising lines on his face indicated that he was a principled man. She knew her father would have approved of him because he was upright and ethical, and she felt lucky to be loved by this handsome man.

'I'm back,' she whispered as she knelt down and put her arms around him, disturbing poor Beano.

'How did it go?' Charles forced his eyes open and pushed himself up so that he could kiss Georgia.

'All good; no problems,' she replied. 'Now, just go back to sleep. I'm going to go and sleep as well and later when we've had a few hours of slumber—the Citabria!' Her eyes danced with excitement.

'Make sure you strap yourself in really tightly,' Charles instructed Georgia as they prepared to take the Citabria up later that evening. Charles was in the front seat and he familiarised himself with the controls before taxiing out for take-off.

'It's got fantastic ground visibility for a taildragger,' Charles shouted back to Georgia as they slowly made their way to the top of the runway. 'When taxiing most taildraggers, you have to zig-zag because you can't see where you're going, but with this aeroplane you can see over the nose!'

It seemed to Georgia that the little aeroplane leaped into the air as soon as the tail was up and she was impressed with the rate of climb. Once they got to altitude Charles did some steep turns, turning stalls, power off stalls and full power stalls to see how the Citabria would react to corrective measures. He then did a spin and recovery before heading back to the airfield where he did several circuits and bumps to get the feeling of the landing. Georgia was longing to have a go and watched the sun going down with apprehension. If Charles didn't hurry up the light would be gone and she wouldn't have a chance to fly before it got dark. But when he asked her if she wanted to see a barrel roll, she agreed immediately. So, Charles climbed up to altitude again and then dove to 130knots and demonstrated the roll followed by a loop to his ecstatic girlfriend.

'Now it's your turn,' said Charles to Georgia once they had landed and returned to the top of the airstrip.

They scrambled out and changed places. Charles was pleased to see that Georgia was wearing trainers rather than her usual flip-flops.

'Now, you'll notice that the throttle is on your left-hand side—so you use your left hand to control it. Your right hand will be on the stick. In all the other aeroplanes you've flown so far, you've had the control column in your left hand and operated the throttle with your right hand, so that's the first thing you have to get used to. The brakes are managed with heel brakes rather than toe brakes, so that's another difference to which you'll have to adapt.'

Once they were ready for take-off, Charles told Georgia to open the throttle and then as they rolled forward to ease the stick forward to raise the tail. Very soon after that she was able to gently exert backward pressure on the stick and the aeroplane leapt into the air. Georgia felt exhilarated as they climbed up to altitude where they did the same turns and stalls that Charles had done before.

'She's very easy to fly, isn't she?' Georgia shouted to Charles. 'And it feels as though she's enjoying every minute she's in the sky!'

Just like you, my darling, Charles thought.

'Can I try a loop now?' Georgia asked.

'No. You have to learn how to walk before you can run,' admonished Charles. 'I want you to join the circuit and we'll do a few circuits and bumps now, so that you can learn how to land a taildragger. You're going to do a three-point landing, aiming for all three wheels to touch the ground at the same time.'

Charles could see Georgia's shell-like ears growing pink as her concentration levels rose on their approach to landing. She was doing well.

'At an altitude of five to ten feet slowly close the throttle and start the landing transition to a three-point attitude while dissipating the remaining altitude,' Charles instructed.

The little aeroplane touched down with the tail wheel slightly before the main gear and made a small bounce. 'Freeze the stick where it is,' commanded Charles. 'Now as the aircraft starts to settle, continue back stick. Good. Okay, maintain directional control with your rudders—don't touch the brakes. Keep her straight down the runway and open the throttle and go around again.'

Once they were airborne once more, Charles patted her on the shoulder. 'Good first effort,' he praised.

After a few circuits Georgia had got the hang of landing the little taildragger and in the gathering twilight they taxied back to the clubhouse.

'You need to be mindful of the brakes on a taildragger,' Charles told her as they tied the Citabria down for the night. 'It's pretty easy to tip the aeroplane onto its nose if you use them wrongly. Never touch the brakes when the tailwheel is off the ground—and never touch them when the tailwheel is on the ground until the landing roll is complete and the aircraft is ready to taxi clear of the runway. As opposed to a nose-wheel aircraft, the brakes will afford less control than the rudder.'

'Oh Charles, I can't bear it that I have to leave for Kilifi on the coast with the family tomorrow,' Georgia lamented when they were back in the club. 'I adore my uncle and aunt, they've been so good to me since Mum and Dad died, and my cousin Euan and his wife Diana are good fun. Their two little boys are little crackers and I usually just love to spend time with them all, but everything I want right now—you and the Citabria—are right here and I wish I could make an excuse not to go!'

'It's only for a few days,' Charles consoled her. 'You've already told your family that you have to get back to work on 28th, and I'll fly down and pick you up on the 27th. How about I fly down in the Citabria?'

'Oh yes! That would be great. I'll find a phone and give you a ring on Boxing Day to confirm that I'll be ready and waiting for you at Mnarani Club airstrip on the morning of the 27th.

'Good. I'll be here at the club on the 26th, so ring here rather than to my home number,' Charles told her.

Chapter 15

Alarming revelations

Charles had been expecting Georgia to ring him on the morning of Boxing Day. He had enjoyed a good Christmas with Howard and Mary, but he had missed Georgia dreadfully during the days that she had been away. He made sure he arrived at the club quite early because he was sure she would be feeling the same and would ring first thing in the morning, but now it was early afternoon and he hadn't heard from her.

It was mid-morning when an enthusiastic young man by the name of Mike Grant had turned up asking if he could sign up for flying lessons. Since everything was so quiet, Charles had suggested that they have their first lesson as soon as all the paperwork was completed.

'If Georgia rings, tell her I'm in the air with a student and she should ring back in about an hour,' Charles instructed Sam.

Charles was disappointed when he got back and Sam told him there had been no phone call. He mooched about the empty clubhouse after Mike had left, wondering why Georgia was taking so long to call him. He had been so sure she would have been impatient to get back and eager to make arrangements for her trip home. Beano seemed pleased to have his company, but everyone else appeared to be celebrating at home or nursing a hangover and the club was deserted. As the day wore on, Charles grew more and more impatient.

It was mid-afternoon when the radio crackled as someone announced their arrival at the Lanet airstrip, and shortly after that a Piper Super Cub landed and taxied up to the clubhouse. Charles saw it was Cade and Benedict Heston.

'Is Georgia here?' Cade asked after Charles had greeted them.

'No, she's in Kilifi with her family,' Charles replied. 'I'm actually waiting for her to give me a ring to confirm that she's ready to come back tomorrow. I promised to fly down and collect her, you see.'

'Well, I guess we'll have to come back tomorrow,' said Cade. Charles noticed he looked rather worried.

'Why don't you have a coffee before rushing off?' Charles suggested. He was tired of his own company and could use some companionship. 'You could even speak to Georgia on the phone if she telephones while you're here; I'm sure she'll ring soon and I know she's anxious to find out if you've discovered anything about her parents' murders.'

'So, Georgia has told you all about her parents' murder and my involvement in trying to find out exactly what happened?' Cade inquired as he sipped his coffee.

'Yes, she's told me everything,' said Charles. 'I know she wants to get closure, but is unable to do so until the murderer is brought to justice.'

'Well, we have a good idea who did it now,' said Benedict.

'But bringing him to justice might be a problem,' added Cade.

'So, it wasn't a robbery that had gone wrong?' Charles asked.

'No, it was way more complicated than that,' said Cade. 'It took us a hell of a lot of time to sort out what happened, but now we're pretty sure that the murder was a direct result of events that occurred during the war. Did Georgia ever tell you that her father was recruited as a spy by British Intelligence?'

'Yes, she told me that his biological mother was German and that although he had been taken to England shortly after her death when he was just ten years old, he spoke German fluently. Georgia said that he moved to Kenya after the war ended, because he thought it would be safer to get away from Britain and Europe due to the danger caused by his activities during the war. '

'That's right. Ian Thorne was a hell of a good chap, but I don't think he would have chosen to be a spy if he could have avoided it. It was the fact that he spoke good German that caused him to be recruited. Ian was more of an action man and espionage and intrigue weren't really his thing. Having said that, he knew he was a valuable asset to British Intelligence because he spoke German like a native, so he threw himself into his role and produced good results for them.'

Cade took a sip of his coffer before proceeding.

'I worked with him when gathering some intelligence and although he disliked what he was doing, he was as tenacious as a rabid dog and wouldn't let go until he had got all the answers. I know he wanted to put it all behind him when the war ended. Moving to Kenya seemed like a good thing to do, but I think that despite this precaution, his past caught up with him and the result was that he and his wife were murdered.'

'But that's terrible! Who was it who murdered them and why?'

'I'll tell you in a little while who I think murdered him. But first let me fill you in on a bit of history that I've managed to excavate. Does the name Walter Rauff mean anything to you?'

The name did ring a bell and Charles tried to remember what he had heard about the man.

'He was a Nazi war criminal, wasn't he?' Charles said after a few moments.

'Quite right,' said Cade. 'He was a ruthless and evil man thought to be responsible for nearly 100,000 deaths during the Second World War. Most of his victims were Jews or Communists, but among their number were people from the Roma population and, more distressingly, people with disabilities. He didn't discriminate between men and women or children. If he felt that they were of no worth, he would make sure that they were slaughtered, and he didn't apparently have the slightest bit of compassion for those he was killing. He was a bad bastard!'

Cade stopped to puff on his cigarette, but his eyes were full of loathing for the man he was talking about.

'In his capacity as a spy, Ian Thorne came across this man and had to compile a dossier on his activities for the allies. It was an abhorrent assignment because he had to work closely with the man and his colleagues and convince them that he approved of what they were doing. Rauff and his cronies knew Ian Thorn as Finn Blosser as that was his alias, and he managed to convince them that he was devoted to Rauff and enthusiastic about working with him.'

'What exactly was Rauff doing?' Charles wanted to know.

'He was involved in the development of what was known as gas-vans. They were mobile gas chambers used to kill by poisoning or suffocation. Rauff supervised the modification of scores of trucks, so that it was possible to divert their exhaust fumes into airtight chambers in the back of the vehicles. The victims, who were deemed by the Nazis to be enemies of the German state, were packed into these chambers and then as the vehicles got underway, they were poisoned or asphyxiated from the carbon monoxide accumulation within the truck compartment as the vehicle travelled to a burial site. The trucks could carry between 25 and 60 people at a time, and Rauff apparently thought that by killing the enemies of the state (as he thought of them) in this way, it would take a considerable burden off the soldiers who would have had to shoot these people and load their bodies into a vehicle, had he not thought of this clever invention!

'Now, most of the people who were put in these vans had been rounded up and forced to leave their homes, taking only what they could carry with them. Many of them, the Jews especially, had brought their valuables with them as they knew that their homes would be ransacked the moment that they left. All their luggage was confiscated by those who loaded the unfortunate people into the vans, and Rauff was the man who had to collect all the valuable items and hand them to the Nazis. But it's my guess that he kept most of the stuff because he had contacts that could turn the booty into cash—and we have proof that he had amassed a small fortune before the end of the war and he had been able to get much of it out of the country.'

'My God, what a detestable man!' Charles exclaimed.

'Yes, well, Ian managed to gather a huge amount of evidence against Rauff and his cronies, and Rauff should have been detained at the end of the war and prosecuted at the Nuremberg trials in 1946 where the other Nazis who were caught were sentenced and brought to justice, but this didn't happen. Rauff managed to avoid being arrested to start with, but he was eventually caught and interned in a camp in Rimini by the Americans. However, he managed to escape and hid in a number of Italian convents, apparently under the protection of a Catholic bishop. Later, he moved on and after more activities in Syria and Argentina, Rauff ended up in Chile, where, as far as I know, he still resides with his wife and family.'

'So, the bastard got away with his crimes?' Charles felt outraged.

'Yes. Ian did his bit and provided all the evidence to get the man and his accomplices convicted, but when Rauff slid through the net, Ian decided he had done enough and left it to the Nazi hunters to track him and the other Nazi criminals down. Simon Wiesenthal, one of the most tenacious Nazi hunters, is on his trail I believe and hopefully he will eventually catch him.'

'So, are you saying that Rauff had something to do with Georgia's parents' murders?' Charles asked.

'No, not Rauff,' said Cade. 'During the war Rauff worked with twin brothers, Alfrid and Danek Wagner, who were chassis builders that worked in Berlin. They were about eighteen years of age at the time and exempt from joining the forces, because they both apparently had a congenital heart defect that was diagnosed shortly after they were born. But it's my opinion that the problem wasn't very serious and probably righted itself as they grew up, because they were strapping young men who appeared to be quite healthy. However, they were able to use their medical problem as an excuse not to fight in the war. These boys stood out in a crowd in more than one way. They were identical and both were blessed with classical Aryan looks. They were blond giants of men with the faces of Greek gods and bodies to match. But at the same time, they were full of malice and malevolence, and although women fell at their feet they very soon ran away when they realised what hatred and wickedness the twins harboured in their hearts. Alfrid and Danek didn't care though, so long as they had each other they were happy.

'When Rauff approached them, they soon understood exactly what was required of the trucks that were to be used as mobile gas chambers, and they were as enthusiastic as Rauff to exterminate those who were deemed to be the enemies of the state—especially the Jews; for some reason they hated them most of all. They often observed the victims being crammed into the trucks and were keen to travel with them to the burial sites to check how efficiently their invention had worked. If any of the unfortunate people showed any signs of life, they were despatched with a bullet in the head, and Rauff would often let the twins do the honours because they so obviously enjoyed killing people. Afterwards, they would often drink with Rauff to celebrate—especially if the latest load had been Jews. According to my information the twins also profited from the murders of those that they had helped to kill, as Rauff put some of the booty that he stole from his unfortunate victims their way. Unlike Rauff, they didn't have the contacts to turn this booty into cash, so they just hid it in their lodgings in Berlin, thinking that after the war it may be easier to exchange what they had into cash.'

Cade drew deeply on his cigarette and then forcibly stubbed it out in the ashtray in a show that indicated to Charles Cade's distaste of the men he was talking about. But then he continued.

'Now, all the while Ian was working with these thugs to all intents and purposes. He was apparently, their dog's body and he had earned their trust, but in reality, he was relaying all that they were doing to the allies. When the war drew to its conclusion and Germany did not win, the twins started to panic. They were aware they would be convicted for their part in murdering so many people and knew they must flee immediately, but they couldn't do that in secret while being encumbered by the valuables that they had amassed, so they asked Ian to hide the plunder for them. They told him about their escape plans and offered him a cut in the profit from their booty if he would hide it for them until they could safely claim and sell it. Ian agreed, but instead he informed the authorities of the twins' escape plan and handed the treasure in to be returned to its rightful owners—or their families had the owners been eliminated.

'The authorities acted immediately on Ian's information and they apprehended Danek, but somehow Alfrid escaped. Danek was subsequently tried and convicted in the Nuremburg trials, where after he was executed for his war crimes. But Alfrid got clean away and he managed to make it to Chile as well.'

'So, another bastard gets away with his crimes,' muttered Charles.

'Yes, but unfortunately it doesn't end there,' said Cade. 'Alfrid and Danek had an unfortunate upbringing but they were as close as only twins can be. They were considerably younger than Rauff, and Alfrid was utterly devastated when Danek was executed. It didn't take him and Rauff long to figure out who it was that had provided much of the evidence against them. Alfrid wanted to go after Ian immediately, but he had escaped with very little money and so he appealed to Rauff for financial help. Rauff refused, he didn't want Alfrid to cause the spotlight to fall on him again—even though he felt safe enough in Chile. He had a wife and children to consider and he refused to give Alfrid the money he needed to enable him to go and seek his revenge. So Alfrid had to buckle down and make his own money before he went off to seek retribution and this took some time.'

'How the hell did you find all this out?' Charles wanted to know.

'I was a spy during the war and in contact with Ian Thorn most of the time, so I knew what was going on during that period. And even now, I still have my contacts and I know how to get answers from the people that I question,' said Cade, and his eyes appeared to be shadowed with the deception that he had had to instigate to get the answers he required.

'So, are you saying that this Alfrid Wagner had something to do with the Thorns' murders?' Charles asked.

'Yes, I believe he did. He had a motive—in fact more than one motive. He knew that Ian Thorn must have betrayed them and was thus, in his eyes, the cause of his brother's death. He also must have assumed that Ian took the stolen valuables that he had stashed for the twins for himself, and Alfrid was determined to get back the value of what had been left for safe keeping with Ian. Thirdly, and more worryingly, after Alfrid had subsequently found out that Finn Blosser's real name Ian Thorn, he investigated Ian's background and discovered that his mother was Jewish, so Alfrid had, according to my sources, sworn that he would get his money back and then he would kill Ian and his family to avenge his brother's death. He said that he would not rest until every last drop of Jewish blood connected with Ian Thorne was completely eradicated.'

Cade was looking really worried and Charles suddenly realised the significance of what he was saying.

'Do you think Georgia could be in danger?' Charles asked.

'Yes, I do,' replied Cade. 'When Georgia asked us to investigate the murder of her parents the first people we sought out to interview were their night-watchman and their house servant. During the police investigation, the Thorns' house servant told them that two men had driven up to the house on the afternoon previous to the night they were murdered. He said that they appeared to be lost and were asking for directions to somewhere, but he didn't take much notice of them. He couldn't identify what car they were driving and said the men were wearing baseball caps and sunglasses, so he didn't really get a good look at their faces. But he could confirm that they were both white men and one appeared to have dark hair while the other man was blond. For some reason, the police discarded this information as irrelevant, even though Maina, the night watchman, later said that the two men who perpetrated the attack were white and one was dark while the other was blond.'

'The police probably thought it would be too much trouble to track these white men down,' said Benedict. 'It would be much easier for them to say that the night watchman was in collusion with whoever did it and arrest him!' He shook his head ruefully. 'The police treated Maina's statement with great scepticism because, they said, it's very rare in this country for a white man to plan an attack on another white man and it just didn't seem plausible. They decided that the night-watchman was probably trying to cover up a botched attack and robbery in which he himself had been involved. Maina vigorously denied the accusation and in the end he wasn't charged for lack of evidence.'

'Anyway, having found out about all this, we wanted to question the house servant and Maina,' Cade continued. 'So far we have been unable to find the house servant because he's disappeared back to the Kisumu area where his family reside, but we did find Maina and although he was unwilling to talk to us at first because he thought we wanted to pin the murders on him, he did open up when he realised that we actually wanted to get to the bottom of the matter, which would ultimately clear his name.'

'The poor chap was still distraught over being accused of the Thornes' murders when we questioned him,' said Benedict. 'He said his life had been ruined, because although he had been cleared of all charges, he couldn't get another job, basically because mud sticks!'

'Well, we were very sympathetic,' Cade continued. 'We assured him that we did believe he had seen two white men at the scene and we hoped he would be able to give us a good description of them.'

'Having someone actually believe him seemed to boost his confidence,' Benedict went on with a laugh. 'He was so happy not to be accused and he was very willing to tell us all that he could remember.'

'Yes,' said Cade. 'We find that Africans have wonderful memories for detail and Maina was no exception. It was Margo's screams that alerted Maina to the fact that the Thornes were being attacked. He admitted to us that he had been sleeping on duty and it was only when he was woken up that he acted to help his employers. He started up the power-generator so that the lights came on and then he ran to help the Thornes. He ran straight into the two men leaving the scene of the crime and was pushed violently aside by the blond man as they ran from the room. Maina knocked his head on the wall as he fell and for a few seconds he couldn't give chase. When he did it was too late and the men had driven away.

'He said that one of the men had dark hair and the other was blond. He didn't get a good look at the dark-haired man, but thought he was considerably older than the blond man. He did, however, get a very good look at the blond man because he was the one who confronted him and thrust him out of the way when he ran to the Thorns' rescue. He said that he would never forget what the man looked like, because he had the face of an angel and the eyes of the devil!'

'So, you got a good description of the bastard?' Charles enquired.

'We did. And on the basis of his excellent description, we

managed to get a photofit of the man,' said Benedict with satisfaction. 'Putting that together with the other information that we had dug up, we felt pretty sure we'd got our man.'

'So, what happens now?' Charles asked.

'If we are correct in out reasoning, Alfrid only accomplished one of the three things that he had sworn to do,' said Cade. 'He murdered Ian and his wife, but he was unable to get what he wanted out of Ian before he died. There was evidence that both the Thorn's had been tortured before they died, presumably because Alfrid wouldn't have believed Ian when he told him the valuables of which he had taken for safe keeping had been returned to their rightful owners. He was probably hoping that there was a safe full of cash on the farm somewhere—or maybe he wanted Ian to sigh something to say he owed him a large amount of money. Ian actually died of a heart attack, so that must have frustrated Alfrid because he could no longer brutalise him into doing what he demanded. Then when Maina started the power plant and all the lights came on, Alfrid and his accomplice had to make a hasty exit before they had accomplished the third thing on their list, which was to exterminate all the family. Maybe they had already looked for Georgia and not found her, so they immediately scarpered and presumably, because they were worried that Maina would be able to identify them, they hastily returned overseas. But we think they'll be back to finish off what they started—and that is a big concern for Georgia.'

'We need to nail the bastard,' said Benedict. 'It's not going to be easy and it'll take a while to make the Kenyan officials accept what we've found out. But first we wanted to bring Georgia up to date with our enquiries and discuss how we could improve her security.'

'Do you think she'll be safe staying here at the flying club?' Charles asked.

'If Alfrid comes after her—and we're pretty sure he will eventually come back—she won't be safe staying here in the flying club. It won't take him long to discover where she's living and she's often the only one sleeping in the club at night. It's quite remote, stuck out almost on the runway, and it would be easy to break into the building at night and find her in her room.'

Cade's words made Charles's blood run cold. He immediately decided that he would take Georgia to live with him. They would have to get married as quickly as possible to avoid any gossip, but gossip wasn't a concern, he just wanted to keep the woman he loved safe.

'When do you think Alfrid will return?' Charles asked.

'It's hard to say, but from what we've managed to find out it could be at any moment. He has interests in Somalia and goes out there from time to time, so it would be easy for him to pop into Kenya from Somalia with the intention of finishing off the business he started when he attacked the Thorns.' Cade was looking worried. 'That's why we were hoping to see Georgia sooner rather than later,' he added. 'I expect she's safe enough with her family at the coast, but as soon as she returns, we need to get her somewhere secure until we manage to nail the bastard.'

Charles was about to tell them that Georgia could stay with him, but the telephone shrilled in the office and he ran and snatched up the receiver expecting it to be his fiancée.

'Hello Georgia,' he said as soon as he had picked up the receiver. But it wasn't Georgia who answered.

'Is that Charles Lenten?' It was the voice of a woman and she sounded shaky and upset.

'Yes, it is; who am I speaking to?'

It's Fiona, Georgia's aunt,' said the voice. 'Look, I'm sorry to tell you this, but Georgia has disappeared.'

'Disappeared? Whatever do you mean?' a frown furrowed Charles's brow.

'Yesterday afternoon she borrowed the boys' little inflatable dingy and rowed out towards the reef. Later, the boat and the plastic oars were found washed up on the beach, but there was no sign of Georgia. We were sure there must be some plausible explanation, and decided she must have rowed back to the beach and then gone to visit one of our friends who live around here. We thought she had left the boat too near the sea and the incoming tide had floated it away again. But none of our friends or anyone else has seen her—she just seems to have disappeared into thin air!'

'But. . . people don't just disappear!'

'I know, but if she had somehow fallen out of the dingy and drowned, her body would have been washed up. We've had absolutely everyone looking for her! We've involved the police, who haven't been especially helpful, but we haven't had even a clue as to what has happened to her.'

'Could she have possibly been taken by a shark?'

'A shark? Good gracious no! She was inside the reef and there are no sharks inside the reef.'

'What's to stop one coming in? It may be unusual, but surely there's a chance one could come within the reef?'

'Maybe, but no-one has ever been taken by a shark here inside the reef. It just doesn't happen. And if it had been a shark the boat would have been punctured for sure and it wasn't.'

'So, what do you think happened?'

'I don't know. No-one has been able to come up with an explanation. I didn't want to ring you yesterday, because I was sure she'd turn up, but now that she hasn't I knew you must be told that she's disappeared. I'm sorry I can't tell you any more than that.'

'Okay, I'm going to fly to Kilifi now; I'll help in the search for her. I may be able to see something from the air that has been missed from the ground.'

'Right. Of course, you're welcome to stay with us. When you land at Mnarani, phone our neighbours—they have a telephone and will let us know you're there.' She gave Charles the number.

When Charles returned to where Cade and Benedict were sitting, they could see from his face that something serious had happened. In a few short sentences he repeated what Fiona had told him and informed them that he was leaving immediately for Kilifi. A look passed between Cade and Benedict that was not lost on Charles.

'What?' Charles asked.

'Her disappearance sounds to us like an abduction,' said Cade.

'And we can't discount that it could be connected to the Alfrid Wagner business,' added Benedict. 'We better fly down to Kilifi as well, Dad, we may be able to help.'

Charles took the club's Cessna 182 since it was the one that could fly the fastest and set off for Kilifi as soon as he had refuelled and done all the pre-flight checks. It was a long flight and fear and anxiety gnawed at Charles's stomach as he flew along. What could have happened to Georgia? Was it an accident or had she really been abducted by the detestable man that they had earlier been talking about? Cade had painted a really gruesome picture of Alfrid, and Charles hated to think of what Georgia might be going through if she had ended up in that repugnant man's hands. Surely, he wouldn't torture her as well? Maybe Cade was wrong and Alfrid wasn't as bad as he made out.

Charles just wished that he had a way of gauging what Alfrid was capable of doing so that he could judge for himself whether it was probable that he had abducted Georgia. If he could only go back in time and learn what had happened during Alfrid's past, he might then have a clearer idea of the man's personality and character and be better able to judge what the man's intentions were now—but for him this was impossible.

Chapter 16

Alfrid and Danek Wagner

After he had finished showering, Alfrid Wagner walked back to the big double bed in which he had spent the night and looked with distaste at the woman who still slumbered there. She was at least twenty years his senior, if not more, and was running to fat. Her peroxide blond hair lay untidily on the pillow. It was brittle and dull and grew out black at the roots. She had the sheet drawn up to her chin, but he could see the outline of her huge flabby breasts beneath the thin material. They rose and fell with each breath she took, and every now and again she gave a little snore which made her lips vibrate and caused a small glob of spittle to form at the corner of her mouth.

Alfrid was a fine physical specimen. At 18 years of age his body was hard and athletic; he worked out to keep in shape and was proud of his beautifully tanned physique. He had been blessed with ash blond hair that was luxuriant and grew in curls, and his wide-set eyes were pale blue and very piercing. He had a strong masculine nose and a good square chin above which his full lips appeared sensuous and sexy.

The woman on the bed suddenly seemed to become aware of his scrutiny and she opened her eyes and looked at him.

'Komm mein kleiner schatz,' she patted the bed next to her and threw back the sheet to expose her nakedness.

With a silent sigh of resignation, Alfrid forced himself to smile as he went forward to do his duty. He had hoped that after all his efforts during night the woman would have been satiated, but it seemed that her appetite for sex was insatiable. As he automatically performed his duty he thought about his twin brother who would be similarly engaged at this moment. Later, they would meet and not a word would be mentioned about the distasteful line of work that they had embarked upon. It was all about the money, after all. They had to agree that doing what they did was a lucrative way to make a living and taking everything into consideration, not too arduous. Neither of them got any enjoyment or satisfaction out of their work, both agreed that to enjoy sex to the full you needed to hurt and humiliate the person with whom you were engaging to a certain degree, and this was not possible when you gave sex in exchange for money.

Identical twin brothers, Alfrid and Danek Wagner, had been orphaned when they were two years old and their aunt had reluctantly agreed to raise her sister's children. Ida had never got on with her prettier sister, Selma, and she had not approved of her marriage to Ivo Wagner. She admitted he was a handsome devil, but she found him arrogant and self-opinionated. He had fought in the Great War and had in some way profited from the conflict. Although Ida was never privy to how he had accrued his wealth, she was pretty sure it was not from honest means. She had tried to warn her sister to have nothing to do with the man, but Selma could see no wrong in Ivo and turned a blind eye to all his dubious activities from the past. She thought he was the most wonderful man in the world and he told her she was the perfect woman to become his wife.

Ivo had married Selma just after the Great War and they had, in Ida's eyes, gone mad, because they then went on a wild spending spree and frittered almost all the money away. When the twins had been born the money was all but gone, and then it was discovered that the boys had a heart condition before they were two years old. It had, apparently, been all too much for Ivo and he suddenly disappeared from home with the remains of their money, without telling his wife that he was leaving. A week later he was found dead on the street not far from a brothel. It was whispered that he had tortured and maimed one of the whores with whom he had been engaging and the other prostitutes had set him up to be murdered, but there was no evidence and his murder remained unsolved.

With no husband or money and two children with heart problems to look after, Selma felt unable to cope and took her own life. It was then that Ida had felt obliged to take on the responsibility for the boys, even though she was by no means a wealthy woman. She was a widow as her husband had been killed in the Great War, and she strove to make a living from the smallholding that they owned and had run together before the war had started. She really didn't want the trouble and expense of raising two young children, especially as she had sheep, pigs, goats and chickens to look after as well as the vegetables she had to tend to in her garden. However, she thought it was her duty to take in her sister's children since Ivo had been estranged from his family and there were no other relatives to whom they could go. She hoped that as they grew up they would be able to help her on the small holding.

Ida did the best she could for the boys and despite being diagnosed with heart problems when they were babies they thrived under her care, their heart problems seemingly rectifying themselves as they grew older. They were beautiful children and matured into handsome, attractive young men. But their disposition left a lot to be desired. Behind their beautiful looks there lurked a malevolent, vindictive nature and try as she might, their aunt could not instil in them compassion or a caring nature. They cared about each other and were very close, looking out for one another and forming an impenetrable bond, but they had no time for their aunt or anyone else.

They both grew up hating the smallholding, it was a lot of hard work and right from a young age they were expected to help their aunt. But they had no respect for her and when they were old enough to learn that she was their aunt rather than their mother, their disrespect turned to hate. They detested the animals on the small holding as well, and agreed that they felt abhorrence when they had to muck out the animal sheds and tend to the creatures.

They also hated grubbing about in the earth growing vegetables, and they despised the way they had to live in a small shack with no luxuries.

It became more and more difficult for Ida to control the two boys as they stuck together and defied her much of the time. And then things came to a head when they were sixteen. Hearing the distressing cries of one of her goats that was obviously in pain, Ida rushed to find out what was happening to the poor thing and found the twins had tied it to the shed wall and were mercilessly torturing it. With a cry of anger, Ida had attacked the boys with the spade she had in her hands. She was so ferocious it was a miracle that the twins avoided being hurt, but they raced away laughing together at what they had done. However, it was the end of the relationship between the boys and their aunt.

'Get out of my sight,' Ida screamed at them later when they turned up for their evening meal. 'Get all your things and get off my land. I never want to see either of you in my house again—I never ever want to set eyes on you for as long as I live. You're the spawn of the devil and no good will ever come from you!'

During the period of time that the twins had been living with their aunt, they had been visited several times by a man called Hanno Bachmann, who had been a close friend of their father. Ida didn't like the man, but she hadn't had any good reason to stop him visiting his friend's children, although she could not figure out why he had taken such an interest in the boys since they had reached puberty. It was to Hanno that the twins went after their aunt had thrown them out, and they arrived unannounced with their worldly possessions in rucksacks on their backs. They didn't know to whom they could turn other than him and were unsure of how he would receive them.

'Of course, you can stay with me,' said Hanno warmly when he heard what had happened. To the twins' surprise, he seemed really pleased that they had come to him. 'I'm just amazed that you stayed with that old prude in her hovel for so long. You're beautiful young men and under my tuition you will flourish and become very rich,' Hanno assured them.'

This sounded like good news to the boys, but they were surprised to hear what Hanno had in store for them.

'You have always been beautiful children,' Hanno told them. 'But when you reached puberty you became outstandingly handsome males, and I just knew that someday I would be able to guide you into a profession that would make you very wealthy. It was my dream to do so and now that you've come to me, I know that what I wished for will come to fruition.'

However, when the boys realised that Hanno wanted them to become male prostitutes, they recoiled in horror. It seemed repugnant to them to go into that profession and it took Ivo a long time to persuade them that the work would not be arduous; it would, however, be very financially rewarding and when they had made their money the world would be their oyster and they could spend the rest of their lives in leisure.

'You can live with me to start with; I'll fully train you and when you are ready, I'll find clients for you.' Hanno told them.

Eventually, the boys agreed, they were young and naïve, they had nowhere else to go, and they felt they had little choice in the matter. But they both insisted that they would only service women, even though Ivo wanted them to agree to go with men as well. Nevertheless, Hanno took great pains to train them how to pleasure a woman and was delighted to find the young men had aptitude and great stamina. Once the twins were fully trained, Hanno produced a stream of eager women for them and very soon word got around that as well as being handsome beyond measure, they had exceptional skill and endurance; they became in great demand. Their main clientele was almost entirely older women who were rich and frustrated, because their husbands were too busy making money to give them the attention they deserved.

Neither of the twins liked what they were doing, but the work was not as hard as it had been on the smallholding and the financial rewards were exceptional, even though Hanno was taking his cut. After some time, the twins were able to buy their own apartment and furnish it with expensive fittings and furniture, but they always worked with Hanno because he had been a good friend to them and they trusted him to find them the right women.

Although the twins were enjoying life to a degree, they both became weary of trying to satisfy one fat old frau after another, each of whom were determined to get their pound of flesh when they had paid for their services. The boys agreed they never got any pleasure out of the liaisons themselves, because they needed to hurt their sexual partners to get any gratification out of the coupling and this was out of the question when they were with paying customers. What they really wanted to figure out was a way to make a huge amount of money quickly, so that they could live in luxury and never have to work again. They wanted to be able to afford a huge chateau and have a stable of fast and fashionable cars. They wanted to wear only the most expensive clothes and have the means to travel wherever they wanted whenever they wanted. They wanted to be so rich they need never be polite to anyone ever again, but they couldn't figure out how to get their hands on that sort of money.

About two years after they had been thrown out by their aunt, they received a letter from her. In it, she had stated shortly that they should come and visit her as soon as possible, because some official business had come to her attention concerning them and she would pass on the details to them when they came. It was the first communication they'd had from their aunt since they had left, and they could tell by the briefness of the note that she had in no way forgiven them for hurting one of her animals. However, they couldn't think of any official business that could possibly concern them coming by way of their aunt, so they decided to ignore the note and had screwed it up and tossed it away.

Now, as Alfrid did his duty with the frau grunting with pleasure beneath him, he thought of the note again. Perhaps it had more significance than they had first imagined. Surely Ida would not have written to them had she not felt obliged to because it was important, since she obviously still despised them. He decided they had been hasty in discarding the note as unimportant, and by the time the frau moaned in ecstasy, Alfrid had decided that he and his brother would go and see his aunt that very day.

The two boys dressed with care before they went to visit their aunt. They wanted her to see that they had prospered since she had thrown them out on their ears without a penny, and prove to her that they were much better off than had they stayed and worked on the smallholding. When they knocked on her door there was no reply, so they made their way around to the farmyard, carefully avoiding the muddy puddles as they didn't want to splash their shiny shoes. The twins were pretty sure they would find their aunt working with the animals there.

'Aunt Ida,' Alfrid shouted from afar when he saw her in one of the pigsties.

'Oh, it's you,' said Ida when she turned to see who had shouted. 'Go into the house, I'll be with you in a moment.'

The twins made their way to the house and let themselves in. Nothing much had changed. The dingy curtains they remembered so well looked even more dusty and worn, while the furniture was thread bear and covered with cat fur. The boys looked at it with distaste and remained standing as they did not wish to get cat hairs on their clothes. Even the smell of the place had not changed, it smelt of dust and wet animal fur.

Danek shuddered. 'This brings back so many bad memories,' he muttered.

Eventually, they heard their aunt arriving back at the house. She pulled off her muddy wellington boots at the back door and shoved her feet into some shabby slippers, slippers the twins remembered so well. When they had been young, Ida had smacked them with those very slippers when they had been naughty!

In contrast to the two young men, Ida looked scruffy and worn. Her hair was much greyer than they remembered and her wrinkles more numerous and deep set.

'A letter came for you from a lawyer,' Ida told them when she came into the room. She did not invite them to sit down or have a cup of coffee. 'Apparently Ivo's father has just died. He died intestate, probably because he had kicked his only child out many years ago. Anyway, he left a certain amount of money and since you're Ivo's sons it's to go to you.' Ida handed the boys a letter.

'This letter is addressed to us, but you've opened it,' Alfrid accused his aunt when he saw the envelope had been slit open.

'To be honest, I nearly just threw the letter into the fire without opening it when it arrived,' admitted Ida. 'But then I saw it came from a firm of solicitors so I thought I'd better see what was inside before I threw it away.'

The twins pulled the pages out of the envelope and skimmed

through them. They were delighted to see that they were going to come into some money, but angry that Ida had nosed into their business.

'Since you're going benefit from a legacy, perhaps you'd like to reimburse me for the years that I looked after you and brought you up,' said Ida in a wheedling voice, but without much hope.

The boys looked at each other and rolled their eyes. Then Danek turned to Ida and said with contempt, 'Yes, I can see that you are very poor and some money would come in handy. But no, we're not going to give you anything. Why should we after all, since we had such a dreadful upbringing!'

'Yes, you almost worked us to death and we've done so much better since we left you,' said Alfrid. 'So, rest assured, dear aunt, nothing will be coming your way!'

'Go then,' said Ida angrily. 'At least now that you have inherited some money you can stop selling your bodies!' She said the words with such contempt it made the twins feel like she had slapped them across the face. How did she know what work they had been doing, anyway?

The twins lost no time and went straight to the solicitor's office when they left their aunt. They were delighted to find that there was a nice lump sum of cash and decided that they would no longer have to prostitute their bodies for money. They resolved to buy an aeroplane and learn how to fly, with the idea of running commercial flights around the country once they had qualified as pilots. It would be a lucrative business they thought, so even though the cost of the aeroplane and their flying lessons used up much of their inheritance, they were sure it would be a good investment for their futures.

The boys had just qualified as pilots when the Second World War broke out. They would have been destined for the Luftwaffe, but Hanno told them that they had been diagnosed with a heart condition when they were babies, and they should be able to dodge being drafted into the forces if they could produce that evidence. Neither of the twins wanted to fight for their country, so they sought out the doctor who had diagnosed their heart condition and asked him to write an official letter to say they both had problems with their hearts. After examining the boys, the doctor said that although he had detected in their hearts a medical anomaly when they were babies, the problem must have remedied itself as they had grown up, because their hearts now appeared to be completely normal. In his opinion, they

were fully fit and could join the forces. But this was not what the twins wanted to hear and they persuaded the doctor to write a letter suggesting that the problem with their hearts remained, which he was glad to do for the monetary inducement he was offered.

The twins had spent most of their inheritance and now the war had put a stop to their plans of running a commercial flying enterprise, which was very frustrating for them. Although they had dodged going into the forces, they discovered that they were expected to help in the war effort nonetheless, and they found themselves working in Berlin modifying trucks for the army. It was there that they had first met Rauff, who wanted them to transform the trucks into mobile gas chambers, and they found him to be a kindred spirit. They developed a strong bond with Rauff and they formed an unholy trinity, all of them enjoying the work they were doing for the war effort. The fourth man who worked with them was little more than a lackey. He was a quiet man called Finn, and the twins regarded him as somewhat dim-witted since he never had much to say. However, he seemed devoted to Rauff and happy to help him in every way possible.

They had all trusted Finn implicitly and after the war when Alfrid had escaped to Chile and found Rauff, neither of them could quite believe at first, that he was the one who had betrayed them. When it did dawn on Alfrid that it definitely must have been Finn who revealed them to the authorities and ultimately caused his brother to be executed, he was incandescent with rage. He had been closer to Danek than he ever could have been to a wife and he was determined to find out where Finn was and get his revenge, but it wasn't going to be easy. Alfrid realised that Finn must be an alias, so he didn't even have a name to start with.

The twins had entrusted Finn with what they termed the spoils of war, and Alfrid knew for certain that Finn would not now be giving anything back to him. Alfrid had had to flee Germany in a hurry to avoid incarceration, so all his legitimate possessions and money had been confiscated in Germany. He was now almost penniless and Rauff didn't seem inclined to help him financially, so it was going to take some time to build up his finances before he could eventually track down the man he knew as Finn and exact retribution.

Chapter 17

Murder

Having the nature that he did, it hadn't taken long for Alfrid to become friendly with other people who looked at moral and honest folk with contempt, and very soon he was embroiled in various schemes that entailed lucrative deals to be made when transporting drugs around the world. This led him to make a base for himself in Somalia, because much of the drug trafficking in which he was involved was up the east coast of Africa from Zanzibar heading north. It was at this time that he bought himself a Cessna 180 and also a beach cottage in Kilifi on the north coast of Kenya, so that he had a bolt hole there away from any of the incriminating areas from which he operated. As soon as he had made enough money, he had employed a private detective to find the man whom he had known as Finn. He also persuaded Hanno to come and stay with him, as the twins had been close to him in the past and Alfrid valued him as a trusted friend.

'Look at this, Hanno,' Alfrid said to his friend when eventually he received a report from the private detective. 'The man who went by the name of Finn Blosser during the war was working for British Intelligence as a spy! He was gathering information, among other things, about the so-called atrocities committed by the Nazi party. I always thought the man was not endowed with too many brains and after the war had most probably been forced to tell the authorities about the time when he had worked with Rauff. He always seemed so devoted to his boss and the cause, but this new information puts everything into a different perspective. I wanted my revenge before, because no one will cross me and not be punished, but in light of what has been revealed my retribution will know no bounds!

'What a bastard!' Hanno exclaimed. 'He stole your wealth and was the instrument of you dear brother's death. Is he still alive?'

'Yes, very much so; he's moved to Africa and is farming in the country of Kenya. I'm going to go after him, Hanno, I will force him to give back the money that he must have got from the proceeds of what he was given for safekeeping, and then I will kill him and his entire family.'

'You need to proceed with caution, my boy. Don't go rushing in full of anger and with revenge burning in your heart. Keep a cool head and plan your reprisal carefully.'

But Alfrid's blood was up and he wouldn't listen to Hanno. He knew Ian Thorne was farming at a place called Njoro in Kenya, and the thought of brutalising the man to make him pay back what Alfrid thought was rightfully his and then murdering him and his family, drove him on in a frenzy.

'Look, Hanno,' Alfrid said in frustration when the older man tried repeatedly to make him slow down, 'I'm not waiting any longer or making any fancy plans. My plan is simple and will be effective. If you don't want to come with me, I'll go alone.'

But Hanno was with Alfrid when they arrived on a commercial flight at Embakasi Airport just outside Nairobi, as he wanted to be a steadying hand for his friend. Alfrid's Cessna 180 was in Somalia, so they hired a car and headed for Njoro.

'How do you intend to proceed?' Hanno asked Alfrid as they drove towards their objective.

'Once we've located the farm, we'll stake it out so that we can see if they have any security; guard dogs or alarms, that sort of thing. We can also ascertain how many people are living in or nearby the house. Then later in the early hours of the next morning, if we think it's feasible, we will go back and break in. And then, at last, I will confront the bastard that had my brother killed and he'll be shown no mercy!'

'It's all too simplistic,' complained Hanno.

'Simplicity is always the best way,' said Alfrid confidently.

When they eventually came to the right area, they started looking for farm tracks leading from the main road. When they spotted one, they slowed down and were pleased to see a sign nailed to a tree with the foliage half concealing the lettering. Alfrid stopped their car so that they could have a good look at it. He could just make out the writing and he whooped with satisfaction when he realised the faded letters spelled out *Thorne Estates*. He had just got underway again when a vehicle came down the farm track and tuning onto the main road it sped past them. But there was time enough for Alfrid to see and identify the man who was driving—it was Ian Thorne. Alfrid whooped again.

'The gods are looking on us kindly today,' he said with satisfaction. 'With Thorne out of the way, we will be able to determine far more easily the way to proceed. We can dispense with the time-consuming surveillance and get our answers from speaking to someone on the farm, since no one else will recognise us.' He turned up the farm track and drove confidently towards the homestead which was about three miles from the turn off.

On the way, they noticed cattle and sheep grazing in the fields and a good crop of maize that was almost ready for harvest. Before reaching the house, they by-passed the farm sheds where they noted some rather ancient machinery stood. It all looked clean and in good working order, but there was no denying it was old and well used. As they approached the house a pack of dogs ran out barking. There were three Alsations, two Rhodesian Ridgebacks and three little dogs of indeterminable breed.

When they came to a stop, a slim, pretty woman with wild curly hair appeared; Margo Thorne was wondering who had unexpectedly turned up at their farm. Ian had gone to Nakuru and had not said that he was expecting anyone to visit. She shouted at the dogs, which were jumping around the car while barking threateningly, and told them to back off when she saw there were two white men in the car.

'I'm sorry to disturb you missus. . .?' said Alfrid smiling at her as he got out of his car when he saw the dogs had lost interest. Hanno remained sitting in the car.'

'Thorne,' said Margo automatically. 'Margo Thorne.'

'Ah, Mrs Thorne, is your husband here—or maybe you yourself can help us?'

Margo noted the man speaking to her was wearing a baseball cap and reflective sunglasses, so she couldn't really see his face very well.

'My husband has gone to Nakuru but should be back later. Maybe I can help you instead?'

'Yes, perhaps you will be able to. We're missionaries from Germany and we're looking for a Mr Rharb whom we understand has a farm in this area. He has generously agreed to let us set up a mission station on his farm.' Alfrid felt quite proud of himself for being able to think on his feet and spin a credible story to deceive this woman, whom he thought would be quite gullible.

'Mr Rharb?' A furrow formed on Margo's brow. 'I know all the farmers in this area and I'm quite sure there isn't a Mr Rharb among them.'

'Oh dear, then maybe we are quite lost and not in the right area at all,' said Alfrid. 'Everything is so vast over here, even your farm for example, it is miles from the beaten track; you must feel very isolated and insecure all by yourselves in the middle of the bush! You don't even seem to have any security—no fences, no gates to lock, not even a security guard!'

It was normal practise to be hospitable to any travellers who rolled up at your house if you were farming in Kenya and invite them to have a cup of tea, but Margo hesitated because there was something about the man who faced her that made her feel uneasy. The fact that Alfrid had the peak of his cap pulled well down over his eyes and he wore reflexive sunglasses preventing her from gauging the expression in his eyes troubled her, because she felt the man had an aura about him that wasn't exactly pleasant. She could feel goose pimples on her arms and instinctively felt something wasn't right.

'Security isn't an issue,' Margo said vaguely, deciding that she would definitely not offer any hospitality.

Although she couldn't see the man's eyes, Margo could tell by the movement of his head that he was looking around. The other man in the car who had not got out also seemed to be scrutinising the place carefully and Margo was beginning to feel more and more uneasy. She wished they would leave.

'I'm sorry,' said the man in the sunglasses. 'We have bothered you for nothing because we are in the wrong place; we must now get in touch with our head office and ask them for more detailed instructions so that we can find Mr Rhrab's farm. My apologies and thank you for your help.'

Margo watched their car drive away. She still felt disturbed without quite being able to put her finger on why she felt that way.

'That wasn't the residence of a man who was wealthy,' stated Hanno as they drove away from the homestead. 'It was a pleasant, thought shabby, farmhouse with no trimmings. I was expecting the place to be more grand, since Thorne had stolen all the booty that rightfully belonged to you and Danek.'

'I know, the same thought occurred to me,' agreed Alfrid. 'Obviously, Thorn hasn't spent the money he stole on his farm. He must still have in stashed away in a bank account or a safe. He most probably bought this place out here in the sticks thinking he could lie low and hide out here until Rauff and I were apprehended.'

'Even so, I notice that the farm looks well run and it makes me wonder why he hasn't spent more money on the place. There should be little tell-tale signs of his wealth, for example, a good car or expensive farm machinery—new tractors and harvesters. The ones we saw were very old and well used. I would expect to see he had race horses or a pedigree herd of cattle, but we saw his livestock was only what would be expected on a fairly low-income farm. Even the farmhouse looked as though it would benefit from a bit of maintenance. I noticed that part of the roof on the house could have done with repair and it just doesn't indicate to me that the man has wealth, secret or not!'

'Of course Thorne has wealth—wealth that should be mine! No man would relinquish what we trusted to him back to the families of those whom we disposed, and if he hasn't spent it on this farm it's certainly somewhere else. Wherever it is, I will get it back and Thorne will pay for double crossing us.'

Alfrid's eyes were murderous and he banged his hand on the steering wheel as he went on.

'We know now where the farm is and what security arrangement it has. Dogs are easy enough to deal with and we have seen there are no security gates on the doors of the farm house or bars on the windows. The woman confirmed security wasn't an issue—in other words, they didn't have to bother too much about the safety of the place, so getting access to the house will be easy. Tonight, I am going to find out where Thorne has put the money he got from selling my treasure and when I have finished with him, he will be glad to hand it over! Then I will kill him and his wife and daughter. I will do it for Danek and every trace of Thorne and his family will be wiped out!'

'He has children?' Alfrid had not given Hanno any details about Thorn's family.

'Just one daughter; I'm not sure how old she is, but she lives with her parents so must still be young. She will also suffer a painful death so that my brother's betrayal will be completely avenged!'

❖

Ian Thorne arrived back on his farm later that afternoon. He was a short stocky man who had a shock of sandy hair and a deter-mined expression on his craggy face. He was a man who thrived on action and positivity and he dismissed incidents that he felt had no bearing on him or his family. When Margo related the in-cident of the so-called missionaries to Ian later that evening, he had shrugged his shoulders. 'There are missionaries popping up all over the place these days,' he said. 'But they must have been miles away from where they thought they were, because I know there isn't a farm belonging to a Mr Rharb anywhere close to here. As to your uneasy feelings about them, my dear, well, they were German, weren't they? Of course, you would have uneasy feelings about any German people turning up here unannounced, be-cause of what they did to Britain during the war.'

The subject of missionaries was dismissed, but then Margo told her husband that Georgia was planning on going to Nairobi for an engagement party that evening.

'She's not going to ride that damn Vespa scooter all the way to Nairobi, is she?' Ian asked, a frown furrowing his forehead. He knew his daughter was headstrong and fearless—rather like him—but he did worry about her riding her scooter around after dark.

'No, she's going to ride it to the flying club and then catch a lift with someone who has a car,' Margo told him. 'I can't imagine she'll be back before the early hours of the morning.'

'Well, at least we know she doesn't drink,' said Ian. 'Small mercies, eh?' He knew Margo worried about their daughter even more than he did, but he accepted Georgia had inherited his intrepid nature and knew it would be wrong to try and keep her safely under his wing at all times.

Alfrid had anticipated that there would be dogs on the farm and he had brought the means to neutralise what he thought was the only security that the Thorns had in place. Earlier that day, he had bought meat from one of the butcheries in Nakuru, and it would be an easy matter to conceal the poison he had brought from Chile in the meat and lay it out invitingly for the unsuspecting dogs later that evening. They planned to put it around the perimeter of the homestead when it got too dark to be observed, and then they would wait until the early hours of the morning before they attempted to enter the farmhouse.

After they had put out the poisoned meat, the two men sat in their car that was concealed in the bushes a little way from the homestead and they waited until they felt the dogs would have consumed the meat and died. They were satisfied that there were no other safety measures in place, because Margo had said security wasn't a problem in this part of the world. However, what she had not mentioned was that they also had a night-watchman—an askari.

Maina had come to work that evening as usual, carrying his spear, knobkerrie and the shining silver torch of which he was so proud. He enjoyed the prestige of being an askari and after starting the engine that ran the generator which served the house with electricity, he strode importantly around the homestead checking for anything untoward. The dogs followed him around because they liked him. He knew when he had started the job that the dogs would be his allies; they would help him in his task to keep everything safe and so he made sure he made firm friends with them right from day one. He always asked the syce, who looked after the horses, to save the clippings he trimmed from the horses hoofs so that he could give them to the dogs. They absolutely loved them and knew that Maina often had his pockets filled with these delicious treats.

'You will be my eyes and ears tonight,' Maina said softly to the dogs in Swahili as he doled out the goodies to the expectant dogs.

Maina thought he had the best job on the farm and he liked his employer. He had nothing but respect for both Ian and his wife, but there was one aspect of his employment about which he disagreed because he could see no sense in it. The bwana and the memsahib had both impressed upon him the necessity for him to keep alert during the night. They insisted that he should not sit in one place for too long, but patrol around so he would discover anything untoward if it were to occur. But Maina knew that this was what the dogs did of their own accord, and that they would immediately warn him if they found anything they considered troublesome or out of the ordinary.

He was quite willing to leap to the defence of his employers if necessary. He had no fear for his own safety and he had his weapons ready for action if needed, but he didn't consider expending his energy on patrolling around the homestead during the night as sensible. He decided he would rely on the dogs to warn him of anything untoward and then he would leap into action if necessary.

Once Maina had started the engine that ran the power-plant, all the lights in the main house would spring on and remain on until the engine was turned off. Maina would know when to turn the engine off, because his boss had instructed him to keep an eye on the window of the room in which he and the memsahib slept, and when he saw the bedroom light go off, he was to shut down the engine. After that, he was supposed to resume his patrols but Maina did not do this.

As soon as the engine was off, Maina went to get the pile of sacks that he had hidden in the garage and laid them down next to the engine that was now silent. It still radiated a welcome warmth and the sacks protected his greatcoat from the oil on the floor of the engine room and provided a comfortable mattress. Having thus bedded down for the night, Maina was quite confident that the dogs would wake him up if necessary. He knew the bwana always rose between 5am and 6am, so all he had to do was make sure that he was up by then and the sacks were once more concealed in the garage.

On the day that the Germans had come to the farm, Maina had had a busy day digging his garden where he hoped to plant maize and vegetables. He felt quite tired when he arrived for his nightshift and was dismayed when he saw Georgia driving off on her Vespa scooter that evening. He enquired of the maid where the girl was going, and the maid told him Georgia was going to a party in Nairobi but she would be back sometime during the night. This meant that Maina would have to be careful not to sleep too deeply, because otherwise he may not hear the dogs welcoming Georgia on her return. He knew he would be expected to greet her when she arrived and shine her way to the house with his torch, after she parked her scooter in the garage.

Alfrid and Hanno had dropped the poisoned meat beyond the boundaries of the homestead to avoid detection from the dogs. They knew that the smell of the meat would soon drift over to the dogs' noses and they would seek out the unusual bounty because they were, in effect, scavengers. When the men felt they had given the canines enough time to find the meat, consume the poison and die, they made their way cautiously back to the homestead on foot. They encountered none of the dogs and no-one challenged them as they silently approached the house. It took only a minute to force the lock on the back door.

The house was a rambling one-story building and the men silently explored the inside of the building with the use of a small pencil-torch. They found that there were four bedrooms, two were obviously used for guest rooms and were empty. A further bedroom appeared to belong to a child as it had pictures of horses and aeroplanes on the walls, but was at present empty. Then they had located the bedroom in which Ian and Margo slept and Alfrid immediately switched off the torch. The two men silently approached the bed and stood over the two sleeping forms.

Ian sensed, even as he slept, that there was danger in the room and he suddenly sat up and reached for his pistol which he kept under his pillow. But he was immediately grabbed and, despite him fighting them like the very devil, he was soon immobilised with cable ties that were secured around his ankles and wrists. Margo was similarly secured as soon as she woke up.

Once Alfrid and Hanno had immobilised their quarry, Hanno switched on a battery powered lantern that he had brought with him. It gave out enough light for Ian to get a good look at his attackers and he saw that one of them was one of the twins. Since Danek had been executed he knew that the man leering down at him was Alfrid. Ian's worst nightmare had been realised.

'You are not mistaken,' said Alfrid in a sneering voice. 'Did you really think you could hide from me when you were the cause of my brother's death? And to compound things, you stole what was not rightfully yours! Of course I was going to hunt for you and not give up until I found you. Now is the time for retribution and revenge—but first you will hand back the money you made from selling the treasure that I gave you for safe keeping.'

'I. . . I don't know what you're talking about,' spluttered Ian.

'Oh, yes you do! You called yourself Finn Blosser when you worked with us; don't try and convince me that this is a case of mistaken identity.'

'Those men are the missionaries I told you about,' Margo suddenly said.

Hanno slapped her across the face and told her to shut up and she relapsed into shocked silence.

'Right, first things first,' said Alfrid. 'I gave you a number of articles of great value for safe keeping. I believe you sold them and I now want the money that you made from the sale, since it is rightfully mine.'

'Okay, I admit that I did work with you during the war under the alias of Finn Blosser,' Ian conceded. 'I really had no option and I hated what you were doing, but it was what I had been detailed to do by the war office and they expected me to do my work efficiently. I did report back to them what I had found out and yes, this did lead to you, Danek and Rauff being hunted by the authorities for your war crimes after the war. I did not kill your brother; he was judged to be guilty at a fair trial and subsequently executed, but I was not part of that. The items that you gave me for safe keeping were handed to the authorities and they ensured that they were given back to the families of those whom you had murdered. I did not profit from what you stole; I'm an honest man and I would never do anything like that.'

Alfrid stepped forward and punched Ian full in the face. 'You lie!' he roared. 'No man would relinquish such valuable items if they got their hands on them, it would not be possible for a man to even think about doing that. Now, you are going to tell me where the money is and how you are going to give it back to me.'

Alfrid started to savagely beat Ian, but he continued to insist that he had handed the items back to the authorities and not made any money out of them. However, Alfrid couldn't accept that as the truth, he was convinced Ian was lying and he worked on the poor man viciously and violently in the hope that he would crack. Alfrid was enjoying himself. Having Ian at his mercy so that he could hurt and humiliate him was like a very thrilling and powerful drug flowing around his veins, and Margo's distress added to his pleasure.

'Stop,' said Hanno in German when he could see that Alfrid's brutality had almost killed Ian. 'He is a stubborn man and would rather die than give back to you what is rightfully yours. However, there is another way in which to make him talk.' Hanno's eyes slid towards Margo.

Alfrid immediately liked the idea; he saw he could add mental pain to Ian's physical agony and in so doing increase his own pleasure. Strangely, at that moment, the money he felt that Ian owed him was almost of no consequence now. The endorphins that had been released in Alfrid's brain from the pleasure of torturing Ian, had flown through his nervous system and given him a high that no drug would have been able to compete. Now Hanno had suggested something that would enable him to rise up to even dizzier heights of pleasure.

But Margo's pain was too much for Ian to witness, and as she lay screaming in agony and close to death her husband had a massive heart attack.

Hanno was frustrated that they hadn't got any information out of Ian before he died and blamed Alfrid for being so heavy handed.

'We must now search the house for a safe or details of Thorn's bank account,' he growled.

They started to ransack the bedroom, but unexpectedly the engine that worked the generator sprang into life and all the lights in the house suddenly illuminated the rooms in dazzling light.

Maina had been sleeping more lightly than usual because he didn't want to be caught napping when Georgia returned, and it was for this reason that he was woken by the faint scream that came from the house. He sat up uncertainly, wondering if he had dreamed it and then there came another louder more agonised scream and he knew it came from the bwana's house.

Maina felt confused; could his employers be under attack? It seemed that they were, but the dogs remained silent. Something was very wrong. He knew he must go to the Thorns' aid, but first he decided to start the lighting plant so that he could see what he was dealing with. It didn't take him a minute to start the engine and then he ran to the house, brandishing his knobkerrie and spear. When he got to the front door, he saw it was open so he unhesitatingly ran in screaming a loud war cry as he went to bolster his courage. He knew exactly where his employers slept, so he ran straight towards their room.

Hanno and Alfrid knew that their break-in must have been discovered when the lights came on and they made haste to depart. But the shrieking of the African was so disconcerting it made their blood run cold and Alfrid hesitated for a second.

'Don't delay,' shouted Hanno desperately. 'We need to get the hell out of here—and fast!' He snatched up Ian's revolver.

They ran out of the bedroom and down the passage where they came face to face with an apparition that hardly looked human. Maina's greatcoat flapped around his knees and his pounding feet were bare, but it was his head that anchored their attention. It was thrown back and his wild staring eyes looked manic, while from his mouth, which was an open round pink hole around yellowing teeth, he was emitting what sounded like strange animal howls.

'Mein gott!' Hanno was leading and he suddenly saw the man was armed. He lifted Ian's revolver and fired at Maina. When Maina saw that Hanno was going to shoot him before he could get close enough to use his own weapons, he ducked to one side which caused him to lose his momentum and balance, and he dropped his spear and knobkerrie as he tried to prevent himself from falling down. Alfrid was onto him in a flash and grabbing him by the shoulders he threw him headfirst against the wall. The impact stunned Maina and he fell to his knees, giving the two Germans the chance to jump over him and escape into the night.

They didn't stop running until they reached their vehicle and then they made a quick exit from where they had been parked. Just after they had turned out from the farm track onto the main road, they passed a Vespa scooter going in the opposite direction. They took no notice of it and didn't see it turn off the main road down the track that ran to the farm that they had so recently left.

'You were too heavy handed,' Hanno accused Alfrid after they had covered a few miles. 'You need to have more finesse if you want to torture information out of someone. Now you have lost the opportunity to ever get back the money that is rightfully yours.'

'No, you're wrong,' replied Hanno. 'We still have the ace up our sleeve—the child of Ian Thorne still lives.'

'What good will the child do us?' said Hanno sounding surprised.

'She will inherit Thorne's estate—including the money he refused to relinquish to us. If she is still young, as we assume she is, everything will be held in trust until she is old enough to inherit, but it will all be there in safe keeping for her. Now, we must leave the country quickly and let the dust settle, but when it has, we will come back for the girl. We will abduct her and demand a ransom. We know the money is there and will be in safe keeping for her until she comes of age, so all the family will have to do is release the money and give it to us.'

Hanno was at first speechless when he heard what Alfrid was planning, but after a minute he said, 'But we were seen by that man who ran into the house—it would be far too dangerous for us to come back and try and abduct the child.'

'We will give it some time,' said Alfrid. 'I'm sure that after a while all the details of the Thorn's murders will be forgotten. Someone else may even be accused of killing them—this is Africa, after all! When I think the time is right, we'll strike again.'

'No, I think the risk is too great.' Hanno looked worried. 'Abduction is a tricky thing to pull off and we may fail. We could even end up in a Kenyan jail—and that is not something that I could endure! You have had your revenge now, so let's leave it at that.'

'Never! My revenge is not yet complete!' Alfrid spoke emphatically. 'I will find the child and demand a ransom for her release. The family are sure to use her inheritance money to pay for her liberation. Release her, I will not. The child has Jewish blood in her veins and she has been spawned by the man who was the instrument of my dear brother's death, so for those reasons she must also die!'

Chapter 18

The Search

Cade and Benedict had departed for Kilifi before Charles, since he had to ring Howard before he left to explain to him what had happened. He had been further delayed because he had to refuel and file a flight plan before he took off, but once he was airborne, he soon caught up and passed the Super Cub because the Cessna 182 was a faster aeroplane. As soon as he landed at the Mnarani airstrip he used the club's telephone to ring the family's neighbours and let them know he had arrived. They were expecting his call and promised to tell Oliver immediately that he was ready to be picked up.

By the time Cade and Benedict touched down, Oliver and Euan had made their way over the creek via the Kilifi ferry and had just arrived at the Mnarani Club. After they had all introduced themselves, they ordered some tea and sat down together so that they could try and figure out what could have happened to Georgia.

'The police have been informed of course, but they haven't come up with anything,' Oliver said.

'They've been absolutely bloody useless,' added Euan bitterly.

Charles could see by their faces that they were deeply troubled and worried sick about Georgia's disappearance.

'Are you sure that no one saw anything untoward on the day

that she disappeared?' Cade asked them.

'No. Nothing much goes on around where we have our cottage. The odd fisherman walks down the beach or sails past in a boat, but on the day she disappeared we didn't see anything that was different,' Oliver answered.

'Did you see any fishermen on their boats or on the beach on that particular day?'

'My wife, Diana, and I went to Nyali to visit friends on the day that it happened,' explained Euan. 'We left Kenny and Brent with their grandparents. When we got back and found out Georgia had disappeared, neither my father nor my mother had seen anything suspicious. I questioned the boys about any boats that they may have noticed and Kenny said he saw an ngalawa going past when he and his brother were making sandcastles, and he thought it was about the time Georgia went out in the dingy.'

'Did he remember anything in particular about the ngalawa or the people in it?'

'I didn't actually ask him, but he certainly didn't mention that anything was different about the ngalawa he saw, or its occupants.'

'Well, we need to talk to him again about it. It could very well be significant and kids often remember things very clearly when they're nudged.'

'But why do you think that a couple of fishermen on their ngalawa could have any significance?' Oliver asked looking mystified. 'You see them all the time sailing past our cottage; they're not that unusual.'

'I think that Georgia may have been abducted,' said Cade flatly.

'Good God, man! Why would you think that?' Oliver looked astonished.

'Considering all the facts that we have at the moment, it very much looks to me that her abduction is a very real possibility,' Cade answered. 'If she had drowned, her body would have turned up and if she had been attacked by a shark, which would be very improbable inside the reef near Kilifi, I have no doubt that the boat would have been punctured. I agree that a fisherman would be unlikely to want to abduct anyone, but he could have been working for someone else, someone who had a good reason to take your niece.'

'But who? And why? I haven't received a letter demanding money or anything, and anyway, to me the whole idea of abduction sounds preposterous!'

'There's still time for a letter of demand to arrive,' said Cade. 'But let me explain—some months ago Georgia asked me to try and find out who had murdered her parents, and from what I have subsequently discovered I think Georgia's disappearance could easily be connected to their murder.'

Cade went on to describe what he had found out and his reasons for suspecting Alfrid was behind the Thornes' murders. He told Oliver and Euan, in no uncertain terms, that he feared Alfrid would seek retribution for the death of his twin brother and this would put Georgia in an extremely perilous position.

'My God, if Georgia's in the hands of the person who viciously tortured my sister and her husband, she's in dire danger!' Oliver had turned very pale. 'We need to find her fast, but we have hardly anything to go on.'

The four men decided to go over the creek and back to Oliver's beach cottage, so that they could talk to Kenny about the boat that he had seen around the time Georgia had disappeared. They found Fiona, Diana and the boys sitting on the veranda; all were in a subdued state.

'If only I hadn't sat with my nose in a book,' lamented Fiona. 'I should have been keeping an eye on Georgia as well as the boys.' She obviously felt very guilty. 'I didn't see anything—I didn't even see the ngalawa that Kenny spotted.'

Kenny felt rather intimidated when Cade questioned him. The man's commanding presence and his light piercing eyes unsettled him, but Cade tried to put him at ease.

'You're a clever little fellow to spot the ngalawa,' Cade told Kenny kindly. 'Now I want you to think if there's anything you noticed about it that you could tell me.'

'It was just an ngalawa,' said Kenny shrugging.

'Okay. Did you notice how many people were on the ngalawa?'

'There were two. One of them stood up and looked about and then sat down again. I thought he might fall off the boat because you shouldn't really stand up when you're in one, but he didn't fall.'

'Could you see what he was looking for?'

'No. . . I don't think so.'

'Could it have been Georgia in your dingy?'

Kenny nibbled the side of his finger as he thought about that. 'It might have been,' he said at last. 'She was out on the water rowing the dingy towards the reef and he might have been looking for her.'

'Was there anything else on the water that he could have been looking at?'

'Well, I thought he might be looking for a place to throw out his net and do some fishing, but the fishermen usually go near the reef to do that.'

'So, he didn't throw out a net?'

'No, he just sat down again. I didn't really look at him anymore because I was busy making a sandcastle.'

'Can you tell me what the man who stood up looked like? What he was wearing?'

'I couldn't see his face really, but when he stood up, I could see he was wearing a red and black kikoi and he had something white on his head.'

'A hat? A cap?'

'No, it was sort of like when Mum washes her hair and puts a towel on her head.'

'A turban, then?'

'I think so,' said Kenny looking at his mother for confirmation.

'I think he means a turban,' affirmed Diana.

'What about the other man?'

'He was sitting down and I couldn't really see him.'

'What about the ngalawa? Had you ever seen it before?'

'Yes, I think I saw it sailing past lots of times?'

'Lots of times on the day Georgia disappeared?'

'No. I mean it sailed past every day that we've been here.'

'Are you sure?'

'Yes, because I remember it had two stripes painted on the sides—a red one and a white one, but the white one was dirty and I thought if it was my boat I'd at least clean it up.'

'Good boy, you've been very helpful.'

'I saw that boat as well,' piped up Brent. 'I didn't see it on the day that Georgia disappeared, but I did see it on other days.'

'Did you notice anything else about it or the men in it?' Cade asked the younger brother.

'No. . . only, well, I usually wave to all the boats going past and mostly the people on them wave back, but the two men on that ngalawa never ever waved to me.'

'You've both been very helpful boys,' Cade told them when he was sure they had nothing else to tell him. Then he nodded to Benedict and his son left the room.

'Where's he going?' Brent asked.

'He's going to find out about that boat and the people in it,' Cade said.

When the little boys had gone off to play, Cade told the adults that Benedict spoke Swahili like a native and he had a way with African people that made them want to help. 'His mother died when he was a baby,' Cade explained. 'He was looked after by an ayah when he was very little and it's given him and affinity with the African people, which has been very beneficial when we've had the occasion to question them about something.'

Charles felt he wanted to go back to Mnarani so that he could take the 182 up and fly around and look for some evidence of Georgia, but it was already getting dark so that wouldn't be possible. He was dreadfully worried about her and found it very difficult to even sit still. All sorts of horrendous scenarios flitted thorough his head and he felt tormented and impotent. When Benedict arrived back a couple of hours later, Charles eagerly went to hear what he had learned.

'Apparently, that ngalawa isn't from around here. It arrived from the south a few days ago and it left the area on the day that Georgia disappeared,' Benedict told everyone. 'All the fishermen I spoke to confirmed that. I thought I wasn't going to get any information other than that when I suddenly struck lucky. An old retired fisherman said he thought he had recognised one of the men on the boat. He said he couldn't be absolutely certain, but he was pretty sure his name was Abdullah and he came from the Funzi area, which is a long way south from here. He said that when he knew him, Abdullah was mixed up in drug smuggling activities from Zanzibar.'

'Was that all he could tell you?' Cade wanted to know.

'Pretty much. He did say that Abdullah was rotten to the core and he wouldn't be surprised if he was still involved in drug smuggling, or doing something else equally as illegal now.'

'Well, we could have a lead,' said Cade thoughtfully. 'Tomorrow, Benedict and I will hire a boat and sail south down the coast and see if we can locate the ngalawa. If we find it, we'll question this Abdullah.'

'Do you think Georgia might be with them?' Charles asked.

'Highly unlikely; there would be no place to hide her on an ngalawa. It's more probable, if it was he who took her, that he would rendezvous with another boat and hand her over.'

'How can I help tomorrow?' Charles wanted to know.

'You can fly up and down the coast and see if you can spot the ngalawa with the red and white stripes on it. We're assuming that Abdullah is going to sail it south, back to Funzi or even Zanzibar, but we could be wrong. He could have gone north or even stayed somewhere quite close. Meanwhile, Benedict and I will hire a fishing boat from a friend of ours and head south down the coast in the hope of coming across the ngalawa. Sword Fish is the name of the boat that we will be on, and if you spot the ngalawa when you fly up and down the coast, come and find us and drop us a note,' Cade told Charles. 'It's a pity we can't be in radio contact, but a message will do.'

Oliver suggested that Charles should take one of the children's inflatable armbands so, if necessary, he could secure a message to it in a plastic bag and drop it near the Sword Fish. 'It's bright red, so will be easily visible and it'll keep the message from sinking.'

That night Charles hardly slept at all. He kept imagining Georgia in the hands of a torturer and his stomach would knot in anguish. She was so small and vulnerable and he couldn't bear to think of the pain that she might be subjected to. Eventually, he got up just as dawn was breaking and went to make himself a coffee. He found Oliver in the kitchen making coffees for himself and Fiona.

'I don't think any of us slept much at all,' Oliver said when he saw Charles. 'Cade and Benedict have already departed as they wanted to get underway at first light. This is a terrible thing that's happened.' He looked grey and drawn as he made a third coffee for Charles.

Charles gulped his coffee down and refused to wait for breakfast as he wanted to start on his search as soon as it was light enough to fly. Euan drove him back to Mnarani and Charles had soon refuelled and taken off. He started by flying south and checking every ngalawa that he came across sailing serenely over the ocean. As soon as he spotted one, he would dive down and fly low, just above the waves, so that he could have a good look at the boat.

'Red and white stripes,' he muttered to himself. 'Man in a black and red kikoi with a white turban on his head.'

Sometimes he made more than one pass so that he could be absolutely sure it wasn't the one he was seeking and the occupants looked at him in surprise, most of them giving him a cheery wave. He also came across Cade and Benedict in their hired fishing boat, the Sword Fish. He flew down and alongside them and shook his head while throwing up his hands to signify he had seen nothing of interest as yet. They nodded and Cade pointed north, indicating that he thought Charles should fly north to continue his search.

All morning, Charles scanned the ocean for ngalawas and meticulously checked each one he came across, but the more he looked the more he felt like he was hunting for a needle in a haystack. Sometimes he came across several ngalawas beached under the palm trees at the top of the beach and he really couldn't get a good look at them. Those he would have to leave to Cade and Benedict, he decided.

At midday, he returned to Mnarani to refuel and have a sandwich and then he took off again and widened his search. There weren't that many ngalawas on the water, so Charles decided to check out any boat he saw in the hope that it could be one that had rendezvoused with the ngalawa. He figured that if Georgia happened to be on board she would definitely try and indicate her presence to him, especially if she saw that the 182 came from Lanet. But he was only met with cheerful waves, or in some incidences gestures of annoyance. Of Georgia there was no sign at all.

As Charles continued his fruitless search, he became more and more despondent. He wondered if they weren't on a wild goose chase—they were, after all, spending a lot of time and energy hunting for a boat on the slimmest evidence given by two small boys. The more he thought about it the more he was convinced that they were on the wrong track.

But where was the right track? The only thing he knew for sure was that Georgia had disappeared and if she was still alive, she must be unable to contact him, because he knew she would be aware that he would be worried sick. He wondered if she was anywhere close and had heard the 182 flying overhead? It was possible that she was being held prisoner on land somewhere along the coast. If she had heard the aeroplane flying back and forth, he was sure she would know it was him searching for her and surely, she would try and signal to him. He started flying over all the houses that were situated along the coastline at a fairly low level and then doubling back and overflying them again to see if he could spot any sort of signal, but there was nothing. At last, when the light was fading and he was getting low on fuel, he flew back to Mnarani and landed. His only hope now was that Cade and Benedict had found the elusive ngalawa and had managed to question Abdullah.

Euan came over the creek on the ferry to collect Charles once again, as soon as the neighbours passed on his telephone message to Oliver's family. When Charles admitted that he had found nothing at all to help them in their search for Georgia, he and Euan drove back to the beach cottage in depressed silence. Euan told Charles that Cade and Benedict had not yet returned, so Charles clung onto the hope that they had had a more productive day than he.

It was well after dark when Cade and Benedict arrived back at the beach cottage and just by looking at the expression on their faces, Charles knew that they had had an unsuccessful day. They had travelled as far as Funzi without success, calling in on many of the little places where they thought the ngalawa might be anchored or beached.

'Don't give up hope yet,' said Cade when he saw the look on Charles's face. 'We've spoken to all the people we came across down the coast and offered a reward to anyone who spots that ngalawa or can give us any information of its whereabouts. We've explained to them that we'll fly down the coast tomorrow in the Super Cub and if they have any information for us, they must signal to us and we'll find a place to land and listen to what they have to say. That ngalawa can't just disappear, so I'm sure we'll find it eventually.'

'But what's happening to Georgia meanwhile?' Charles said miserably. 'They could be torturing her like they did her parents—and the longer we take to find her, the worse it will be for her!'

'If my information is correct, Alfrid Wagner wants to reclaim the money he thinks Ian must have got for the items that were left with him for safe keeping,' said Cade. 'He'll probably ask Georgia for it but she won't know anything about it, so he will then contact the family in the hope that they will be able to procure it and pass it on to him. I imagine he'll offer Georgia in exchange for a large sum of money. It wouldn't be in his interest to torture or kill her until he gets what he wants, so I think we can be reassured that she won't be harmed—not immediately anyway, because he will assume that the family will need to know that she's alive and well before they give him anything.'

'But what will happen when they find that Oliver doesn't have the money? Won't they kill her then? Alfrid will probably kill her anyway, because it's part of his revenge for Ian getting his brother executed!' Charles looked utterly miserable.

'When they make contact they'll leave some clues,' said Cade. 'You can gather a lot of information from a letter of demand and it'll give us something else to work on. If I'm right about my suppositions of what they're going to ask, we can stall them, delay them, and work on the clues and that will give us a chance to find Georgia.'

'It all seems so vague,' sighed Fiona and Charles was inclined to agree with her.

'Why haven't they contacted Oliver already?' Charles wanted to know. 'If Georgia obviously doesn't know about the money, why would they delay in getting into contact with her uncle?'

'For two reasons,' explained Cade. 'Firstly, the longer they wait before contacting Oliver the more anxious they expect him to become, and that, they hope, will make him more willing to cough up the dough. Secondly, they could need time to get Georgia to a more secure location before making contact. At the moment, they may be holding her in a boat or a beach chalet somewhere close to here and they may feel it would be prudent to put more distance between us, especially if Georgia is behaving like a little prickly pear—as I assume she is, knowing her!'

'Well, I'm going to resume my flights up and down the coast at first light,' said Charles. 'Because, if she's able, I'm sure she'll try and signal to me when she realises that the club's 182 is flying around.'

'Try flying further out to sea as well,' suggested Benedict. 'They may have her on a boat of some sort, holding her some miles off the coast as a safety measure.'

Charles went to bed feeling very depressed. He couldn't get it out of his head that Georgia may already be dead and he just couldn't imagine facing the future without her. He knew he would keep hunting for her until he found her, but what if she was to be transported away from the area by road? He couldn't possibly try and fly low enough to check every vehicle he found driving away from Kilifi. And what if she had already been moved far away by one means or another? It didn't seem possible to locate her by just flying around in the hope that somehow, he'd come across her.

Charles was exhausted and he eventually fell into an uneasy sleep in which he dreamed that he could see Georgia being transported across the ocean in a dhow to be sold to a wealthy Arab sheik for his harem. He woke up bathed in perspiration, and seeing that dawn was breaking, he got up and went to wake Euan so that he could ask him to take him back to Mnarani.

By mid-day Charles had already flown a good few miles looking for any clues that might lead him to Georgia. He had checked out a number of boats he had seen and had even tried to fly low enough to see into some of the vehicles that were travelling away from Kilifi. He knew he was contravening the air laws of Kenya with all his low flying, but he didn't care, he would do everything he could to try and find the woman he loved even if it meant breaking the law. But in his heart, he knew it was all futile. There was not one single clew that gave him a glimmer of hope and when he returned to Mnarani to refuel and have a drink before resuming his search, he was quite certain that he would never see Georgia again.

Chapter 19

Georgia's Ordeal

On the morning that Georgia had disappeared, she had been sitting on the beach watching her cousin's two little boys building an elaborate sandcastle. She had spent a lovely Christmas with her family and they had, as usual, eaten and drunk too much and now she felt bloated and lethargic. But bubbling away under the sluggish physical symptoms of her body, her mental activities were working at full pace. She couldn't wait to get back to Lanet, to Charles, to the Citabria, so that she could resume her life. Suddenly she felt she couldn't just sit around anymore, she needed to be doing something active. Georgia was all about being energetic and lively and sitting around never suited her for long.

'Boys, would you mind if I borrowed your dingy for a while?' she asked her two cousins. They had received a little inflatable blue and yellow dingy with two plastic oars for Christmas and Georgia felt like going out for a row.

'Yes, that's fine,' said Kenny, 'We don't want to use it right now.'

Georgia first went to tell Fiona what she was going to do, so that the boys' grandmother could keep an eye on the lads in Georgia's absence.

'Make sure you take your hat and put on some more suncream,' Fiona instructed her niece. 'Your shoulders and the top of your thighs are already looking rather pink.'

'Okay; actually, I think I'll put a T-shirt over my bikini as well to prevent me from getting any more sunburnt.'

Before she went, Georgia selected an oversized T-shirt she had that was so long it fell half way to her knees, so it would protect both her shoulders and her thighs; but before doing this, she also rubbed on a generous amount of sun-cream for good measure. Then she picked up the little dingy and the oars and walked to the edge of the ocean.

'Have a good time,' shouted Brent.

'I will,' Georgia called back as she launched the dingy and started rowing.

Georgia decided she would row vigorously out towards the reef and then drift back to the beach on the incoming tide. It was lovely out on the water. A slight breeze cooled her body as she rowed briskly away. When she began to get tired of rowing and felt she had gone far enough, she shipped the oars, leaned back so that her head was comfortably placed on the back of the dingy and let her legs dangle over the other end so that her feet and legs were in the water.

The bright sun dazzled her eyes even though she was wearing her sunglasses and she moved her hat forward so that the brim covered her eyes. It was peaceful bobbing about on the ocean and this calmed her restless spirit. She could hear the cry of the seagulls and the splashing of the water against the side of the dingy, and occasionally the voices of Kenny and Brent floated over to her when the breeze blew from their direction. Georgia's thoughts soon turned to Charles and she wondered if he was longing to see her as much as she was longing to see him. She anticipated learning how to do aerobatics in the Citabria, and then she tried to imagine what it would be like being married to Charles. She knew she was floating towards the beach and she relaxed to the gentle rocking of the boat. It made her sleepy and she found herself drifting into a doze.

Suddenly, some instinct made her aware that danger was imminent. She snapped awake and pushing back her hat, she turned her head to see an ngalawa approaching from behind. It seemed to be silently honing in on her and a large dark-skinned man wearing a kikoi and a dirty white turban was standing in the bow with a club in his hands. Lying prone in the little soft dingy as she was, Georgia was not able to move quickly when she saw with horror the man bringing down the club. She heard the thump as it hit her head, but there was no pain. Then through the dimness of diminishing consciousness, she felt rough hands pulling her into the ngalawa. She fought to stay cognisant, but someone pushed a bit of cloth under her nose that has a strange smell and she suddenly slipped into oblivion.

'Did anyone see us?' the man with the club asked the other man who was sailing the ngalawa. He was speaking in Swahili.

'No, we're too far out. Anyway, the boys and the woman with them are the only ones on the beach and they weren't looking this way.'

'Are you sure?'

'Yes. The woman is lying down reading a book and the boys are busy playing in the sand.'

Georgia didn't know what time it was when she eventually regained consciousness or how long she had remained comatose, but she could see it was getting dark and thought it must be evening time. She realised she was lying on a bed in a place that she didn't recognise and she struggled to remember what had happened. It didn't help that she had a thumping headache, worse than she had ever experienced before. But slowly it all came back to her and she realised that someone had forcefully taken her from the dingy and she was now, apparently, in a strange house.

Gingerly, she sat up and the room seemed to spin around her, so she lay down again feeling very nauseous. It was no good, she couldn't do anything while she felt like this, she couldn't even think straight. She shut her eyes in an attempt to relieve the dizziness and tried to relax so that the spasm of nausea would diminish. She felt a bit better lying still with her eyes closed, so she stayed like that until she drifted off to sleep.

When Georgia next awoke, the sun was filtering into the room through heavily barred windows and she knew it was morning. She felt a bit better now, the headache was still there, but it wasn't as fierce as before and she found she could sit up without becoming too dizzy. She desperately needed to use the loo and looking around she saw an open door leading off the room in which she was lying, behind which was a bathroom. She made her way unsteadily there and after using the toilet, she went to the basin and splashed water on her face. There was a mirror above the basin and she could see that she had dark circles under her eyes and her hair was a complete mess. She ran her fingers through her hair in an attempt to remove the tangles and she encountered a painful lump on her skull and a mass of dried blood clotting her hair around it.

'Bastard!' she muttered as she remembered someone hitting her over the head. She bathed the wound as best she could with the cold water, but there was nothing to be done about her appearance. She didn't have a hair brush or anything with which to tie back her hair, so she just had to leave it as it was.

After leaving the bathroom, she inspected the room in which the bed stood. It seemed to be a standard bedroom that was situated in a rondarvel that stood a small distance from some other buildings. The solid wood door was securely locked and there were heavy bars on the windows, but Georgia guessed these had been fitted to keep people from breaking into the room, rather than for imprisoning someone within. Other than the bed, there was no other furniture except a small bedside cabinet. Georgia spent a bit of time trying to find some way of escape, but it was obvious that without any tools there was no way of breaking out. Eventually, she went to the window and looked to see exactly what was outside.

There were palm trees with their fronds rustling in the gentle breeze and a bougainvillea bush that was covered in bright pink flowers. Just beyond those there were similar buildings to the one she was in and beyond them she could hear the waves breaking on the beach, so she knew that she was still somewhere on the coast. She made her way back to the bed, wishing that she was dressed in more than a bikini and outsized T-shirt. Her lack of clothing made her feel very vulnerable.

Georgia sat on the bed trying to think what she should do. She had obviously been abducted and imprisoned, but why? And by whom? Escape seemed impossible, so she wondered if she should bang on the door and demand to be released. It was while she was still deciding what to do when she heard someone approaching. The door rattled as it was unlocked and then a man stepped through the doorway and closed the door behind him. He was tall, muscular and beautifully tanned and when Georgia saw his face, she though it was the most beautiful face she had ever seen on a man, but then she noticed his eyes and she gave an involuntary shudder. They were of the palest blue and very piercing, but they glinted with malice and cruelty. Right now, the man was trying to compose his face into a pleasant smile, but Georgia could feel the malevolence behind the façade.

'Don't be frightened, little girl,' the man said in heavily accented English. 'I'm not going to hurt you.'

Georgia immediately realised that the man thought she was a lot younger than she actually was. She had a short stature and obviously the oversized T-shirt she was wearing concealed her womanly curves, while she knew her face, when unadorned by makeup, gave her the appearance of a child. Instinctively, she knew that if she kept quiet about her age, she could perhaps use this misconception to her advantage, so she didn't reply but just kept staring at the man.

'You have been sleeping for so many hours I was worried you were not going to wake up,' said the man. 'But now you are awake and I think you must be hungry, yes? I will send someone in with some breakfast for you.'

'Why am I here?' Georgia whispered.

'You don't have to worry about that,' said the man. 'It is an adult problem that has led to you being kept here, but don't worry, very soon we'll get you back to your family. All you have to do is be a good girl and not worry about a thing.'

Georgia didn't reply and the man then turned a left, securely locking the door behind him.

When he had gone, Georgia sat on the bed wondering what all this was about. She must have been abducted for a reason, but what could it be? Her uncle wasn't a rich man, so she couldn't have been kidnapped for a ransom, but what other reason could there be? She was still trying to think of a motive for someone to abduct her when the door opened again and a little wizen African with a cap of white curls on his head and a kind face came in with a tray on which there was a bowl of cereal, some toast and a cup of tea.

'Your breakfast, Memsahib,' he said graciously.

'Asante, Mzee,' Georgia replied politely. Then, still speaking in Swahili, she asked him where they were.'

'I'm not allowed to talk to you,' replied the old man sadly, speaking in the same language.

'Please,' begged Georgia. 'I just need to know where this place is.'

'I'm so sorry,' the old man said. 'I can't tell you, but I can tell you there is an electric fence all around this property, so even if you escaped from this room, you would not be able to get away.'

Georgia ran her fingers through her unruly and matted hair in despair. 'It's so unfair,' she said in English. The old man nodded in agreement, but didn't say anything else. Then he turned and left, locking the door behind him.

Georgia no longer felt nauseous and when she looked at the tray the old man had left, she suddenly realised she was quite hungry, so she sat down and ate the breakfast while she thought about her situation. Who was the handsome man who had the evil eyes of the devil? Why had he abducted her? What was going to happen to her in the end? Then her thoughts drifted to Charles who was waiting for her phone call that wasn't going to come. And her uncle and aunt and Euan and his wife, who must all be worried sick and wondering what on earth had happened to her. Perhaps they would think she had somehow drowned and were now looking for her body.

Georgia just couldn't think of a good reason for her abduction. Surely, it must be a case of mistaken identity, she decided in the end. After all, they thought she was a child, so they must have somehow mixed her up with someone else. She wondered if she shouldn't just tell the man with the evil eyes that there must have been some mistake, so that he would let her go. But then on reflection, she knew this wouldn't be a good idea. It wouldn't be lost on the man that she had seen his face and if he let her go, she would definitely be able to identify him. She shuddered to think what he might do to her if he thought she would be any danger to him. It would be better, she decided, to go along with things as they were for the time being and try and find a way of escape. She thought that her best option was to work on the old man who had brought her breakfast. He looked kind and sympathetic and she might just be able to get something out of him if she persisted.

As the time went slowly by, she heard the sound of a light aeroplane that seemed to be flying up and down the coast. It sounded like a Cessna 182 to her and with a start, she wondered if it was Charles looking for her. If only she had some means of signalling to him, but there was nothing she could do to attract his attention and she remained in an agony of suspense due to her inability to do anything.

At lunch time the old man appeared again to bring her a sandwich and another cup of tea. He retrieved the breakfast tray at the same time, but although Georgia tried her best to draw him into a conversation, he remained resolutely silent. She found it incredibly frustrating and scowled at the man in her irritation. However, after he had left the room and she turned her attention to the lunch tray, she saw he had placed a comb and a length of elastic next to the plate. She realised he must have noticed that her hair was annoying her and had thoughtfully provided her a means of at least sorting out that problem. Georgia immediately felt gratitude for that small kindness and wished she hadn't glared at the old man because he had obeyed orders and not spoken to her.

After eating her sandwich, Georgia decided to have a shower and wash her hair. She found there was soap and shampoo in the bathroom and she felt a lot better when she was clean and wrapped in a towel. She combed the tangles out of her hair, carefully avoiding the painful bump on her skull, and tied it back with the elastic. Then she looked at her bikini and T-shirt and grimaced. She would have loved to put on some clean clothes, but those were the only ones she had and she didn't want to be scantily draped in a towel if someone came to her room, so she dressed once again in her dirty clothes. At least her hair was out of her face and it felt nice and clean.

Later on, after she had eaten her supper—which was delivered by the old man who once more remained studiously silent even when she had thanked him for providing the comb and elastic—Georgia could smell cigarette smoke and she went to the window to see if she could spy who was smoking. It was dark, but as she squinted into the darkness, she could see the glow of a cigarette end at the corner of a building that she could just see from the window in her room. Then she heard words spoken in a low voice and another voice answering. Two men were having a conversation, but they were not speaking English. Georgia strained her ears and suddenly realised that the language spoken was German. Her brow furrowed as she struggled to understand the words.

'We need to get her away from the area before we contact the family,' said the first voice, which she now realised was the voice of the beautiful man who had mistaken her for a child. 'Already there are two aeroplanes flying about looking for her and you can be sure questions are being asked. We can't be absolutely sure that no-one saw Abdullah take her off that dingy, despite what he says.'

'So, what do you plan to do?' the second, deeper voice asked.

'Tomorrow I'm going to move her to our base near Kismayo in Somalia. As soon as I leave you can deliver the letter, but not before. I will go alone with the child, but on the way, I'll stop off at the Tana delta to collect Fritz who wants to return to Somalia.'

Georgia could understand the gist of the conversation if not every word. She strained to hear some more of their words.

'What if the family are unable or unwilling to give you what you want?' The deep voice asked.

'The child is the spawn of a traitor and has Jewish blood running in her veins,' answered the beautiful man. 'Whether the family give me what I want or not, the girl is destined to die. I will reap the revenge of my brother's death in full, you can be sure of that!' The two men then moved away.

Georgia felt her heart rate increase when she heard those words. At first, the only thing she could think about was her imminent death and it made her mouth go dry. Now she knew for sure that it wasn't a case of mistaken identity that had caused her abduction. She knew she definitely had Jewish blood in her veins, and surely the traitor the man was referring to was her father for his involvement in spying for the British during the war. She felt absolutely terrified, but slowly she managed to get her racing emotions under control and she was able to gather her thoughts and decide what she should do. She knew it would be impossible for her to break out of the room she was in—and even if she managed to push past the old man who brought her food and made a break for it, there was an electric fence around the property to consider.

Georgia decided it would be best to try and escape on the long trip to Somalia, since that appeared to be where they were going to take her. Surely, she should be able to find a means to get away from her captor then, especially if she was alone with him. He couldn't possibly keep his eyes on her all the time, there had to be times when escape would be possible. He thought she was a child and if she played along with that and pretended to be acquiescent, he would surely let his guard down at some stage and give her a chance to get away. She was very aware that if she didn't escape she was going to be killed, so it was vital that she at least made an effort to break free, even if she died in the attempt.

Georgia thought that they would probably be making the trip by boat, since Somalia lay to the north of Kenya and had a long coast line. She hoped, since she was a strong swimmer, that she might get the chance to throw herself overboard once they had got underway. She would try and do it before they got too far from land and if she swam underwater for as long as possible, she might be able to avoid detection. If they went by road, on the other hand, it would be a trip of more than 700 miles and would take them a couple of days to complete. They would definitely have to stop for petrol and rest, which hopefully would give her a chance to escape.

Georgia was absolutely determined to at least try and break free. Her trump card was that they thought she was much younger than she actually was, just a little girl in fact, and hopefully when it appeared she was docile and trusting, her captor would be less vigilant and she would get her chance. She was very aware that she needed to escape before they reached their destination, because once she was locked up again, she would have no chance of getting away. She also wondered how long they would keep her before killing her—probably just long enough for them to prove she was alive to her relatives before demanding whatever it was they wanted from the family.

Once Georgia had thought out how she might escape, her thoughts turned to the words she had heard at the end of the conversation between the two men: "I will reap the revenge of my brother's death in full!" Was it possible that her own father had been the cause of the death of the German's brother? It certainly seemed that way. Then it suddenly dawned on her that her captor may very well have been the person who had tortured and murdered her parents and she started shaking. Surely, he would torture her to death as well if he was out to avenge his brother's death in full? Facing death was bad enough, but facing torture was too horrendous to contemplate. Desperately, she tried to think of something that would disprove her theory, but she could only think of her father saying that he had moved to Africa because he was worried that he and his family wouldn't be safe in Britain or Europe after the war. He had obviously thought Kenya was safe enough, but it seemed that there had been nowhere safe in the world for him.

Georgia slept fitfully that night. She had thought, after her parents had died, that she would never be completely happy again. But during the last few weeks things had changed and she realised that she had been wrong to think that, as she had never been so happy in her life. She thought of the wonderful future she had been planning with Charles, but now in another twist of fate, it all seemed to have been cruelly snatched away. How could life be so unfair? She felt the tears gathering in her eyes, but suddenly she dashed them away angrily. I'm not going to let them win, she decided. I have a future worth fighting for and I'll do everything I can to get away from these evil men. I already have a couple of advantages over them. I know what they're planning, because unbeknown to them I can understand German. Also, they don't realise that I'm a woman with a good brain—not a child who can be led to the slaughter like a lamb! At the very least, I'm going to give them a good run for their money!

The old man brought Georgia's breakfast very early the next morning.

'You are leaving today,' he told her quietly in Swahili. 'God go with you.'

Georgia had hardly time to finish her breakfast before they came to fetch her. The beautiful man was accompanied by an African man whose skin was as dark as charcoal. Georgia didn't think he could be a Kenyan because they generally had much lighter completions. He was large and muscular and as ugly as the other man was beautiful.

'We are leaving now,' said Alfrid. 'You will come with us and not make a fuss, yes?' Georgia nodded, making her eyes big and innocently trusting. 'Good girl.' Then he turned to the African and said in German, 'You must take charge of her and make sure she doesn't escape, Hanad.'

Hanad grinned, showing a mouthful of big yellowing teeth. 'She won't escape, boss,' he said in the same language. 'You can see she's too scared to do anything and anyway, even if she should run, could she expect to outrun the "black panther"?'

Georgia was led outside to a carpark where a long wheelbase Land Rover stood. Unlike her own Land Rover, this one had a hard top and looked quite new. She was told to sit in the front on the middle seat so that she was between the two men. Georgia was surprised that Hanad was coming with them. She had thought from the conversation she had eavesdropped the previous evening that she would be alone with the beautiful man. Maybe she had misunderstood, she thought, or maybe, if they were going to go by sea, Hanad would not accompany them on the boat.

Georgia tried to see if she could figure out where they were as they left through the gate of the property. She had no idea whether they were still in the Kilifi area or had moved to another spot on the coast. She didn't recognise the road on which they were driving, but it was quite obvious that they were travelling inland from the coast, so she deduced that the trip was to be done by road. She thought that the track they were taking would lead them to the main road, but they continued bumping along it, over the coral that ridged along the track and through some stretches of thick sand. It was very hot and Georgia could smell the rancid sweat on Hanad. She suddenly wondered if they were going somewhere remote where they could murder her and dispose her body without anyone seeing. It made her feel sick with worry.

After a while, they came out of the plantation of palm trees in which they had been driving for the past few minutes, and the open land in front of them was flat and had little vegetation growing on it. Then rounding a corner, Georgia suddenly saw a windsock fluttering in the breeze and her heart started to beat faster. Was it possible that they were going to fly to Somalia?

Chapter 20

Escape Attempt

For some reason the prospect of flying to Somalia had not crossed Georgia's mind before, but now she suddenly realised that her chance of escape had increased if they were to go by air. As they got closer to the windsock, she saw that next to it there was a large building, obviously a hangar that was constructed mainly with sheets of corrugated iron.

Alfrid stopped the Land Rover next to the building and Hanad indicated that she should get out.

'Keep an eye on her,' said Alfrid in German. 'She might try and make a run for it.'

'She's going nowhere!' Hanad propelled the girl towards the building and told her to stand next to the windsock pole. Someone had planted a small border of Sansevieria Trifasciata, more commonly known as Mother-in-laws-Tongue, around the windsock and Georgia's sharp eyes noted that there was an edging of stones and lumps of coral around the spikey plants.

'Stand close to the pole,' Hanad commanded and he pushed her through the plants so that she was touching the pole. Then he removed a chain from his pocked, secured it tightly around her waist and then padlocked it to the pole, so there was no chance she could escape.

Meanwhile, Alfrid was opening a padlock that locked the door to the hangar. Hanad went to help him open the door and as it swung back, Georgia could see there was a Cessna 180 inside. The men went into the hangar to push it out and Georgia knew that this was her chance to select some sort of weapon. She had already decided on a smooth rounded stone slightly larger than a tennis ball, that formed part of the edging of stones around the windsock and plants. She quickly lifted up her outsized T-shirt and slipped the stone into her bikini bottoms, hoping that the weight of it wouldn't tug them down when she moved. Once the T-shirt was pulled down again, it completely concealed the bulge in her knickers and Georgia was hopeful that the men wouldn't notice anything untoward. She moved the coral and other stones around to hide the mark when her stone had been, and scuffed the earth around to make it seem natural.

The two men were busily pushing the Cessna 180 out into the open and Georgia noted it was one of the older models and it looked very well used. Furthermore, the white paintwork was scuffed and very dirty and Georgia had to wonder how well it had been maintained. Hanad rolled a drum of petrol outside so that they could refuel the aeroplane, and Georgia noticed that they had a hand pump similar to the one that was used at Eliye Springs. Alfrid left the pumping to Hanad and when they had finished the refuelling process, he started to do the pre-flight checks while he gave Hanad instructions. He spoke in German, but Georgia could understand most of what he said.

As soon as I take off, you must go back to the house and ring Fritz. Tell him I'm on my way and I don't want any delays, so he should be ready and waiting for me on the runway when I touch down. Then you must decide how you're going to deliver the letter I've written to the child's relatives. Obviously, you need to get it to them without being seen, but I'll leave that to you.'

'Yes boss, you can depend on me,' said Hanad with a grin.

'Right, I'm ready to roll,' said Alfrid when he had finished the checks. 'Bring the child and put her on the back seat. I want to leave the front seat free for Fritz.'

Georgia felt a rush of relief when she heard she was to be seated in the back. As she had waited under the windsock with the stone uncomfortably stowed in her bikini bottoms, she had deliberated how she was going to manage to retriever the stone and hit Alfrid over the head without him seeing what she was up to and stopping her. If she sat in the seat behind him, it would make things much easier.

'Come on,' Hanad said to her when he had released her from the windsock pole. 'You're going for a ride in the aeroplane.'

Georgia walked meekly to the 180, the stone in her knickers almost pulling them down as she walked, but she couldn't adjust them without being noticed. Luckily, she didn't have far to walk and Hanad opened the door and indicated that she should climb in.

'Get in the back and just move all that stuff to the other seat,' he told her.

There was a clutter of things strewn across the back seats and Georgia cleared a space for herself so that she would be sitting directly behind Alfrid. She noted that there was a dog-eared instruction manual, a dirty looking toilet roll, a large fan-belt, a few cable ties, a packet of nuts and bolts that was spewing its contents out through a hole in the packet, and a rusty tin that had a red cross painted on it.

'Let me show you how to put on your seatbelt,' said Hanad. Georgia had deliberately left it off when she had climbed in, because she didn't want them to realise that she had flown in light aeroplanes before. 'See that plastic bag in the pocket in front of you?' Hanad pointed to it once the seat belt had been secured. 'If you feel sick you can be sick into it, okay?' Georgia just nodded. She was feeling very apprehensive because she knew she would only have one shot of knocking Alfrid out and taking control of the aeroplane, but the two men thought the nervousness they could see in her eyes was due to her being scared of going up in a small aeroplane.

'Don't be scared, you'll be okay,' said Alfrid. 'Just sit quietly like a good girl and everything will be all right.'

Georgia had no intention of sitting quietly and being a good girl, but she knew she must wait until they had taken off and gained some altitude before she made her move. She noted with satisfaction that the aeroplane was dual controlled, so once she had rendered Alfrid unconscious she would be able to fly it from the right-hand seat. She knew that she would have no trouble flying the Cessna 180, but since it was a taildragger, she thought landing it could be difficult for her as she had had little experience on landing taildraggers. However, she had flown and landed the Citabria, which was also a tail dragger, so she more or less knew what she had to do.

Georgia was surprised that Alfrid did not make a radio call to let aeroplanes in the area know he was about to take off. The radio was situated on the far-left side of the instrument panel and he had not even bothered to switch it on.

After take-off, Alfrid headed north and flew along the coast line as he gained height. Behind him, Georgia was sweating and shaking as she waited for him to gain altitude. She had never hit anyone in all her life and now she was going to have to clout this man so hard with the stone that she had selected for the purpose, that he lost consciousness. But how hard would she have to hit him to achieve that? The last thing she wanted to do was hit him so hard that she killed him and then have it on her conscious for the rest of her life. Would it even be possible for someone of her size to kill anyone by hitting them on the head with a stone, she wondered? She didn't want to just stun him for a few seconds, because then he would retaliate violently and she wouldn't have another chance to get out of his clutches, but how hard was hard enough?

Abdullah had known exactly how hard to cosh her over the head when he abducted her, but he'd probably had lots of practice of hitting people over the head! Also, he had chloroform or something to make her remain comatose. Georgia vaguely remembered being dragged from the dingy onto the ngalawa, so she would have to hit Alfrid much harder to make him completely comatose she decided.

As they gained height, Georgia looked to see what there was to secure Alfrid once she had knocked him out. She realised that in all probability, he wouldn't remain unconscious long enough for her to get back to Mnarani and land the aeroplane. So, she needed to tie his hands and feet so he couldn't get at her or try and take over control of the aeroplane again. She pulled the tin box with the red cross on it to her and eased off the lid. Inside there was a tube of antiseptic that looked as though it had seen better days and a couple of bandages and a roll of Elastoplast. The bandage and Elastoplast could be useful, Georgia decided.

When Alfrid reached his cruising height he throttled back and re-trimmed the aeroplane. Georgia had already removed the stone from her knickers and had chosen a spot in Alfrid's bright curls where she was going to aim for. The back of his head looked so vulnerable and innocent it took all her courage to lift the stone and bring it down onto his skull. But by that time, she had psyched herself up and was so full of adrenaline she used all her force and the audible crack as the stone made contact with the head made her feel sick. Immediately a red stain blossomed in Alfrid's hair as he grunted and fell forward onto the control column pushing it forward. The aeroplane immediately went into a dive, and Georgia had to haul Alfrid off the control column and pull it back to get the aeroplane out of the dive and onto an even keel once more. The nose of the aeroplane rose again, but Georgia knew if she let go of Alfrid he would fall forward once more and the same thing would happen.

Reaching over to the front and holding Alfrid with one hand and the control column with the other, Georgia looked around for something with which to keep the man from slumping forward again. Her eyes fell on the fan-belt and she let go the control column and grabbed the belt. Quickly, she pushed it over Alfrid's head and shoulders so that it was looped around the top of his backrest as well and thankfully, although his head lolled forward, it held him more or less in the upright position and kept him clear of the control column. By the time she had finished securing Alfrid, the aeroplane had dropped a wing and was about to go into a spiral dive, so Georgia leaned forward into the front of the aeroplane again and grabbed the control column so she could get them back on an even keel once more.

Alfrid jerked convulsively and Georgia was sure he was regaining consciousness. Letting go of the control column, she pulled the man's arms behind his seat where she thought to tie them with the bandages from the red-cross box. But suddenly her eyes fell on the cable ties and she decided to use those instead. She managed to secure his left arm to the metal of his seat with a cable tie before having to dive forward again and right the aeroplane that was once again teetering on the edge of a spiral dive. When Alfrid groaned, she flung herself into the back once more and proceeded to secure his right arm behind the seat with the help of a cable tie. She saw that there were two left in the packet and decided to use one more on each of his arms to make doubly sure he couldn't move them, but first she had to quickly lean forward into the front and right the aeroplane again.

Now Alfrid was muttering incoherently and Georgia was terrified he was going to regain consciousness before she had got him properly secured. Grabbing the bandages and Elastoplast she wiggled her way over the seats so that she could sit in the front right-hand seat of the aeroplane. Once she had the aeroplane on an even keel again, she leaned over Alfrid and tied his left foot to the metal at the bottom of his seat. It was really awkward because she had to almost get down on the floor to do it, but at least when she bobbed up, she was in a better position to control the aeroplane than she had been when she was in the back. She decided to put Elastoplast around the foot as well to make it more secure, but after going around the foot a couple of times the Elastoplast ran out.

Alfrid was twitching again and Georgia hastened to secure his right foot in the same way as his left, but although she wrapped the bandages around and tied them as tightly as she could, she wasn't sure that they would hold. She wished there had been enough Elastoplast to go around this foot as well, but there wasn't, so she just had to hope the bandages would be enough. It was the best she could do, so now she had a good look out of the window to try and locate where they were. It appeared that they were still flying north, but had drifted quite far out over the ocean. She banked the aeroplane around and headed back to the coastline where she planned to turn south. She wasn't sure where they were exactly, but if she just followed the coast line she knew that sooner or later they would arrive over Mnarani.

Georgia then thought about making a mayday call on the radio to notify anyone flying in the area that she was coping with an emergency, but that would mean leaning over Alfrid to switch the radio on and then fiddling about to find the right radio-frequency. She glanced at Alfrid, the blood from his head had run down his neck and stained his collar and the top of his shirt red, and Georgia suddenly wondered if he was bleeding to death and pondered whether she should be giving him some sort of first aid. But then, to her horror, he snorted, his eyes opened wide and he looked around in confusion.

'What the. . . what has happened?' he muttered in German. He stared at Georgia with a perplexed expression in his eyes and then he seemed to gather his scattered wits and attempted to move his arms so that he could take control of the aeroplane.

'What. . .? Why. . .?' At first, he was unable to understand why he couldn't move his arms, and then he seemed to realise he'd been tied to his seat.

'Help me or we will crash!' he yelled in a panic-stricken voice. He pulled desperately at his bonds.

'We won't crash,' said Georgia quietly, hoping to calm him down. 'I'm flying the aeroplane now.'

'You. . .? You are a little girl. . . you can't fly an aeroplane!' Alfrid's eyes protruded out of their eye sockets because he couldn't believe what was slowly penetrating his brain.

'Just relax, it'll be okay,' Georgia said.

Georgia was terrified that Alfrid would free himself before she could get to Mnarani, because he was struggling so desperately and he was obviously a very strong man. After she had hit him on the head with the stone, she had let it fall out of her hands and it now lay out of sight under Alfrid's seat. Georgia didn't know where it was, but she wished she had kept it handy so that she could give him another good clonk if he seemed to be getting loose. It was a bad mistake and it might be a costly one, she realised.

Alfrid was frantically trying to break loose and glancing at his right foot, Georgia was horrified to see that the bandages that held it to the seat had stretched and it had given him room to wiggle his foot around. She realised that it would only be a matter of time before he was able to kick his way free of the bonds that now held his right foot to the seat. Desperately, she searched the horizon with her eyes looking for the Kilifi creek, because she was under no illusions what would happen if Alfrid managed to free himself.

Suddenly, she saw the creek materialise out of the haze and she opened the throttle and pushed the nose down, while trimming the aeroplane to go into a shallow dive. She needed to get there as soon as possible. Alfrid could see what she was doing and it was at this point that he seemed to truly comprehend that the girl could undoubtedly fly the aeroplane. Before, in his still rather befuddled brain, he had thought she had somehow managed to tie him to his seat, but was then clueless as to how to get the aeroplane back to earth. But watching her quick, precise movements on the controls made him realise that she did, indeed, know how to fly an aeroplane. Before, he had been struggling because he was terrified that they were going to crash, but now his terror turned to anger. Looking at Georgia he was amazed to see that the little girl he had kidnapped who had frightened eyes and a trusting nature, had now turned into a calculating, confident young madam who certainly seemed to know her way around an aeroplane. Anger made him buck against his bonds even more violently.

'This I will *not* permit!' he shouted. 'You will do as I say or I will kill you! I will do it slowly so that you will suffer very badly if you do not do what I tell you!'

'You were going to do that anyway,' said Georgia. Then she spoke in German and quoted what she had heard him say that first evening she had been taken captive. "*The child is the spawn of a traitor and has Jewish blood running in her veins, she is destined to die—I will reap the revenge of my brother's death in full!*"'

For a moment Alfrid was speechless. This little vixen was able to speak and understand German, so what else had she eavesdropped? He realised he was in far greater trouble than he had realised and it made him even more furious and determined to get free of his bonds. The cable ties kept his hands securely tied behind his seat, but he could feel the bonds around his ankles were loosening. The right one, in particular, was slackening and he concentrated all his power in getting his right leg free.

Georgia was terrified. She could see it would be a race with time to get down on the ground before the enraged man got himself free, and she pushed at the throttle that was already in as far as it would go. Mnarani was looming up quite quickly now and she had to turn her thoughts to landing the Cessna 180. The radio had remained switched off as she hadn't had time to turn it on and find the correct frequency, so she couldn't announce her arrival at the airstrip. Also, she couldn't join the circuit in the normally approved manner because she needed to get down as soon as possible, so she hoped that there would be no other aeroplanes flying in the area. The Cessna 180 was a tail dragger and she would have to do a three-point landing. The strip at Mnarani wasn't particularly long and she would have to land on her first attempt—there would be no going around for a second try with this angry man at her side. To add to her problems, Georgia could see by the windsock that there was a fairly stiff cross-wind blowing and she would have to contend with that as well. She tried hard to concentrate her thoughts on landing and ignore the violent struggling of the man next to her.

Georgia was descending fast on the final leg of the circuit when Alfrid suddenly managed to free his right leg from the bandages. He immediately kicked out sideways at the girl, but secured as he was to his seat the kick was pretty ineffectual when it made contact with her leg, but it did cause Georgia's foot to slip off the rudder peddle for a moment.

'Don't do that,' she screamed at Alfrid. 'Do you really want to make me crash this aeroplane?'

What Alfrid wanted was to prevent Georgia from being able to land the aeroplane. If he could only get her to open the throttle and go around again, he would have another chance to free himself of his bonds and take control of the aeroplane once more. However, he was so angry, he was prepared to take the gamble of her crashing the aeroplane because of his interference, so when kicking at her leg didn't producing the violent action he had hoped for, he pressed hard down on the right rudder peddle that was on his side of the aeroplane. It immediately made the aeroplane yaw in an alarming manner. Georgia instantly took corrective measures, but then he lifted his foot and the aeroplane swung like a pendulum.

'Stop it!' Georgia shouted. But Alfrid kept pressing down hard first on the right rudder peddle and then on the left rudder peddle, making the aeroplane swing about in an almost uncontrollable manner. His face was now set in a grimacing rectus and his eyes were wide and shone with a manic gleam.

Georgia fought with all her might to keep the aeroplane on an even keel as it descended towards the ground swinging violently from side to side. Every muscle strained as she tried to countermeasure every wild movement that Alfrid was creating with his rough use of the rudder. She was absolutely determined to land on their first attempt—do or die! The alternative was to open the throttle, climb back up to height and give the maniac beside her a chance to get control of the aeroplane—and that wasn't going to happen!

The palm trees at the end of the airstrip were now beneath her and the threshold of the runway was coming up fast when Alfrid suddenly tried to lift up his knee and hook it under the control column. Georgia saw what he was attempting to do and for a moment she was so incensed that she let go of the control column and, with all her strength, punched him in the eye. The sharp and unexpected pain of her blow made Alfrid pull away for a moment, and for a couple of seconds he wasn't interfering with the controls and she was able to steady the aeroplane a little.

Chapter 21

Crash

Charles had been up since dawn and had already flown a good few miles looking for any clues that might lead him to Georgia. He had checked out a number of boats he had seen and had even tried to fly low enough to see into some of the vehicles that were travelling away from Kilifi, but in his heart, he knew it was all futile. Now he had returned to Mnarani to refuel and have a drink before he resumed his search.

Having refreshed himself by drinking a bottle of Coke after supervising the refuelling of the 182, he was about to get into the aeroplane and taxi to the end of the runway when he heard the approach of another aircraft. Looking to where the sound of the engine was coming from, he was amazed to see a Cessna 180 descending in a terrifyingly erratic manner. It slewed from one side to the other and swung about alarmingly as it plunged towards the threshold of the runway.

'My God, it's going to crash!' Charles muttered as he ran to the edge of the runway to get a better look at the aeroplane. He thought the pilot must be drunk or ill, or maybe there was some sort of mechanical failure that was making the aeroplane difficult to handle. He watched with his heart in his mouth as the aeroplane veered from one side to the other, while the wings seesawed in an alarming manner.

Just as the aeroplane passed over the threshold of the runway it seemed to steady a little, but the pilot had not compensated for the cross-wind and the aeroplane drifted off the centre of the runway towards the right side. As it shot over his head, Charles could see by the movement of the rudder and ailerons that the pilot was fighting the controls to get it back on course. It touched down with the right wheel on the edge of the runway as the pilot closed the throttle, but it was going fast and bounced up again.

'Go around again,' Charles found himself shouting. He didn't think there was room for the pilot to correct the bounce and still have enough runway on which to land.

But instead, the pilot hauled back on the control column and now the tail wheel came down and touched the edge of the runway before it slipped completely off the tarmac. The left main wheel then made contact with the right side of the runway, followed quickly by the right wheel that touched down just off the runway. It was still a retrievable situation, Charles thought, but the pilot, whose feet were obviously dancing on the controls in a Fred Astaire impression, made matters worse and the aeroplane started to ground-loop to the right.

'Don't use your breaks,' Charles muttered, anticipating the pilot's next move, but that's exactly what happened. The pilot was obviously scared that they were going to end up in the palm trees and pushed hard on the brakes. The aeroplane seemed to hesitate for a second and then it tipped forward onto its nose, the propeller making an ear-splitting clanging noise as it hit the ground. It slewed around causing a great deal of dust and then came to a standstill with the nose on the runway and the tail stuck up in the air.

Charles was already running towards the crash when the right-hand door suddenly burst open and Georgia tumbled out, he could hardly believe his eyes! She was barefooted and appeared to be wearing only a T-shirt as she looked about wildly.

'Georgia,' Charles shouted.

Georgia heard his voice and started to run towards him. When they reached each other, she fell into his arms and burst into sobs. 'Charles, he's still in the aeroplane,' she gabbled between her sobs. 'Don't let him get away—he's an animal, he was going to fly me to Somalia and kill me. I managed to knock him out for a little while and get control of the aeroplane. I tried to tie him securely to his seat, but he got his foot loose and he kept kicking the rudder pedals when I was trying to land and that's why we crashed.'

Charles was trying to process her almost incoherent words in his brain so that he could get the picture of what had happened, and he suddenly realised that whoever had abducted Georgia must still be in the crashed aeroplane. He gave Georgia a quick hug and said, 'Stay here, I'll go and get him out.'

'Charles, be careful,' shouted Georgia after Charles as he sprinted towards the crash. 'He's a dangerous man!'

By this time, other people were running up to see who had crashed the aeroplane, but Charles was the first there. He thought that the man still in the Cessna might be injured due to the crash, but apart from a wound on his head and blood all over his shirt, he seemed unhurt. However, his face was contorted with fury and he snarled out a number of words spoken in German, which Charles was in no doubt were not complimentary to Georgia!

'Get me out of here,' the man demanded in English when he saw Charles's face peering at him.

'I will, but first I want to know why you abducted my girlfriend,' Charles replied, ripping open the door.

Alfrid's only reply was a string of German swear words that Charles didn't understand.

Several people had now arrived on the scene and one of the guests who had been staying at the Mnarani club, Felix Harrison, tried to assume control of the situation because he was the chairman of a large company and thrived on being the focus of attention in any given crisis.

'Good Lord!' Felix Harrison exclaimed. 'The poor man is tied to his seat and it appears that he's hurt.' He sounded appalled. 'Let's get this unfortunate fellow out so that we can help him.' Harrison went to release Alfrid from his bonds, but he stopped abruptly when Charles spoke.

'*No!*' Charles's tone was sharp and emphatic. '*No one* is going to get him out before he tells me why he abducted my girlfriend! In fact, he's going to sit right where he is until the police have been called to arrest him.'

'But his head is bleeding,' objected Harrison pompously. 'I don't know what's going on here, but common courtesy demands that we should get him out and treat his wound!'

'Common courtesy is not something this man understands,' said Charles savagely. 'And if anyone tries to go near him, I'll punch them on the nose!' Charles looked straight into Harrison's eyes and it was obvious he was not joking!

'Now, if you want to be useful, go back to the Mnarani clubhouse and ring the police,' Charles instructed Harrison when he saw the man backing down. 'This man is a dangerous criminal and the police are the ones who should release him from the crash so that he can be arrested.'

'There could be the danger of fire,' suggested someone else, glancing uneasily at the fuel that was dripping from one of the tanks.

Charles had already noted with approval that, despite her hasty exit, Georgia had turned off the fuel and the magnetos. He thought there was little chance of the aeroplane catching fire now, but he didn't like to say that it would actually be a damn good thing if the man who had kidnapped his girlfriend was burned to a cinder. Instead he said, 'It won't go up in flames as long as no-one lights a cigarette or does anything silly.'

Felix Harrison strutted off to ring the police. He was of the opinion that Charles was the one who should be arrested and he made this clear to the policeman who answered his call.

A police van arrived very soon thereafter and the sergeant, a little fat officious man who took his duties seriously, was very soon escorted to the crash by Harrison. He took in the scene and frowned.

'Why is this man tied to his seat?' the sergeant demanded of Charles. 'Why hasn't he been removed from this crashed aeroplane when there could be a risk of fire?' He glared at Charles while Harrison stood by, revelling at the reprimand that the sergeant was handing out to Charles.

'This man abducted my girlfriend,' said Charles. 'He was going to fly her to Somalia and then kill her. Luckliy, she managed to tie him to his seat and take control of the aeroplane, but unfortunately, they crashed when she landed it here. I wouldn't let anyone free him from his seat because he's a very dangerous man. I thought it would be better to wait until you got here so you could take charge of him and arrest him.'

'Oh yes. We have been looking into the incident of the missing girl,' said the sergeant importantly. 'Is this the same girl of whom you now speak?'

'Yes. I'm not sure how she did it, but she must have managed to overcome the man when they were flying to Somalia and then she flew the aeroplane back here.'

'Wheee! That girl, she must be very strong and very clever,' said the sergeant looking mightily impressed. 'Where is she now?'

Georgia had not returned to the crashed aeroplane with Charles because she felt she just couldn't face seeing Alfrid again. Also, the reaction to her ordeal had made her legs feel like jelly, so she just sank down at the side of the runway where she was and sat in the sand, hugging her knees.

'Erm, there she is sitting over there,' said Charles pointing to Georgia's diminutive form.

'But that is a child,' objected the sergeant looking confused.

'No, she just looks younger than she is,' Charles assured the man.

'Are you sure that it was her? Was she really able to overcome this man?' The sergeant indicated Alfrid. 'And then fly an aeroplane? It seems impossible to me!' He looked sceptical.

'I know, it's unbelievable, isn't it? But they were the only two in the aeroplane when it crashed, so I think that proves that she somehow overcame the odds and got back to safety.'

'Wheee!' The sergeant was obviously very impressed. Then he laughed out loud. 'First I must shake this lady's hand, and then we will get this scum out and detain him.' He glared at Alfrid who was now beginning to look apprehensive, and then he glared at Harrison whom he felt had misinformed him right from the start.

Harrison, realising that he was not going to emerge from this little drama covered in glory, silently slunk away. Meanwhile, Charles followed the fat little sergeant over to where Georgia sat. When she saw them coming, she scrambled to her feet and pulled her T-shirt down in an effort to make herself more respectable.

'Madam, I must congratulate you!' The sergeant held out his hand. 'You are a very, very brave lady even if your flying skills are poor,' he glanced back at the crashed aeroplane. 'Very soon we will have your abductor locked up securely in Shimo la Tewa maximum security prison and you will be safe. Please, madam, take some time to rest and recover, and then could you come and make a statement at the police station?'

Georgia nodded. She was very pale, but Charles noticed two spots of colour appearing in her cheeks when the sergeant had suggested that she was a rubbish pilot. However, she didn't vocalise the retort that Charles was sure was on the tip of her tongue!

The fat little sergeant walked back to the crash and ordered his men to release Alfrid from the wreck and arrest him. Charles and Georgia stood together and watched from a distance the German being pulled roughly from the aeroplane, manacled, and bundled into the police van.

'Will I be in trouble for hitting him over the head?' Georgia asked.

'No, of course not,' Charles reassured her. 'And that little tap that you gave him is nothing compared to the beating he's going to get in Shimo la Tewa. They don't treat their prisoners well in that prison, so he's certainly going to reap the rewards of his reprehensible behaviour. But come now, my darling, let's get you back to Oliver's beach cottage so you can have something to eat and drink and freshen up. You look all in and I'm guessing you've had a terrible ordeal. We've all been out of our minds with worry and Oliver and Fiona and the others will be so glad to see you safely home.

'What about the chaos I've caused on the runway?' Georgia asked. 'Shouldn't we arrange to have the crash taken away?'

'No, the police said they will have it removed and taken to the police station. I guess it's part of the evidence now.'

The manager of the Mnarani club was more than willing to drive Charles and Georgia back to the family beach cottage on the other side of the creek, and Oliver and the rest of the family could hardly believe their eyes when Charles walked in with Georgia. They were overjoyed to have her back safe and sound! However,

Fiona saw at once that Georgia looked traumatised, so she insisted that the girl have some time to herself to shower and change before she was obliged to tell them all what had happened to her. Georgia appreciated her aunt's kind consideration, as it gave her a chance to pull herself together and arrange her thoughts in a coherent manner. She was still feeling shaky, but a hot shower, a hair wash and clean clothes all helped to make her feel more human and in control.

Georgia related to the family what had happened to her while she tucked into a ham sandwich and a cup of coffee, and then she was told of Cade's findings in his investigation of her parents' murders.

'Cade told us that Alfrid Wagner was the person who murdered your parents,' said Fiona. 'He had a vendetta against your father and he also thought Ian had sold some items that he had been given for safe keeping and kept the money for himself. He was determined to get his money back, but his main objective was to get his revenge on Ian for being the instrument of having his twin brother, Danek, executed for his war crimes. He abducted you in the hope that we could get hold of the money that he felt sure your father had made by selling the items he was given for safe keeping. He thought we would gladly pay for your release. It was a dreadful situation for you, Georgia, but I doubt very much that he could have been so evil that he would have murdered you—just an innocent young girl.'

'Oh yes he would!' Georgia assured her. 'I overhear him say that I was—"the spawn of a traitor who had Jewish blood running in my veins". He also said I was destined to die because he wanted to reap the revenge of his brother's death in full!'

Everyone was silent for a few seconds as they digested those chilling words. Then Georgia asked, 'Where are Cade and Benedict now?'

'Well, they got a lead on the ngalawa that apparently was used in your abduction and they've been trying to find out where it's gone, but I expect they'll be back this evening,' Oliver told her.

After Georgia had finished her snack, she wrote out a detailed statement and then Oliver and Charles took her to the police station so that she could present it to the police. They had just parked their car when they saw, with surprise, Cade and Benedict walking out of the station.

'Georgia, we heard you'd managed to escape from your abductor!' Cade said looking mightily pleased to see her. 'What happened?'

'Well, I'm just on my way to give a written statement to the police,' said Georgia. 'You can read if you like, and then you'll be in the picture. But first, why are you here at the police station?'

'Well, we managed to locate the ngalawa we've been looking for and we apprehend a man called Abdullah who, it turns out, has had his fingers in all sorts of illegal pies! He's been squealing like stuck pig in an effort to clear himself of as much blame as possible when it comes to your abduction, so all the evidence is stacking up against the German. We let the police know what we had found out about Alfrid, so I think he'll be in jail for a long and very uncomfortable time—that's if he survives the harsh conditions for more than a week of two!'

Georgia had written into her statement that Alfrid worked with a man called Hanad and also he had a colleague named Fritz who lived north of Malindi in the coastal area, so the police would also be able to round up those members of the gang as well.

When they all got back to the beach cottage, Cade and Benedict told Georgia in detail what they had found out about Alfrid and why they were certain he was the one who had murdered her parents.

'He wanted avenge his brother's death, we know that for sure,' said Cade. 'We also know he wanted the proceeds from the sale of his booty that he was certain Ian had kept for himself. Obviously, Ian was unable to give him the money he was demanding, but he was still sure it must be sitting somewhere and he was determined to get it for himself. That's why he abducted you, Georgia, and his plan was to murder you as well, had you not been brave and clever enough to escape from his clutches!'

Georgia shuddered. 'Hanad was supposed to deliver a letter of demand that Alfrid had written to Oliver,' she said. 'I heard him tell Hanad to be careful not to be seen when he delivered it.'

'Well, no letter has been received,' said Oliver.

'I guess that Fritz would have rung back to the house where I was kept prisoner and told Hanad that Alfrid had failed to turn up,' said Georgia. 'They wouldn't know what had happened, but maybe they thought we'd crashed en route to where Fritz was waiting for us, so Hanad probably decided to wait to deliver the letter until the circumstances became clearer.'

'Hopefully, the police will find the letter in his possession,' said Oliver. 'It will be more evidence against them.'

'How will the police even know where the house was where I was kept prisoner?' Georgia wanted to know. 'I was only able to tell them it was close to the beach and sea because I could hear the waves breaking.'

'Oh, Alfrid will tell them soon enough where it is,' said Cade. 'The methods of interrogation are very robust in Kenya, so he'll very quickly confess everything,' he added grimly.

'So, what'll happen to him?'

'The legal system is quite slow, but I'm sure he'll be found guilty of murder in the end and he'll swing for it,' said Benedict.

Georgia got up and walked away. She hoped that Alfrid would be handed the death penalty for the murder of her parents, it was what he deserved. But she didn't like to think of him or anyone else being hanged.

'Are you okay?' Charles had followed her as she walked down the path towards the sea.

'Yes,' Georgia assured him. 'I'm fine.'

She allowed him to catch her up and take her hand and together they walked to the top of the beach. It was high tide and the waves were running up the sand in a flurry of foam and bubbles.

'I'm just feeling a bit overwhelmed at the moment,' Georgia admitted after she had sunk down and sat in the warm sand at the very top of the beach. She picked up a bit of drift wood and tossed it into the waves as Charles squatted down beside her. 'Ever since Mum and Dad were murdered, I've lived for this day when the person who did it was caught and put in prison. Now that it's happened, I don't feel happy and victorious as I thought I would. I feel empty and sort of deflated. Alfrid will probably die for his crimes and so he should, but it won't bring Dad and Mum back, will it?' She put her head on Charles's shoulder and he put his arm around her.

'Unfortunately not,' Charles agreed. 'But I do think they would have been so proud of you for managing to escape from that man—and not only that, for getting him apprehended as well! The odds were stacked against you, sweetie, but you used your head and the skills you had and accomplished something remarkable. I feel nothing but admiration for you when I think of what you achieved.'

Georgia didn't reply, she seemed to be seeped in melancholy and unable to appreciate the feat she had accomplished against all the odds. Charles wanted to shake her out of her dejected state so he added mischievously, 'In fact, I would be in total awe of you had you not completely ignored my instructions and applied the brakes to a taildragger before the landing roll was complete!'

'Charles, that's not fair!' Georgia snapped out of her despondency and as she pulled angrily away from him, Charles could see the colour rising in her cheeks. Then she suddenly noticed his wicked grin and she slapped him lightly on the arm. 'Don't you *dare* tease me about that,' she said. 'I was under extreme duress and it's a wonder I got down without killing myself and the German.'

'Exactly! And you need to keep that in mind, my sweet girl. You achieved your escape in a completely mind-blowing way! You deceived the German about your age, you had the guts to knock him out and tie him to his seat and you even managed to get the aeroplane down onto the ground when he was kicking the controls and making things impossible. Your parents may not be here now, but I can virtually hear them clapping and cheering you! We all are!'

Chapter 22

Congratulations

'Pick a landmark before you start the manoeuvre so that you have a reference point on which to keep the aeroplane straight,' Charles instructed Georgia.

He couldn't help notice her ears had become a delightful shad of pink as she concentrated on performing her first ever loop. Her long hair was tied up in a ponytail and Charles fancied it trembled a little in excited anticipation as Georgia followed his instructions.

'Now, go into a shallow dive and ease the throttle open; when you get to 130 pull back on the control column, that's it, back, back, back. . . now you're at the top of your loop ease off the pressure slightly so that your loop is nice and round. Good. . . good, now over you go. . . back pressure on the stick again and look for your landmark so that you keep straight.'

The aeroplane bumped slightly as it flew through some disturbed air. 'Did you feel that?' Charles asked. 'We just flew through our wake, which is a good sign that your loop was nice and straight.'

Georgia whooped in delight as they came out of the loop. 'That was awesome! Can I do another one?'

'Climb back up to height,' said Charles, 'and then check for other aeroplanes. Don't forget your checks in your euphoria.'

After Georgia had had a couple of days to get over her ordeal, she and Charles had flown back to Lanet in the Cessna 182, leaving the rest of her family to finish their holiday at the coast. When Georgia had put up a fierce argument as to why she should be the one to do the flying on their return journey to Lanet, Charles felt relieved because he knew for sure then that she had regained her equilibrium and was picking up the threads of her life once more.

'Okay,' said Charles with a laugh. 'You can be the pilot and fly us home, but I want to stop in Nairobi on the way back, so please file your flight plan accordingly.'

'Why do you want to stop in Nairobi?' Georgia wanted to know.

'Because when we land at Wilson Airport, I want to hire a taxi to take us into the city where I'm going to buy you the biggest diamond engagement ring that I can afford!'

'This means so much to me,' Georgia said as she admired the ring on her finger that was flashing with sparkles of iridescent light. 'Just a few days ago, I thought that this was never going to happen. I thought that I was going to die and everything I'd been looking forward to was going to be terminated before it had even begun.' Her eyes looked haunted and Charles immediately took her hands in his.

'But that's all in the past now, my darling. Thanks to your bravery, tenacity and adeptness you have regained your future and I'm so happy to be part of it! I also thought the worst when you disappeared and we couldn't find any clues as to where you were—those were definitely the most appalling hours I've ever had to live through, but we can put all that behind us now and look forward to a wonderful future together. Now, let's order a sandwich and something to drink.'

They had decided to have lunch at the Thorn Tree Restaurant in Nairobi before taking a taxi back to Wilson Airport.

'Does everyone at the club know what's happened?' Georgia asked as she ate her lunch.

'Yes, pretty much. Well, they don't know all the details of course, but I've filled Howard in with much of what's been going on and he'll be sure to pass it on to everyone else. I've also told him that we're flying back this afternoon and will be ready to start instructing again tomorrow.'

'You didn't tell Howard we were going to stop in Nairobi to buy an engagement ring, did you?'

'No, of course not! You said you wanted to keep it a secret and make a big announcement, so I didn't tell him about the ring.'

'Good. I'll have to take it off before we land at Lanet in case anyone notices it. Then we'll have to decide when to make the big announcement.'

As they winged their way towards Lanet bumping gently through the up and down draughts, Georgia turned and smiled at Charles. 'It feels nice to be going home,' she said. 'The members of the club feel as much my family as Oliver and Fiona and I'm looking forward to seeing them all. And then there's the Citabria!'

Charles was amused to see how her eyes flashed with passion when she mentioned the new aeroplane. 'What about the Citabria?' he asked mischievously.

'Aerobatics!' Georgia said with a laugh. 'Look, I know you're an old hand when it comes to aerobatics, but to me it's a very exciting prospect to be able to learn how to do them. I've wanted to for ages and very soon you're going teach me everything you know!'

Georgia took the ring off her finger and slipped it into her pocket just before she touched the Cessna 182 onto the runway as gently as thistledown at Lanet. As she taxied towards the clubhouse, she suddenly noticed that a crowd of people were standing on the veranda looking in their direction. For a moment she wondered if they were waiting for someone important to arrive and then suddenly, she realised that they had congregated to welcome her back.

'Seems like you're a very popular lady,' said Charles with a laugh. 'You carry on and show everyone that you're in one piece and I'll tie the aeroplane down etcetera.'

Georgia was received with many hugs and kisses.

'We thought we'd lost you,' said Mary with tears in her eyes. 'I'm so glad you're back safe and sound.'

'I'm sorry that we both deserted the club and left no one to do the instructing,' Georgia said to Howard when he greeted her.

'No need for apologies, my dear,' Howard said, giving her

another hug. 'Here you are now, and I can assure you the booking book is full, so as soon as you feel ready you can get stuck in again.'

'I'm ready now,' Georgia assured him.

'Good, then you can start first thing tomorrow,' said Howard. 'Now, Mary and some of the other members have organised a "welcome home" meal for you this evening, so you can just sit back and enjoy. What would you like to drink?'

'A Coke please, Howard, in the bottle with a straw.'

Everyone was so pleased to have Georgia back safely and she had to relate to them all that had happened to her in great detail.

'That poor bastard that abducted you didn't have a clue what he was letting himself in for,' said Randy when he had heard her tale. 'Had he known what an annoying little kitten you are with your sharp mind and innovative ideas, he would have run a mile! Good on you girl, don't ever change!'

Before the meal was served Georgia managed to have a private word with Charles.

'Charles, everyone is here—do you think that this would be a good time to announce our engagement?'

'Yes, good idea,' said Charles. He took the ring from Georgia and slipped it into his pocket.

Just before the meal was served and everyone was sitting waiting for the first course, Charles stood up and tapped his glass with his spoon to get their attention.

'Georgia has asked me to thank you for all for your kind concern and for organising this fantastic meal,' he said. 'Many times, she's told me that she regards you all as her extended family.' He paused while everyone clapped and then when the noise had died down, he continued. 'So, we both though it would be a good time to share some exciting news with you.'

Georgia stood up at that point and Charles took the engagement ring from his pocket and slipped it onto her finger. 'We're engaged to be married,' he said simply, as Georgia held up her hand so everyone could see the flashing diamond on her finger.

Everyone clapped and cheered and congratulated the young couple, delighted to hear their exciting news.

'Champagne,' shouted Randy. 'I'm paying! But I'm not paying for Coca Cola, so don't you dare ask for it, Georgia!'

END

Also by Janet E. Green

Janet Green has enjoyed writing novels for a number of years. She was born and brought up in Kenya, East Africa, and also lived in central and southern Africa for many years. Now living in England, she draws on her memories of Africa, where her heart still remains, for inspiration. Most of the books she writes are sagas and some of them are seasoned by her strong Christian beliefs. You can find out more about Janet Green by visiting her website and blog at www.janetegreen.org.

A
HABARI
PUBLICATION

Sharba is only too aware of the calamitous consequences of a relationship that has soured, and she is determined never to be ensnared in a liaison that could end in physical or psychological abuse. When she embarks on a holiday romance in Australia, Sharba has no intention of letting things get too serious. However, due to circumstances beyond her control, she suddenly finds herself engulfed in a relationship that has all the warning indicators of what she has been so careful to avoid in the past. Disentangling herself from the man she has come to fear takes courage, but Sharba takes the initiative and thinks she has freed herself from him for ever as she hides away in a corner of Africa where she is positive he will never find her. But unbeknown to Sharba, she has landed herself in a situation that she could never have perceived and has, in fact, added to the danger that is already stalking her.

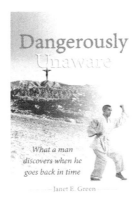

Dangerously Unaware

What a man
discovers when he
goes back in time

—Janet E. Green

As Josh hurried down the passage away from the dentists' rooms and towards the lifts, he felt a sense of relief. Although he was now a confident young adult, he still disliked going to the dentist for check-ups. He hated the feeling of vulnerability as the dentist tipped the chair back so that he was lying almost horizontal. It made Josh feel at the mercy of the dentist and his middle-aged assistant who hovered over him with their instruments of torture in their hands. He detested the sharp things that were poked around his teeth and gums and the shriek of the drill set his nerves on edge, while the sight of the dentist coming towards him with a syringe in his hand made Josh feel very apprehensive.

God's Timing

Lucy has suffered a crushing sorrow and now, to her, the world seems to be a place of chaos and disharmony. She is convinced that she or her family will sooner or later be caught up in some disaster and longs to know what the future holds so that she can be prepared. Although she is holidaying in one of the most beautiful places in the world, her dark thoughts drag her down to the point where she is almost overwhelmed.

Is it by sheer coincidence that she is introduced to someone who has the knowledge and absolute proof of what the future holds? Lucy finds herself going on a journey of discovery that almost blows her mind. And at the end of her holiday, there is one last surprise. . .

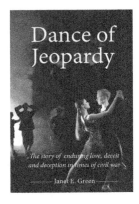

The man in my arms was the most important person in my life. Right from the time that I first met him when I was still very young, there had been a spark between us —a connection that had never been completely broken. It was there all through the years when he was seeking adventure in other parts of Africa—it was there when his life took a turn that excluded me completely, and it had lain dormant until the time was right for it to ignite once again. It seemed to me that too many years had passed while he was away striving to accomplish his dreams—the dreams of a man who craved action, danger, and adventure. His quest for adventure had, for so many years, seemed to draw us further and further apart, but now, at last, the man I loved so much was in my arms.

The Lunar Rainbow

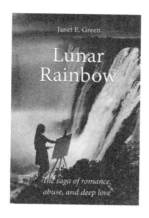

Janet E. Green

Lunar Rainbow

The saga of romance, abuse, and deep love

It was one of those very rare days in England when the weather was decidedly un-British. The unusual pressure system that swirled over the British Isles that early summer's day drew in hot moist air all the way from Africa, causing the sun's rays to become magnified as they filtered through the moisture-laden atmosphere. It was so different from the normal British sunshine that would usually seep over a cool bracing dawn and highlight the countryside in fingers of bright warmth. This heat was humid and heavy, it felt like hot syrup, and I could feel my arms prickling as the fierce rays burned into the exposed skin. The sky was a steely blue, but to the east there was a huge build-up of cumulonimbus clouds under which the sky was almost black. Ominous growls of distant thunder rumbled every now and again.

Jigsaw

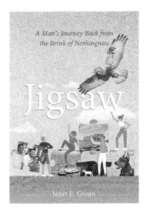

It is a terrifying experience to wake up and find that you are blind, deaf and cannot move. But for Mike, the worst is yet to come. As he lies completely immobile in his bed, the only thing that he can do is try and remember how he came to be in this state. However, the memories of his past only come back to him randomly in bits and pieces that he must try and put together to get a whole picture of his life. Frighteningly, much of what he remembers is almost too distressing to contemplate. Did he really do the things that now float into his mind? What could have driven him to act in such a despicable manner? He remembers that he had been a Christian in his early life, but something terrible must have happened to so dramatically change his way of thinking. What could it be? And is there any way back from the physical and mental torment in which he now finds himself?

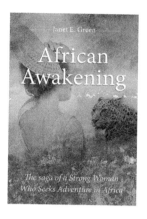

Kate drove her hire car at snail's pace down the dusty track, bumping over the crunchy coral bones that ridged on the surface of the narrow road, and she turned up a lane that was marked with the sign 'Bougain Villa'. With every metre she covered her heart seemed to pump faster and faster. She had searched for so long that she had almost despaired that she would ever find what she was seeking. But now after months of research and a trip half way around the world to Kilifi in Kenya, East Africa, she was sure that she was on the threshold of finding the person that she had sought for so long.

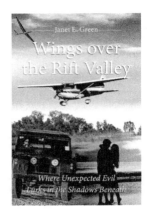

Having been subjected to a heartbreaking incident, Georgia is now determined to move forward, concentrate on her future, work hard at her chosen career and make a success of her life. She does not expect to find the happiness that suddenly and wonderfully comes her way. But unfortunately, lurking in the shadows beneath, there is evil that unexpectedly takes her by surprise.

Hosea served as a prophet in remarkable and challenging circumstances in Ancient Israel's Old Testament times. His interactions with the people he encountered—including Gomer—are explored imaginatively in this novel. Publication date: 2024.

Printed in Great Britain
by Amazon

35961920R00145